DECEIVED BY FAITH

Jean Hendy-Harris

CHALKPITS PRESS

Copyright Jean Hendy-Harris 2019

Other Titles by this Author

Chalkpits Press
CHALK PITS & CHERRY STONES

EIGHT TEN TO CHARING CROSS

IN DISGRACE WITH FORTUNE

MORE THAN JUST SKELETONS

SUNDAY'S CHILD

Hodder & Stoughton
PUTTING THE JOY BACK INTO EGYPT

Ashton Scholastic
CREATIVE PATHWAYS (I&II)

ISBN: 9781098509071

Fiction: internet fraud, revenge, psychological thriller

ONE

It all started long before I really understood what was meant by the term obsession. I had never been obsessed with anything in particular unless you counted the idea I harboured from childhood of becoming rich and famous – as an actress perhaps, or a dancer, maybe even a writer. But back then those misguided ideas were really more a passionate wish than anything else, the sort of thing I whispered to myself when pulling the chicken wishbone or sometimes when lighting a candle in church. Anyhow as I grew older and by that I mean out of my teens, I became more pragmatic about stardom in any field whatsoever. Celebrity simply didn't happen to girls like me though of course notoriety sometimes did. You only had to look at Mandy Rice-Davies to see that.

Back in those long-gone days before cell phones and simple internet searches we seemed to know much less than we do these days. For instance we didn't know what 'grooming' meant except where it applied to poodles at the newly emerging pampering parlours, and ponies if we happened to be more middle class. There was little likelihood that we would have realised we were being groomed should we find ourselves in that unhappy position. Now of course, courtesy of the massive and world-wide publicity that has heightened the profiles and the wrongdoings of individuals such as Rolf Harris, Michael Jackson and Jimmy Savile not to mention a raft of Roman Catholic priests and bishops, it would be hard to find a twelve-year-old still confused as to the practice. But that was then and this is now and a lot has changed in the interim. In any case the grooming process is by its very nature more likely to be welcomed and appreciated by the object of the exercise rather than rejected. This is generally the case whether the victim be seven or twenty-seven years old. And simply speaking for myself there would have been few twenty-one-year-olds as predisposed to the charms of flattery and attention as I was. You could say I was ripe for the plucking.

I was similarly programmed for jealousy in all its various guises and years later even my brother said that girls like me, those who had lost a father at a significant age, and in my case that had been eleven, were particularly prone to the torment of mistrust. He was likening this unhappy state to ornithology at the time, explaining how flocks of birds will isolate one they perceive to be an outsider and from that moment the unhappy outcast will not have the protection of the group.

I was struggling to understand how this metaphor worked but what was clear was that Vanith Lefarge actively encouraged suspicion and distrust. It was almost as if he sought to make these emotions a fundamental part of his relationships not only with those women who fell in love with him but in every aspect of his dealings with people. He talked a great deal about the folly of possessiveness but was never happier than when two women were involved in an emotional skirmish concerning him. Causing pain to others, forcing friends and family to face the distressing choice of either doing his will, or accepting the fact that they would be torn from all contact with him, seemed to afford him enormous pleasure. It was a game he never tired of and each woman who loved him was drawn into it so it was no surprise to find years after the unsavoury events I now write of that there had been no very good reason why Persephone Faith became so hated by Christina.

Though she was to become central to my life for over a year in a time that was very much yet to come she had begun somewhat slyly, furtively simply as an unusual name in a fragment of a letter written in 1961 or thereabouts, by poor beleaguered and aggrieved Christina. It was her name that had caught my attention in the first place, as out-of-the-ordinary names so often did and I blamed my mother for that preoccupation. I wondered if she had found growing up as Persephone difficult. For me growing up as Bernadette had never been easy, surrounded as I always seemed to be by more sensibly named Shirleys and Wendys and Marjories. As a child although constantly told I had a saint's name, which in itself made me shudder, I did not even realise that it was French and had I done so I might even have been more accepting of it.

I stumbled across that initial mention of Persephone back in the days long before home computers and email correspondence, significant attachments and simple text messages, at a time when people were still in the habit of writing notes to others. Vanith had made a somewhat half-hearted attempt to destroy such correspondence and so the more salacious paragraphs had rather disappointingly well and truly disappeared by the time I got to it. *'...I have begun to truly hate Persephone...I detest her so much that when I think of her I can smell myself, smell the hatred...'* Most definitely written by Christina, whose hand I recognised at once from her more homely messages directing him to the whereabouts of the milk or cereal. He should have taken the precaution of destroying all such notes as I invariably happened upon each one in my hurried routine searches of his pockets. Yes, I recognised the writer at once and felt a small surge of triumph that at last he was out of her clutches, away from the free bed and board she had offered him for nearly two years, and was now mine alone. But I did wonder exactly who Persephone was, a woman Christina hated so much, though strangely enough not why because I could totally understand the rapacious animosity of her possessive love.

The torn fragment was disposed of in the household rubbish and several weeks elapsed before I began to understand that the mysterious Persephone was in fact the alter ego of Christina's one time flat-mate, Faith, and was the name she had adopted when writing the children's stories she every so often tried her hand at, with some success it must be admitted. It seemed that these two women, once good friends, were now sworn enemies and all because of love for Vanith Lefarge. For if he was to be believed, both were or had been in love with him and although Faith was possessed of many of the qualities he desired in a woman, Christina was sadly lacking.

But that was all in the past and not of any great importance because I was now the prominent woman in his life and working hard at remaining so. And there was a great deal of work to be done in order to maintain my position. It was not just as simple as being a good cook and keeping a tidy home, nor even being an intelligent conversationalist or exciting in bed. I was a good cook in any case and about to become even better if the Cordon Bleu course worked its magic. He was not interested in me keeping a tidy home and in fact there were times when I fervently wished he was more so. He seemed to prefer an untidy home and if he placed bits of rubbish in odd places then he definitely expected to find them there even three or four weeks later. He said he found housework disruptive to his train of thought and so I had to do it furtively and as quietly as possible. We did not own a vacuum cleaner so that was a bonus of course as far as general silence of execution was concerned. He likened himself to a cat in this respect and said he wanted as little distraction of his daily routines as was possible.

In many ways he was less demanding than the average man. For example he cared little if he ate at regular times – in fact he cared little if he ate at all though he was fond of spaghetti Bolognese. I was not therefore expected to provide regular meals. Having said that, the availability of refrigerated treats such as smoked fish roes or slices of air-dried beef put him in a very good mood indeed. He was also quite fond of poached chicken from time to time. You could say he was easy to please in this respect and not a roast beef, two veg and gravy man at all. He never ate breakfast and lunch only seldom but he did like to be wakened with a baby bottle full of warm milky coffee with lots of sugar. This was only a slight eccentricity I decided at the time though later the idea disturbed me.

I had a problem with intelligent conversation but I tried to be amusing and appear well read and erudite. I attempted to have opinions on current affairs and so a rapid perusal of the *Times Leader* was a daily must but I found it difficult to retain the information for any length of time. It was an uphill battle. There was another disappointment when he told me that I was not a terribly exciting sexual partner and this was something else that needed to be worked on. It was not as if I lacked experience in this area because before meeting him I had been rather liberal with my favours, always hoping for love in exchange for sex and if that was not realistic then at the very least for someone I liked well enough to actually like me sufficiently to want to pursue the relationship. Until meeting him I had been generally disappointed.

Looking back from the benefit of four decades of distance it seems obvious that the problems in the relationship were never going to be overcome. On one side was a young and desperately needy woman, more than willing to sacrifice good sense for what seemed almost like love and on the other was a self-absorbed, egotistical thirty-five-year-old man utterly determined not to deviate in the slightest from achieving those things he needed in order to make his life as pleasant and amusing as possible. Even at the time I was sensible enough to understand most of this but somehow or other it was impossible to withdraw from the situation. At that time I had never heard the word masochistic but even had I been familiar with it I doubt if it would have made much difference. And despite his obvious shortcomings of personality he was at the same time extraordinarily kind and attentive to me, at times almost showering me with helpful consideration. So I wonder once again, if I had known about grooming back then would I have realised I was being coached, prepared, primed and mentored for my future role? My best friend Stella certainly seemed to have some reservations about him and pointed out that he was indeed incredibly kind but that at times it was almost as if his sudden and startling bursts of savagery were simply to see if a process of some kind was working. And although I scorned that comment at the time, privately I understood precisely what she meant.

It's sobering to realise that I might never have stumbled across Vanith Lefarge at all and none of the events about which I write would have happened had I not given in to the thrilling madness of taking a job at the Ace of Clubs night club in Brewer Street, just beneath the Raymond Revuebar. And that decision would never have been made in the first place if I had not been sacked from my typing job at the Bond Street recording studio for being late back from lunch three days in a row. This was in the days when sackings routinely occurred for non-conformist behaviour.

The job at the Ace Of Clubs was theoretically that of a dancing partner and this made it appealing as dancing was something of a passion with me at that time; not ballroom dancing in particular, but doing what my mother would have called showing off in public. I suppose I was an exhibitionist though a somewhat timid one and I gained confidence as time went on. The night club job suited me. I found living somewhat on the edge exhilarating and after only three weeks in the job I realised that I would be unlikely to ever return to typing. For one thing the financial remuneration was much greater as a good evening's work could bring in a five pound hostess fee. What is more, we did not seem required to declare this money or pay tax on it or so it seemed at the time. To be fair I had not totally realised that the job would also entail what the club manager termed Greener Pastures and so I resisted this for all of a fortnight before agreeing to go back to the hotel room of the business man from Manchester who was offering ten pounds for extra services.

As we waited in the rain for a taxi he asked me if I would stay with him all night. I readily agreed. I had been earning ten pounds a week as a typist so the arrangement seemed more than reasonable to me and in any event it was after three am before we got to the hotel so not a great deal of the night remained. The next day my co-hostess colleague Marie who had accompanied the business man's friend to the adjoining room demanded to know where I had disappeared to the night before. She looked incredulous when I explained the arrangement I had come to with my punter. She explained that decent hostesses did not demean themselves by under charging and an All Night Job demanded thirty pounds. I soon realised that the other concession I had made, not to use a condom, had also been unwise, because within a week or two I found that I was pregnant. A calamity and oddly such a development had never crossed my mind because pregnancy was something that happened to other people and even then in those days mostly after the wedding ceremony. Naïve to say the least but almost immediately the full horror of the situation dawned and plunged me into the deepest despair. I did not stop for an instant to debate the rights and wrongs of termination but began a frantic search for an abortionist. A few weeks later it was the club's newest dancing partner, Miriam, who pointed me in the right direction. I had been directed by the manager to leave the table by the dance floor that I had until then shared with Marie and Joanne, and go to the table closer to the entry stairs to sit with the new girl who introduced herself as Miriam. She lived in Edgware Road she told me, in her own flat close to the corner of Praed Street, with a Siamese cat called Bamboo. She was twenty-six years old and had worked in clubs since she was seventeen and she had a friend who did abortions. She would speak with him and ask him if he was prepared to do mine. The cost would be twenty-five pounds. What a relief.

And that is how I met Vanith Lefarge the sound engineer, moonlighting as an abortionist.

I wouldn't say it was love at first sight because my first impression was that he was decidedly odd and out of the ordinary in that he was foreign for a start, a German. But he seemed kind and certainly not the run of the mill abortionist because he stayed with me during the three days it took to dislodge my twelve-week fetus with injections into the uterus of first of all glycerin, then soapy water During that time by way of diversion for us both he also seduced me. It was not an altogether comfortable seduction but as I said before he was kind and for most of the time he told me stories about his past, made cups of instant coffee for me on the gas ring, persuaded me to walk briskly in Kensington Gardens in order to hurry the termination process along, and slept on the floor with just a raincoat over him. It was Easter 1962, a particularly sunny and warm Easter and the invigorating walks up Queensway left me hot and sticky and slightly breathless but the slower circle of the park was somehow tinged with excitement and the promise of a more hopeful future.

The poor little would-be baby, cruelly halted in its development, appeared on Easter Sunday along with a great deal of physical discomfort. Oh what total elation to be suddenly free of it! And still Vanith did not leave, but cleaned me up, gave me painkillers, made more coffee and curled up again on the floor to sleep. No-one had been as kind and considerate towards me for a long time and by Easter Monday evening, eating fish and chips out of newspaper, I was just a little bit entranced. Just like that! And as previously documented I went on to discover that concern and consideration formed part of his general modus operandi and this technique worked very successfully as far as the young and emotionally needy were concerned. He did not seem to take much interest in women closer to his own age. In fact I was at the very cusp of that which interested him, being already out of my teens and somewhat overweight so you could say I was lucky to have caught his attention at all. I had been economical with the truth, telling him that the extra pounds had only appeared with the pregnancy. Had I been aware of his preference for teenagers I would have taken a few years off my age at the same time but how was I to know all his likes and dislikes then? These were only revealed to me little by little over the following months as I advanced further and further into his arc of influence. And of course by that time I was unable to pay any reasonable attention to the mounting evidence that pointed towards his real nature, and in any case the next few months were the happiest of my entire life to date. I was ecstatic to have this cultured and educated man by my side, in awe of his intellect and daily more astonished that out of all the women in Bayswater he had chosen to be with me. Well, not quite of course because he was still living with Christina, but that I knew to be a platonic relationship, though she would have preferred it to be otherwise; she was simply offering him a place to live free of charge because he had struck difficult times.

He explained to me in some detail how he had reached this sad impasse. It had all started when his business began to go wrong and all his recording equipment had to be put into storage. He lost the flat where he had been living with someone inconsequential called Irena who came from Peru and made wonderful salads. It was then that Christina, good old reliable Christina who had been dumped some eighteen months previously in favour of the said Irena, had swiftly come to his aid by offering the spare room at her flat in Ladbroke Grove.

'Perhaps she hopes you will return to her,' I suggested and he explained to me that was a silly idea because Christina was only too aware that their relationship was over and how it had really come to an end long before Irena happened upon the scene. It came about when Christina had taken in an old friend from Dublin called Faith who had recently left her husband and come to London to seek her fortune as a writer. In fact he had known her in Dublin himself years before when he had studied medicine at Trinity

College. He was rather attracted to Faith as Christina knew and she sensibly agreed to allow him to pursue his interest in her whilst they all lived together at St. Mary's Mansions in Paddington. A ménage a trois and very enjoyable it had been. Faith had been remarkably sensible and adult about this arrangement but after a while Christina began to take it badly and make silly demands which finally fractured their relationship. He quite understood that she had become jealous but sadly he was unable to totally trust her again.

I nervously enquired what had happened to Faith, wondering if she might be hovering close by, another benevolent ex-girlfriend waiting in the wings to claim him with offers of rent-free living when I finally managed to completely prise him away from Christina. It was then he told me how she went off somewhere to write under the pseudonym of Persephone somebody or other and he had not heard from her since. What a relief.

I had expected him to leave Christina's care and supervision much sooner than he did but he was exceedingly cautious, sleeping at Ladbroke Grove from Monday to Friday and only spending weekend nights with me just a few miles away in Leinster Square, Bayswater. She fed him on those weeknight evenings, after I had departed for the Ace of Clubs in silver lamé dress and high heels, on nourishing stews made from beef with lots of barley and vegetables. It was not gourmet food of course but as I said before he was fairly indiscriminating in that respect. The amount of time he still spent with her though was of considerable concern but there was little I could do to insist upon his exit. We talked a lot of when we would live together, how he would be able to get his equipment out of storage and how I would help him re-establish the business. Thank heaven for my typing skills and for the time I had spent using them in Denmark Street in music publishing offices. He quickly realised that my somewhat tenuous connections might be of use to him and I fervently hoped he was right. And to be fair in the end they were of use because most of his future business would come directly from them and most especially from a DJ, Stan Douglas, with whom I had a brief fling a year or so before, just before I had an even briefer fling with the technical director of the pirate radio station in the North Sea they both worked for. None of these details are really important.

Vanith had inculcated within me an overwhelming desire to do my very best for him in every way I could. I was quite confident I would not let him down and the only thing that concerned me to any extent was the fact that I was still not very exciting as a sexual partner. I tried, but I did not really know how to improve and my newly developing work as a professional via the Ace of Clubs did not actually help that much. Maybe I was not a natural as far as sex was concerned and that might have been because of all the uncles and older cousins who had tried to initiate me in these matters when I was still a child, but that's another story altogether and we won't go into it here. Anyway, whatever the reason, although I was very keen on sex with Vanith, and he seemed very keen too, the matter of my overall rating was still an issue. It was certainly a worry. Looking back I feel that this was because he tried to introduce me to group sex, orgiastic sex, rather alarming sex, far too early in the relationship, but that was simply a miscalculation on his part. It is just possible that he was not quite as seasoned a groomer as I now believe him to have been.

I was most reluctant to become involved in these practices and fervently hoped he would abandon the disagreeable ideas but he didn't. He did, however, modify his initial suggestions and soothingly suggested that for the time being and only in order to spice up our sex life we should simply take another man into our bed occasionally. Not on a regular basis of course because that would become humdrum, just from time to time. How would I like that? Well I didn't much like it but it certainly seemed to be the lesser of several evils and so I agreed half-heartedly and he began a search for someone suitable.

In discussion with Stella years later, when the relationship was seriously fractured, she pointed out that the situation I had found myself in with Vanith Lefarge had not been all that uncommon and if I should be able to discuss it with the much reviled Myra Hindley whose face adorned every newspaper in the country at the time, she would undoubtedly have been in a position to sympathise. Then she added that in Myra's case, with the demands placed upon her by the astonishingly evil Ian Brady being so many light years in advance of what Vanith Lefarge stipulated, several years might need to pass before she would find herself in a position to be of much emotional support. And even as she spoke the greater part of what remained of my inner pool of common sense acquiesced quietly.

Vanith found a forty-year-old dress designer called Rene who came from Berne and who clearly found him a much more attractive proposition than me which had been immediately obvious to me and allowed just a small sigh of relief. After the Rene episode I felt just a little more relaxed. After all, had I not demonstrated that I could if necessary, be as orgiastic as the next woman? Maybe a single date night with Rene would be all that was necessary to improve my rating. It did not work out that way and within weeks he had re-introduced the three in a bed idea but this time we would apparently select someone suitable from a girls' club in Bayswater.

The girls' club was a real surprise as I had never been to one before – in fact lesbian activity of any kind was only just on the periphery of my personal radar. Among the crowd of women, some with names like Steve sporting short hair and men's suits, others remarkably feminine, we found a very odd young woman called Veronica who wished to be known as Rabbit. She had not yet decided upon her overall sexuality and was experimenting with smoking a pipe. She cautiously agreed to Vanith's love triangle when he promised vodka to accompany it and possibly also pizza. He was full of bounce although he said she wasn't perfect by any stretch of the imagination but she would do. Rabbit's heart wasn't in the idea and it did not prove to be a success. It was in fact a rather embarrassing little troika that thankfully did not last forever and Sunday evening saw us back to normal, eating strips of air-dried beef in front of the gas fire in my Leinster Square bedsitter. He said he was pleased with me and I was beginning to meet his expectations. He promised that in the future we would attend real orgies and have the most wonderful life together. I wished fervently for us to be slow to locate those real orgies but a small pocket of contentment was also burning in my heart and I began to feel tiny shivers of bliss.

Warning bells should have been ringing in crescendos, shrieking danger in the ears of all but the most naïve, the most trusting and the most guileless. My early sexual experiences and my subsequent rapid turnover of one-night-stands and five-day lovers had taught me very little and so instead I began to actually believe that once we two had settled down to live together we would undoubtedly live happily ever after.

I came to the conclusion that I should give up my night club job and go back to typing, revert to a more conventional life style. Surely it followed that henceforth all and sundry, including he, would treat me with true respect. Surely I would be less likely to find myself under the constant threat of threesomes, foursomes and multiples of same. I was quite surprised when the idea was greeted with some horror. He thought it was a very silly idea. For one thing I was earning far more in a night club than I ever would do in an office, and perhaps even more importantly, the nightclub sex was good for my development and most important of all, he found my nightly activities there a very sexy idea and liked to fantasise about my work. No, it would not be a good idea to make any radical changes and so I didn't.

Instead Miriam and I decided to change our place of work and we toured the nightclubs of the West End one Saturday evening applying for jobs and were hired almost immediately at a Turkish-owned place in Swallow Street called unimaginatively, The Swallow. The move brought a new set of problems with it and a rather steep learning curve for me as I was toppled headlong into the more sinister side of nightclub life where club managers extorted fees from hostesses and various threats were made to ensure they were forthcoming. Miriam, more accustomed to the practice, advised me to get over myself or get a job in a shop.

It was late summer and Regent Street was still warm each evening and swarmed with lazy Londoners and tired tourists as we made our way through them in flimsy cocktail dresses from the bus stop to the club. On such evenings I felt happy, convinced that life ahead would be good because had I not won the affection of the fascinating man I had fallen precipitously in love with? Certainly there were snags in the relationship but surely nothing that would prove insurmountable.

Sometimes at weekends, making the most of the Indian Summer, Vanith and I and went for long walks together up Queensway, through Kensington Gardens and along Knightsbridge all the way to the museums in South Kensington. Often we stopped for coffee and cake at Gloriette's in Knightsbridge and he told me stories of Vienna and of his strange, nomadic childhood where he seemed to move from one grand European hotel to another and not have a proper home. They were fascinating tales and ones I had cause to wish I had paid more attention to later when trying to recall the details for his son.

And blissfully over the months of that glorious summer I lost a great deal of weight, dwindling down to a mere seven stones and naturally he believed that I had always been slender and told me again and again that was the way he wanted me, that he was averse to fat women. During the time that I knew him I remained painfully and dutifully thin.

It was during this summer idyll that he first broached the idea of introducing ongoing infidelity into our relationship. Again, for some reason I was shocked although a young woman only slightly more worldly would have recognised the warning signs. We should not remain faithful to each other, he told me, because that was boring and so we should each be free to seek other sexual partners and for me he felt, for the most part they should be black. He found the idea of me copulating with what would these days be more appropriately called men of colour, enormously exciting. And when I paused to ask where I could find these men he said I could pick them up on the street, offer myself to them, telling them I had an overwhelming urge for intercourse, I was a woman possessed of a voracious sexual appetite. They would no doubt be surprised at first, but then interested and it would not take them long to act upon their impulses.

The first man I approached was an African priest on his way to Mass who circled around me, made the sign of the cross, and said he would pray for me. The next was a rather tall schoolboy who warned me to leave him alone and that he was going home to tell his Mum. I gave up at that point and would have despaired until I realised that there was always the power of invention. I called my black lover Percy, made him hail from Guyana and he filled the bill very nicely. Vanith was extremely pleased with me and that made him most attentive towards me so my heart nearly burst with satisfaction and love because I knew that it would be several weeks before I would need a further assignation with Percy. You could say I was learning fast.

I was very, very upset one day when he proudly announced that whilst I had been hard at work in the club the previous evening he had spent the night with an ex-girlfriend called Lucy whom he had re-met accidentally. He told me that he knew that with my new sexual maturity the thought of him penetrating

Lucy would excite me greatly. I think he was genuinely surprised when I burst into tears.

Vanith was patient and explained the things he had already explained more than once in the past. There should first of all be no petty sexual jealousy between us because he found being with a jealous woman almost impossible. In any case a Real Woman would not be jealous over such a minor matter and my distress was a sign that I had not yet quite grown sufficiently in this respect. It should be obvious to me that he preferred me to Lucy. He had the very greatest regard for me and that should be self-evident and he likened me to his favourite smoked salmon. He loved smoked salmon, he said, it was probably his favourite food, but that did not mean that from time to time he would not accept a fish paste sandwich, and really that was all that Lucy was – fish paste! He partook of fish paste at least twice weekly during those autumn months of 1962. At least he was honest about it. Well that is what I chose to believe at the time but now I tend to believe that his motivation was more complicated than simply telling the truth and that there was more than a small element of sadism involved. Vanith Lefarge took delight in observing the emotional pain he caused in others and it was this aspect of his nature that was totally at odds with the fact that he was at the same time capable of enormous kindness and concern and overwhelming gentleness.

But these opposing perceptions regarding his psyche were far from my grasp in those early days and I could only cope with the misery of the moment and wonder if I would be able to retain his undivided love and attention. Had I been just a little more detached I would perhaps have realised that he found my earning capacity enormously attractive along with my woeful inexperience and very great desire to please. My fear that he would disappear from my life if I did not immediately become the woman of his dreams was not altogether sensible.

TWO

It was over a year and a half before he finally left Christina and he said that it was because it had been so difficult to find a suitable flat for us to share together. We had looked at a great number of places but the moment we found something that seemed to be just right he decided there was something wrong with it. A large part of me was continually disappointed with this lack of progress and a much smaller part simply accepted it and was relieved at the delay in becoming involved in the extensive financial implications of helping him re-establish his business. I knew that I was going to have to be totally responsible for all the bills for a while. He had been quite honest about that.

The move was preceded by a hard, cold winter during which I had made three smaller bedsitter moves. One, chosen by Vanith, had a private telephone and bathroom and had seemed far too expensive at nine pounds a week but he was so thrilled with it that I weakly acquiesced. Often when I left for work each evening he stayed behind in my expensive little home for an hour or two to make telephone calls to mysterious friends to whom I had not yet been introduced and to take long baths. Once I believe him to have actually entertained a Fish Paste woman there whilst I was working because later I found long red hairs in the bed and in the bathroom. But by that time I had learned to keep my jealousy to myself and by way of retaliation invent assignations with Percy with which to titillate him. I believed that once we lived together properly all the infidelity nonsense might well cease.

That winter there were times when the weather was positively arctic but we were cosy with gas fires to sit by and new-fangled duvet style quilts to wrap ourselves in. The latter had been his idea and I had elected to pay for them. He spoke at length about himself and I compliantly listened and from time to time asked what I hoped were intelligent questions. Vanith loved to talk of his life, his views, his feelings and outlooks so it was not too difficult to pass those long contented winter hours.

His was a most unusual story by any stretch of the imagination. His mother, he told me, had been brought up in a castle, just a small castle, in Saxony towering above a little village where her family reigned supreme. She had married young to a wealthy man, a distant cousin of the Hapsburgs of whom I knew nothing, who died tragically on the honeymoon in Egypt. During the First World War she met Vanith's father, a man already advancing sixty, a prosperous silk merchant. When she became pregnant with Vanith's older brother, Rudy, the pair married and began to live a nomadic life in European Grand Hotels, never acquiring a proper home together. According to Vanith his mother had difficulties with giving birth and had been told she must not have a second child but when Rudy was almost seven years old she became pregnant with

Vanith. She was in her early forties and her husband in his seventies. They decided to terminate the pregnancy and went to Switzerland to the most prominent gynaecologist of the day who performed the operation. However, for some reason it did not work and the pregnancy proceeded. It was some time before they realised this and then it was too late to rectify matters and so it was said that therefore this particular child was one meant to be born, perhaps even destined for greatness.

He laid a very great emphasis upon this story, telling it to me more than once, with great solemnity. At his birth, he told me, his mother had been aware that something quite extraordinary had occurred, a totally unique being had entered the world. He did not tell me what his father had thought of the situation although many years later Rudy related that he had in fact totally abandoned the family when Vanith was four years old, unable to tolerate his second son's unruly behaviour.

Overall, it was a tale full of pathos and drama and of course I could not but be impressed and felt privileged to be very nearly sharing my life with such a significant person. The uncontrollable early behaviour that drove a wedge between his parents seemed only to confirm how very special this child was. Vanith substantiated this with tales about his school days when several junior schools in succession asked his mother to enrol him elsewhere because he refused to conform to rules. He proudly related how whilst only eight years old he had told the headmaster of a most prestigious private academy in Berlin what he could do with his bloody establishment. And I admired his audacity and compared it with my own lack of similar courage at the same age. At ten years of age he sustained a skull fracture and because he was therefore supposed not to be subjected to any stress that might cause him to become angry, from that moment on school was out of the question and private tutors were engaged. He and his mother lived together in hotels. His brother was elsewhere at boarding school and his father had long since disappeared first to New York and then to England and never lived with his family again.

At first I was told very little of his brother's life but bit by bit I learned that Rudy was a well-known yachtsman having circumnavigated the world a number of times in increasingly small craft, something that in the early 1960s had definitely become in vogue in yachting circles. Vanith felt his sibling had always sought fame and fortune rather than what he described as 'the path to enlightenment'. This path was mysterious and difficult to comprehend. It seemed to have something to do with Eastern mysticism, that of Tibet in particular and a lot of it apparently revolved around what a woman called Alexandra David-Neel had achieved during her journeys through Tibet early in the twentieth century. Apart from these rather scattered facts I grasped very little. He talked long and earnestly about her and about Tibet and about enlightenment and much of the time I daydreamed pleasantly because apart from a vague feeling that Tibet had some connection with China I barely knew where it was on the planet. Mysticism in general terms seemed to loom large to him, almost equalling the prominence he placed upon unusual sexual behaviour. An interest in matters mystical ran in his family. His paternal grandmother, hailing originally from Ireland, had apparently studied magic under a French magician, Eliphas Levi and a woman called Madame Blavatsky was said to have been a friend of the family and visited the castle in Saxony on a regular basis. At the time I had only the vaguest notion of who these people might be.

Occasionally he wanted to know about my own life and background, urging me to tell him everything about myself. Some difficulties were posed here because having listened for hours to the stories of his most illustrious family I was most reluctant to reveal certain details concerning my own, being as they were of the less savoury working class variety with a strong criminal element thrown in for good measure. However, he seemed quite thrilled when he heard about my gin drinking, palm reading, diddicai grandmother, once he understood the term and realised that she had burst triumphantly upon the palm reading and lucky heather selling scene, as a half breed from a distant and decidedly errant tribe of horse dealers. The fact that even semi decent travellers avoided her if they could did little to quench his ardent desire to meet her. He quickly decided that it was this somewhat distant Romany heritage that made me what he termed 'fey and capricious'. Having never been described in this way previously I was more than a little flattered and when he urged me to hone the skills of second sight I must surely have, I promised to do so. I was uneasy though as I had no idea how it could be done and working towards improving my sexual appeal was taking up a fair amount of emotional energy at the time. But his request went dutifully on the list of improvements I must make.

It was during that hard winter, when we spent many hours inside avoiding the frozen wasteland of Queensway and beyond, that he made two propositions that worried me. One was that we should try taking LSD and the other was that he should hypnotize me in order to set me free from some of my inhibitions. Both these suggestions left me feeling unenthusiastic. During the first few weeks of our relationship he had very kindly purchased some good quality marijuana for me to smoke and instead of making me feel sexually liberated as intended, it had caused me to sink into a mini depression and sob for an hour about the sad state of the world. Vanith had not been pleased and so when we tried it again I developed convoluted techniques for not inhaling the smoke if at all possible whilst rapidly appearing to ascend to the verge of nymphomania. This had to some extent appeased him for which I was grateful because I had always been far too cowardly to try drugs of any kind even when those around me were doing so and urging me to join them. Consequently the LSD suggestion filled me with panic and I quickly opted for hypnotism. As luck would have it, it turned out that he was somewhat of an expert in the art of hypnotism and had deftly hypnotized a number of his lady friends over the past ten years or so, mostly in order to free them from a range of irksome inhibitions. He told me a great deal about how it worked, how important the subconscious was, and went on to reveal even more about the lives and work of Freud and Jung together with more than I ever thought possible about dreams and what they really meant. If you dream of losing your teeth, he said, then it was a sign of serious illness and if you dream of riding a horse, in particular a black stallion, then it means you are at last in control of your sexuality. I determined to get to that happy state by degrees and perhaps via a piebald mare. The sum total of these lectures took up more than a week of frozen afternoons and so put action of any kind nicely into the future.

However, the initiation into hypnotism came long before the thaw and though I approached it with some trepidation I very quickly discovered that either I was a very poor subject and a very good actress or the whole hypnotism business was complete nonsense. Vanith seemed to accept that he had 'put me under' with no problem at all and he also accepted that I later recalled nothing of our conversations whilst in that happy state. The truth was somewhat removed from this perception. The conversations were naturally enough primarily of a sexual nature and I was careful not to reveal anything to him of the unpleasant incidents with uncles and older cousins that occurred after the death of my father. Those matters stayed in the closet, growing ever dustier among the many secrets and lies of a seriously dysfunctional family. To explain away my mysterious inability to be a truly sexually developed woman I had to invent vague fears which he readily accepted. The good thing was that he believed the therapy to be working. The bad thing was that the LSD idea was not going to go away and although I tried hard to avoid the experience, Vanith's friend Max, a jazz musician with time on his hands, helpfully accessed the drug for us and before I knew it I had consumed it on a sugar lump placed into my cup of instant coffee. We were on the way to the tube station before I realised that something odd was happening, and it was long afterwards that I came to know that Vanith himself had not joined me in this particular exciting little weekend interlude. I alone experienced the joys and delights of a spoonful of sugar laced with Lysergic Acid over the next thirty-six hours or so. At best it was mostly unpleasant and at worst terrifying. None of it felt real and though the hours inevitably passed, time itself took an odd and dreamlike quality as I fought to escape from a series of traumatizing delusions such as imagining I could halt the buses on Bayswater Road simply stepping in front of them as they hurtled into the wintry night. I have since taken great care to never again add sugar to hot drinks.

That winter eventually passed but before it did so completely we finally found the perfect flat to live in together as a result of Vanith's friends the Bycrofts buying a house in what was then a dilapidated part of Clerkenwell, and offering to let us rent the top two floors. I was ecstatically happy that at last we would be together properly, that Vanith would be able to re-establish his business, that we could perhaps become just an ordinary couple, living an ordinary and predictable life. What utter bliss that would be.

I realised that I would have to continue working at night in order to finance this longed-for state but strangely I had come to accept the night club life, even enjoy the glamour a little and it was certainly well paid. In any case there was not much point in disliking it as Vanith had made in abundantly clear that club hostessing was his career of choice for me. It was not as if I had ever expected more and in any case he explained kindly, in order to get into a proper career structure I would have to have some kind of university degree and of course that was out of the question. It did not occur to me to argue this point; some older members of my family were totally illiterate, having never attended school at all, the younger generation attended mostly but certainly not a day past their fifteenth birthdays. None of us were ever going to set the world on fire academically and that seemed good enough to me.

He had described his four years at the Medical School in Dublin in some detail and I knew that for reasons which were complicated and which I promptly forgot, he then transferred to the School of Music to study piano. The whole saga of his university studies was just that – a saga. He had on several occasions regaled me with the extended version of the story but always, halfway through the events, I stopped listening and so I never truly grasped what took place. Briefly he claimed to have been a student of some considerable ability and certainly interested in the subject of medicine, surgery in particular, which was evidenced by his continuing interest in providing an abortion service throughout the network of his friends; he simply had not had quite enough interest at the time to finish his degree. He wanted to switch to his true love – music. Even that did not work out well for him in the end, mostly due to the treachery of his mother and an aunt in America, 'Nothing on earth is as malevolent as a treacherous woman,' he observed, slowly shaking his head from side to side in a manner that was to become comfortably familiar over the years.

Although he made it abundantly clear how he felt about his mother, who had clearly treated him very badly and tried to control him completely throughout his life, I could never rationalize in my own mind what the true relationship had been between Vanith and his father, who had been born so long ago that he was a very little boy at the time of the American Civil War and had lived in America for many years when it was still an exciting place to be and cowboys fought Indians on the plains. His father seemed to have had much more to do with brother Rudy than with Vanith but possibly that was simply because he was seven years older and in any case his behaviour as a child had never been out of the ordinary. There were parts of the family story that were confusing but what I did understand was that for years old Mr Lefarge lived in a large house in Surrey, moving later to another house in Devon. In his latter years he employed a full time nurse, a Miss Mackay, who looked after him until his death in the late 1950s. Vanith's mother had fully expected that she and her sons would inherit the house in Devon or the proceeds from its sale but in fact in a confused state he left a final Will leaving all his possessions to Miss Mackay and she being a feckless and stupid woman, prone to drunkenness and gambling, simply spent the lot in a very short space of time and ended up living in a broken down caravan on Exmoor. I absorbed much if not all of these domestic chronicles during the time before we lived together and it seemed to me that Vanith's family was that of which fairy tales are made. It was possible that although I later discovered most of what he had told me was true, at the time I only half believed the stories, so improbable did they seem. I did not imagine him to be telling lies because he had frequently impressed upon me that he never, ever told lies, but rather I viewed his tales as emerging from his own perception of family events, rather like a small child's re-telling of an episode that looms important in his life.

I was more focused on the future, living in our Clerkenwell flat as a contented couple where we would be too busy working to build that future to get side tracked by drug taking, hypnotism or Bayswater girls' clubs. I would work hard towards becoming the kind of woman he so clearly desired, no matter how difficult it might be to discover what the elusive secret to real womanhood was. If I succeeded then things would undoubtedly change between us and he would be proud of me. It was worrying that despite his often attentive behaviour towards me, he was still very critical, and he definitely kept large parts of his life from me. Miriam, who had known him since she was fifteen years old, told me that he had always been secretive with people, observing that he did not even like to tell people what he had for breakfast and it was best not to enquire.

It was true that he hated questions of a personal nature and it was at times quite difficult to know in advance what might actually constitute a personal question. He was quick to anger whenever I asked what he had done on particular evenings whilst I had been working, belligerently querying why on earth I needed to know. I obviously couldn't admit that I wanted to know because I was jealously wondering if he had spent the evening with a rival so I would murmur something about just making conversation and he would advise me not to speak at all if that is what I thought reasonable conversation consisted of. And so I was silent sometimes for hours.

The fact that he had friends he was unable or unwilling to introduce me to niggled much to the forefront of my mind and once when I had momentarily abandoned all caution and reason about upsetting him, I courageously brought the subject up and told him how unhappy it made me to be a secret. Was he perhaps ashamed of me I ventured to ask. To my surprise he did not get angry but explained quite soothingly that there were some people he simply was not able to introduce me to no matter how much he might wish to and this was because of the work I was doing in nightclubs; it was just too difficult to explain something like that. I said that there was no real reason to actually tell them all the gory details and he said that he did not like to be dishonest with people. He added that my constant questions and resentment about his friendships were becoming a burden and he was beginning to have doubts about our ongoing relationship. A jealous woman was an emotional encumbrance he explained. And so amid many tears I apologised and vowed to do a better job at curbing my insatiable desire to know everything about him and his friends, because once we actually lived together as a couple I was sure that these things would undoubtedly sort themselves out. He could not, after all, keep me a secret forever.

We moved to Clerkenwell in November of that year and although the expense involved in setting up the sound studio on the top floor was considerably more than I had anticipated, he became totally immersed in it and for a while we lived an almost average and routine life there together. I was supremely happy that he no longer went home to Christina each evening but instead was still there working in the upstairs studio when I came back from work at three or four in the morning. And at weekends we could be together all the time and I even began to cook regularly, roasting chickens and once even a rib of beef. He inspired me by talking a great deal about the kind of food he had eaten as a small child and his favourite dishes ordered in hotel dining rooms, Crayfish Tails in Butter Sauce, Chicken Fricassee, and something called an Emperor's Omelette, filled with fresh fruit that spilled out onto the plate. I scoured the library shelves for cook books and worked diligently at reproducing these dishes for him. And when Saturday evening came and he perceived the aroma of tender chicken pieces simmering gently alongside sliced mushrooms in a creamy lemony sauce he would sometimes whoop with delight and sit down to consume a large quantity. Irrationally I began to think that good food might even cure him of the odd sexual desires and fixations. They had abated a little during the move to Clerkenwell and for a few weeks following it, but after a while emerged again bright and bushy tailed as ever.

I had tried my best to develop an interest in the aberrant practices without much success. Though he told me often enough that I was verging on frigidity in some areas of my development, a larger part of me now sensibly disbelieved this. I was not attracted to other women, I did not care to be in bed with more than one person – preferably Vanith – at any one time, I could not work up much enthusiasm for wantonly picking up Jamaican train drivers or ticket collectors on their way to work and offering myself to them for a few minutes in a dark alley. Furthermore, watching him have oral sex with another man did nothing much for my libido either. You could say that I was conservative in this respect though Vanith told me it was more to do with being brought up a Roman Catholic. He also believed that my ambivalent attitude to my dead father was odd.

Looking back on this period of my life from the safety of only twenty years into the future as I cooked for my New Zealand family, I allowed myself to wonder at my total lack of good sense. The fact that I was obsessively in love with him no longer appealed as an excuse for my ongoing acceptance of what was a very bad situation rapidly getting worse as we escalated towards the weekend orgy scene.

However, the lowest point of all for me came just before we stepped upon that carousel of regular Saturday night revellers. From the safety of my Auckland kitchen that early evening of reverie in 1983 it still sent tiny shivers of disbelief through my consciousness. I recalled the details of the Saturday when Vanith decided it would be fun to hire a couple of Bayswater streetwalkers to join us in bed for an hour or two. We could walk up and down Queensway he said and I could approach likely girls and proposition them. When I pointed out faintly that we would have to pay them his response was, 'Of course – but if it's not worth a few pounds it's hardly worth going out at all for the evening is it?'

I knew without question that I really did not want to do this both for myself and also for the other women who would have to be paid. I also felt extreme anger at the absurd and bizarre idea that I should work from Monday to Friday as a paid sexual partner in order to hire sex workers on Saturday for the titillation of the man I loved so desperately. But he was insistent. We had not been anywhere much or done anything much for weeks, he said, and it would be a lot of fun. However, it was not much fun and an hour or so later it half occurred to Vanith that Sheena from South Shields and Mitzi from Wolverhampton were not in our flat to enjoy themselves and extend their sexual horizons. He observed with some degree of surprise once they had left, 'I don't think either of them were really interested in sex, do you? Both of them seemed as repressed as you are yourself. And I agreed.

THREE

We burst upon the Saturday evening orgy scene shortly after the depressing episode with Sheena and Mitzi and although I have thought long and hard about exactly how it happened and who it might have been who introduced us to it, I cannot pinpoint the facts. Of one thing I am certain: you needed a proper introduction into this sacred little circle because they certainly did not admit just anyone. Lone men most certainly could not 'belong' because you needed to be a proper couple and the female part of the partnership should if at all possible be young and attractive. Naturally enough this was not always achievable because for the most part men attended with their wives and the wife of one Essex sub-postmaster was decidedly overweight and looked unsightly in her purple underwear. At least that was my opinion at the time when the flesh of my own thighs was not as frankly flaccid as it became years later. But to attend with a female was of such great consequence that it seemed to matter less than one would imagine if she was of the not altogether attractive variety. Not all the women were of the sub-post-master's wife's ilk in any case but conjuring up the memories all these years later immediately brings her to mind though I have long forgotten her name.

It would be true to say that most of the men were pushing middle age to its outer limits and more than slightly balding and a high number of them represented the professions being doctors, lawyers or accountants or military men. Clive was a barrister of some renown and at least three Saturdays out of five he was our host in his tall, imposing house in Campden Hill. He did not have a wife or female partner but he was allowed to deviate from the established rules because not only did he have a very pleasant venue for the parties with resident staff who prepared splendid dinners, he was also happy to hire at some expense a number of extremely attractive young women, often two or three at any one time, who were described as 'models'. Even taking into account the fact that he could well afford to do so, he more than pulled his weight. One of the hindrances regarding accepting his hospitality was the fact that his sexual preference revolved around sadomasochism and he owned a wide collection of whips and canes which he used with skill and dexterity. This was all very well if you happened to be an actual run of the mill masochist or even if you had been hired for the evening, but if none of this applied then there was a problem for some. But not a problem of any great proportion because Clive was a charismatic and charming man, generous in the extreme, and the women around and about him did their best to please. Once I recovered from the shock of being regularly caned or whipped in public for the entertainment of the guests, I found I got used to the pain and all in all I began to find the orgy weekends preferable to Vanith's previous entertainment ideas.

On the whole they were more predictable and the people involved reasonably pleasant.

Generally the women were considerably less keen on deviant sex than the men, except the models of course who were always enthusiastic. I was simply relieved that after a number of false starts, Vanith and I had at last found a hobby we could share, one that filled those perilously unoccupied Saturday evenings, and that once I got used to it, seemed to be relatively harmless. I did not expect to enjoy the activities and by and large I was not disappointed. Vanith was totally thrilled for many months, to have sexual access to the young models in particular, but also to meet so many pillars of the community – a couple of whom were interested in the same intellectual ideas as himself concerning quantum physics or the thoughts of Nietzsche. For instance, Clive himself had read *Thus Spoke Zarathustra'* with total understanding and was not fearful of robust discussion.

The situation deftly kept the man I so obsessively adored from Fish Paste women, minimizing the secrets between us. I was still naively confident that slowly his interest in all these activities would fade and he would become as keen as I was to have a monogamous relationship, a cosy home and perhaps at some stage even consider the idea of parenthood. Well I did point out didn't I that I was trusting to the point of hovering on the cusp of simple-mindedness. That was how things were.

In those far off days of the early 1960s life was different. With no internet, virtual sex and pornography sites available to all at the flick of a finger, men like Vanith, and even run of the mill respectable sadists such as Clive, had to make their own amusements, provide as best they could and according to their means, for their own sexual amusement. Back then many of the ideas we now take for granted now such as Gay Rights and High Street Brothels, were simply unavailable at whim because certain activities were actually illegal. This meant that homosexual men without a support network were forced to trawl the public lavatories of London suburbs to meet others of the same ilk and the exciting details of a brothel were passed on in a most clandestine and unsatisfactory manner. Deviation houses such as Sophie Sanderson's in Pimlico where I later worked once Daniel was born, were hush-hush affairs and even knowing someone who knew someone who had firm knowledge of one was astounding. They certainly did not advertise in the columns of local newspapers as they do today even here in socially backward and morally distant New Zealand.

So many things have changed in the intervening years, such as smoking in restaurants and allowing pet dogs to foul the pavements with impunity. You could say as one set of freedoms increases, another diminishes. Nowadays the revelations regarding the parties attended by Stephen Ward would not raise an eyebrow but should he still be with us and be unwise enough to light a cigarette whilst waiting for his fish course at Rules Restaurant, now that would be a totally different matter. Life changes and if we are under the age of fifty we barely notice that we are absorbing and accepting a new set of social parameters such as abortion on demand and gay marriage. Just a few old fogies and a proportion of the unworldly cling on to the social customs and traditions of past decades. Strangely enough I find myself numbered among that unbending sub-group of society, regularly offended to be casually addressed by my Christian name by all and sundry whilst I still call the plumber Mr Smith, and astonished by the acceptance of others of my age group who cheerfully embrace the idea of their daughters producing lesbian partners and sets of test tube twins. In short I could not in any way be described as forward thinking or permissive and my children would heartily concur with that.

Even in the sixties I was never really as liberal as I would have liked to appear and at the time that was one of the personal characteristics I worked diligently towards changing. I believed it was admirable to be possessed of progressive views on life and partnership, to be non-judgmental and tolerant, to not care one iota if Vanith went off for an hour or two with Fish Paste. The modern equivalent would be to support the mores of global warming I suppose, or devote time to saving whales from beaching. After all a great many people do and are described by others as Right Thinking. These days I shudder and shy away from anything that might move me closer towards that repellent group of sanctified citizens .

Vanith and I were 'swingers' in one way or another for the next two years. Mostly we attended swinging parties in inner London and at times hosted them ourselves in Clerkenwell. Sometimes we were invited to weekend events on country estates. Despite my initial hopes, I probably do not need to elaborate upon the fact that nothing of the connubial harmony and togetherness I had so fervently wished for actually came to pass between us and had I been just a little more worldly I would have foreseen the way things would develop.

During that time Vanith bought a car, a green Mini station wagon with a smart wooden trim, and somehow or other I elected to pay for it. I didn't mind too much, reasoning that it would be fun having our own transport. I thought he might drive me to work some evenings so I could avoid the bus journey from the stop outside Sadler's Wells Theatre, and the trip down Rosebery Avenue, along Clerkenwell Road, New Oxford Street and Shaftesbury Avenue all the way to Piccadilly. It did not take too long once I was actually on the bus but the walk to the stop took six or seven minutes, and invariably I had just missed the No.19 and the wait for the next one was always another six or seven minutes. This was not too arduous in summer but in winter in the rain in six inch heels it could be very unpleasant, even hazardous, and after all we were now car owners. But he never suggested that he might provide such a service, unless he was

46

on his way out to visit a friend when, should he be driving vaguely towards the West End, he might suggest dropping me off. I did not complain because at least he did teach me to drive and maybe I would never have got around to learning had he not done so. Once I had passed my test I was sometimes allowed to take the wheel if he was also in the car, though never trusted to do so entirely alone. Still, the skill stood me in great stead when I settled in New Zealand where at the time there was no reliably established transport system and waiting a mere seven or eight minutes for the next bus would have been deemed a first class service. At the time the buses from the suburb where I lived into the centre of the city operated Monday to Friday only, were two hours apart and even then could be anything up to twenty-five minutes early or late at the whim of the particular driver. No wonder even fifteen-year-olds held driving licenses. These days the service is more frequent and reliable but even so most people still drive to their designated destinations if they are serious about actually getting there at all. It was, and still is, a different way of life and to be honest one I never imagined myself taking part in, dedicated Londoner that I always was and to digress a little, still am. The abiding love for a city was something that would only become evident for me in the future. The only love I knew of then whilst still in my twenties, was that which I had for Vanith Lefarge and the only misery was in the thought that I might lose him completely at some stage. This notion plagued me together with, and to a lesser extent, that of reaching thirty because he had so often told me that he viewed women over thirty as past their prime and unspeakably unappealing. I worked towards staying as youthful and alluring as was possible although in those days nobody concerned themselves too much about diet and exercise, and most of us smoked, often to excess. I smoked because I thought it made me seem more sophisticated and l was able to dismiss the resulting nicotine-stained teeth, sallow complexion, and wardrobe hopelessly impregnated with stale tobacco odour. In fact I never gave these matters a thought and Vanith himself smoked Turkish tobacco, and later rolled his own to save money, therefore these effects upon his person were heightened and accentuated. We gave little consideration to the cost of our combined smoking habit because it was simply a necessity, and neither of us was in the habit of drinking much, a habit that made a considerable dent into the budgets of some of our contemporaries. Miriam for example drank a great deal, usually vodka, and also smoked a great deal, and worried a great deal about her diet, spending a significant part of her income on health foods from a shop in Baker Street because, she explained to me, their produce was generated largely without harmful additives or pesticides. I could never work up much enthusiasm for health food outlets. Their goods looked bland and unattractive to me and I did not care much for the look of most of the customers, earnest young women with cane baskets, no make-up and grey headscarves, sometimes carrying toddlers with names like Edith and George that were only to become re-popularized thirty years later. Miriam in her high-heeled boots and tightly belted black leather coat was something of an exception among the general clientele. From time to time she entertained us to intimate dinner parties in the flat on the corner of Praed Street and talked at length about the totally organic farm in Lincolnshire her potatoes came from and how different their taste was from those in the Praed Street greengrocer. I could never distinguish the difference myself.

There were at least some stable periods for us during this time, and we did not spend all of our spare time attending swinging parties. Clive the arch swinger himself often had interludes when he seemed to abandon sadistic orgies and instead cooked magnificent dinners for friends – often those he termed 'straight' friends, which meant that they did not attend the entertainment he put on for his swinging friends. Vanith and I were in the happy position of somehow falling into both categories though I never quite worked out how it was we came to be so favoured. Clive's dinners invariably followed the opening of the shooting season when he spent time at his estate in the North and returned with a selection of game to be hung in his game larder adjacent to the kitchen. He enjoyed cooking on these occasions although of course he always had the help and assistance of his live-in staff. It was he who introduced me to Jugged Hare and taught me much of what I know now about preparing it. He also served us grouse, partridge, guinea fowl and once some spectacular roast venison. His game dinners were usually served with red cabbage and followed by Old English Fruit Fools such as gooseberry or apple and blackberry. His wines were first-class, a good time was had by all, with Clive himself regaling us with exaggerated and hilarious stories of his early days as a Barrister. There was never a mention of whips, canes or sexual deviation of any kind and it was often during these evenings that I was able to begin to believe that my life was a prosaically normal one, pretend that Vanith and I were really a couple, even married perhaps and attending a social activity in that somewhat mundane capacity. It is with considerable horror that I now examine the depth of my pitiful attachment to him. At times it seemed that the deeper my distress became, the greater was his pleasure in increasing my level of misery which he did month by month in small increments in a variety of ways, the details of which have mostly been lost but which were invariably humiliating.

These were techniques that could only result in a robust desire for revenge and even then there were times when my mind sifted through a variety of reprisal scenarios, all of which I then discarded as impractical. His death seemed to be the only conclusion that would help to assuage the torrent of wounded feelings but I could not visualize how this could be prudently achieved. I did not believe I could be capable of murder except by poison but the only poisons I could think of would be hard to come by and even if I did manage to procure something effective, there was still the possibility I may be called to account for the death. Hiring a hit man was a reasonable idea and one I gave some consideration to but even in those heady days of the 1960s, there was considerable expense involved. A death by accident would be most welcome but he was not prone to accidents, indeed he was a careful driver for example, never putting himself at risk. He was most unlikely to succumb to an illness and in fact seemed always to be in vigorous good health no matter how poor his general diet and how many cigarettes he smoked and how little exercise he took. Of course all this was long before he developed the series of health problems leading to events that would culminate in his death forty-five years later. Even had I known what lay in store for him I could not have easily utilized the information at that time. In any case, luckily for Vanith Lefarge, I had not yet matured completely into the bitter and unforgiving person I was ultimately to become as far as all matters concerning him were concerned. I would have been startled by the future depth of my animosity because although my life to that point had not been always comfortable or stress-free, I had not had occasion to feel open-ended hatred for anyone. Vanith was destined to occupy a position in my future recall where even the hint of memory of my years with him would produce an almost physical response that descended into misery and desolation so strong that I would have to actively fight to dismiss it from my mind.

I could perhaps have dealt with all the unhappy emotions of the following few years far more effectively had I known that an acceptable revenge would eventually emerge and take place, but my Romany links were at best tenuous and I did not know anything of what lay ahead. The particular technology that finally facilitated retribution was very much in the future, the dark wasteland of the 1960s being devoid even of cordless phones and therefore all forms of electronic messaging were a very long way distant.

Admittedly there were also occasional good times when Vanith concentrated his entire attention upon me, spending a great deal of time talking to me about himself, his life and his beliefs because he loved an audience, particularly one as receptive and undemanding as myself. He spoke about occult philosophy or Magic and the people in his family, on both his mother's and his father's side it appeared, who had harboured an enormous interest in the subject. When I told him of my grandmother's remedy for warts and other minor physical problems, he immediately said she was a witch and that she had passed on to me her knowledge and that therefore I was something of a witch myself. I accepted this evaluation though I had considerable doubts. Oddly enough, I found I still did not believe everything he told me. He said that magic always worked effectively because 'all thoughts have a tendency to materialize and therefore we must all of us at all times take care when thinking deeply, most particularly when wishing harm to others...'

'But,' I ventured, 'If we wish them harm – possibly because they have done us harm, isn't it more than reasonable that those harmful thoughts should materialize and bring them bad luck?'

He told me that where Magic was concerned, there was great danger that such harmful thoughts would bounce back and harm the person they emanated from – those practicing Magic must take extraordinary care to protect themselves.

'How can a person take adequate care?' I wanted to know. Of course I wanted to know.

'The protection exercises are far from easy to absorb and understand,' he said, 'and exhausting to put into practice. None of this should be undertaken lightly. Magic is both magnificent and potent but it can so easily go drastically wrong and cause enormous harm.'

With more enthusiasm he taught me about music. His love of music at times transcended even his love of sex and it was impossible not to become immersed in his excitement. Later I knew that it had been because of his influence that I learned so much about Paganini, Chopin and Beethoven and eventually could easily distinguish between the voices of Caruso and Gigli and the playing of Menuhin and Heifitz. This preoccupation with music was something that was passed on to his son in whom it was to become an even more overwhelming passion.

When Vanith first claimed to be Fully Enlightened I had little idea what such a happy state entailed. He talked about the last Buddha and how to reach a full understanding of knowledge and I came to grasp a little more, enough to realise that the state he spoke of would never be something I would personally have to grapple with. Life as a Fully Enlightened One was clearly not easy and demanded a great deal of innate ability to absorb and process unusual information. If human intelligence was what it needed then I was never going to make the grade. This was something of a relief.

During the second year we lived together he revealed in greater detail the path he had to struggle along to achieve his present state of knowledge and explained that although it had awarded him power so that he could recognise evil when he came across it, that had not made the path any easier. He now leaned further and further towards Eastern Mysticism rather than any kind of Western religion and whilst doing so had developed something akin to extreme hatred towards the Catholic church, hurling regular abuse at Jesus Christ but saving most of his odium for what he called 'that harlot, Mary, mother of God.' As a lapsed Catholic who at one stage had more than toyed with the idea of life as a nun, this quite understandably was somewhat shocking to me. I waited for the thunderbolt from above that most lapsed Catholics wait for in the presence of such naked blasphemy and when it did not eventuate I was surprised. One way or another Vanith managed to instil a great deal of fear into me. Two or three years later when he was insisting that our child be aborted, I was only too aware of the possible consequences of violating his instructions but it is surprising how resolute a woman can be when protecting a child.

And it also came as a surprise decades later when he failed to realise that he was in daily correspondence with an imposter. On the other hand fraudsters pull the wool over the eyes of lonely old men on a daily basis. It's even possible that he had been more than half in love with Persephone Faith Callahan and his greatest desire was that she should be returned to him.

FOUR

I did not consciously set out to become pregnant, or at least that is what I always claim in any discussion about what happened. More truthfully I do not now choose to think that I did. In any event the constant parade of sexual partners both workwise and socially seemed to have led to a series of low-grade gynaecological problems and I was finally told at the tender age of twenty-six, that I needed a hysterectomy. Understandably this was something of a shock, and whereas I cannot say I had been previously much preoccupied with having babies, once faced with the prospect of being totally barren, the pregnant state seemed suddenly highly desirable. These days I am certain that a responsible gynaecologist would not contemplate removing the uterus of a young woman with quite such thoughtless abandon. Today I do not believe the reply to my tearful, 'Isn't there any hope of me ever having a baby then?' would be a shrug followed by, 'Well I daresay pigs might fly.' But like it or not that's how it was then before political correctness and patients' rights took a firmer hold. I was advised that in preparation for my operation I should stop taking the Pill as the high dosage variety interfered with the process of blood clotting and might have negative effects from an operative point of view. I did not understand much of this at all but I dutifully stopped taking it anyway.

It was during this period that I went upon a whim to Madame Sandra in Oxford Street with my friend Stella. Madame Sandra told fortunes on the second floor of a building close to Tottenham Court Road on Thursdays, Fridays and Saturdays from eleven am until four pm with a break for lunch. She told me that I was unhappy about a man to which remark I remained resolutely silent, determined not to give her clues and she added that I would leave him soon anyway and by Easter the following year would give birth to a son who would be a great comfort to me. The child would give rise to considerable concern at birth, she added, but he would come through all his problems very well indeed and I was therefore not to worry too much.

Given the fact that in order to give birth by Easter 1968 I would have to be already pregnant at the time of my consultation with her in September 1967, my silence grew ever more determined. She said that within just a few years I was going to leave England altogether and go to live in a land of sunshine and white buildings with a man I already knew, a man with initials GH. I left feeling extremely disillusioned with those who proclaim an ability to see the events of the future and though I sifted through all my friends and acquaintances I knew of no-one with the initials GH. Stella thought I ought to keep an open mind and although I might not be pregnant right now, who knew what tomorrow might bring?

Vanith had greeted the news of my proposed hysterectomy with attentive awareness bordering on cheerfulness. With his keen interest in all things medical he liked to be kept fully informed of such developments. He also advised me that not being able to become pregnant would be quite wonderful for me and I should be grateful because there were a lot of women who would positively envy me.

In fact I had become pregnant almost immediately I stopped taking the Pill, possibly within days of the consultation with the politically incorrect gynaecologist. Having been pregnant once before I was well aware what the strangely unsettled and nauseous feeling assailing me a few days later was likely to mean. An overwhelming revulsion at a whiff of roasting coffee beans in Shaftesbury Avenue as I stepped from the bus confirmed it. I began to feel warmer and more positive towards Madame Sandra and when I phoned Stella she said well she had told me to keep an open mind hadn't she?

I rang the surgeon and told him that I did not think I should have the operation as I was now pregnant. He gave me a new appointment to discuss what he said was Quite Impossible and when I sat before him he became much nicer than before and told me stories of patients who had believed themselves to be pregnant when about to have a hysterectomy. It was not that unusual, he explained quite kindly, and I would come to understand it in time but in the interim he would refer me to the hospital Psychiatric Department where they would be able to counsel me more efficiently than he could.

My feelings at this stage were ambivalent to some extent but I was well aware that any decision I made would be of supreme significance to my future mental stability and I therefore wanted the decision to be made within my own time frame rather than Vanith's or that of the hospital medical staff. For that reason I decided not to tell Vanith and he, for his own good reasons, was never able to quite forgive me.

I kept my appointments with the Psychiatric Department which were on a weekly basis and each time I seemed to end up with a different doctor. I even took the pills they gave me at first but was made so dazed and weak by them that after a week or two I threw them away instead. Now I know more concerning the harm powerful drugs can do to a fetus I am shocked at the possible damage that could have been done to Daniel, who seems, despite some deficiencies in his personality, to have dodged a fair proportion of the bullets.

I decided to preserve rather than destroy my baby. My reasons were pedestrian, run of the mill. If I was to believe something of what the surgeon had found when examining me and recommending a hysterectomy, then this child might be the only one I would ever have. And if I was to have a child at all, my father of preference was Vanith, with all his shortcomings and already realising only too well that he would be most displeased at the prospect. I still retained the small hope that he might by some miracle undergo a dramatic change of thinking, and whilst not electing to be father of the year, might come to enjoy his son or daughter. And should I be totally wrong and have to part from him, then at least I would have his child to emotionally sustain me. It would be easier, I decided, to face a future without him if I was left with at least a part of him in the shape of his child. And the more I thought about this the more determined I became.

Neither the surgeon nor the various psychiatrists gave any consideration to the possibility that my pregnancy might be real rather than imagined. I was still treated with sympathetic understanding on my weekly visits to St. Bartholemew's Hospital where some of the unpleasant facts of my relationship with Vanith were listened to with disbelief. I was advised to leave him as soon as possible, given more pills and sent off with a white card on which was written the time of my next appointment. I spent less time in the flat and more time in Clerkenwell Library studying the various stages of fetal development which began to fascinate me as I marvelled increasingly at the prospect of becoming a parent. You could say that I was now sadly out of touch with reality.

When I was eighteen weeks pregnant a new and rather more pro-active psychiatrist told me that if I was pregnant as I still insisted, then by this time the baby would be developed sufficiently for us to both see the spine in outline and he proposed to send me down to X-ray in order that I should be convinced of the error in my thinking. I cheerfully agreed because I knew I would be thrilled to see the child's spine and the possible harm an X-ray might do to the child did not of course occur to me. That was the day they began at last to believe me. I felt a bit sorry for the psychiatrist as he glumly held the film up to the light, screwing up his eyes and commenting on the curve of Daniel's spine, '...there it is all right.'

I was ecstatic to see my baby, curled up and absolutely real. I wondered if it was a boy or a girl and even began to consider names as I sat there somehow inert inside a golden bubble of delight that was so warm and all-comforting that the discomfiture of the doctor was all but lost. I celebrated with coffee and an almond slice in the hospital cafeteria and I wondered how long I could stay with Vanith before he discovered my exhilarating secret. I vowed to be as helpful as possible over the next few weeks and avoid any conflict with him. Luckily he was at this stage in the process of working with my DJ friend Stan Douglas on a project which entailed taping weekly radio request programmes where homesick Jamaicans were interviewed and sent love messages and favourite pieces of music home to Jamaica. So focused was he on this work that we even attended fewer swinger parties than usual and I could turn my attention once again to the kitchen. I cooked his favourite meals from a German cookbook borrowed from the library and did as I was bid around the upstairs studio. The pregnancy seemed to make little physical difference to my overall shape and although I had a fair amount of morning sickness, as Vanith was rarely awake until eleven am he managed to miss most of the drama, and indeed by twenty weeks that phase had well and truly passed.

And life could have progressed in a fairly satisfactory manner if it had not been for the excruciating bouts of abdominal pain I suddenly began to experience, usually in the middle of the night. It is not easy to resign oneself to simply endure severe pain, or at least it was not easy for me to do so and I began to panic. Later, the obstetrician who finally delivered Daniel told me that he thought it was all due to damage done to a fallopian tube during my previous abortion but that was only an assumption. One night the pain became so severe that Vanith was fearful and took me to St. Bartholomew's Hospital where I was asked if I was pregnant and I said I was not but inevitably of course found to be lying.

It is now quite difficult to remember the sequence of events that followed because the only thing that emerges with any clarity even after forty years is the extent of his terrible rage. Once the pain subsided and I left the relative safety of the hospital ward a day or two later, he told me quite clearly and without any obvious rancour that I had become pregnant against his will and that he would be forced to undertake a terrible reprisal against me if I did not have an immediate abortion. When I suggested that rather than abort the child I would leave, he said that was not really an option. I tried to explain that because of my pelvic problems this might be the only child I was ever likely to have and he told me that he was not interested.

'If you do not get rid of this child,' he said, sitting cross legged on the bed and picking idly at the flower print on the duvet cover, 'you will force me into actions I do not want to take.' His quiet tone made me very afraid, but still I wondered if he proposed to commit a murder in the middle of a Clerkenwell winter day when the trees in the square outside were stark and bare and everything seemed normal, ordinary. He continued to explain in calm and conversational tones, 'I will curse you and your child into all eternity...I will place a demon on your shoulder that will never leave you...you will have bad luck wherever you go...you will never rid yourself of my curse.' It was a promise he would repeat hourly during those days, often hissing it into my ear as I slept. But he was not actually proposing to physically do me harm. Good news! Nevertheless I was uncertain about the reality of his demons or the extent of his power.

'I will protect myself with prayer,' I suggested. His reaction threw me into a new dimension of terror. 'You might think that your fucking Virgin Mary can help you but you will soon find that particular whore is powerless against my magic... you can never escape, never, never, never... and should you try to get away on a vessel as big as the Queen Mary it will sink!'

He was packing to go out of London for a week on a pre-arranged visit to his mother in Munich as he spoke and I knew he was attempting to paralyse me with fear so that I would simply obey. And had I been able to do so, I would probably at that stage acquiesced. In fact I think I promised I would have the child aborted during his absence and before he left some hours later even told him I had made telephone contact with an abortionist; at least that is how I remember it now. And after he left I sat for a long time and wondered what to do because by that time I was very, very afraid but no longer capable of just disappearing from his life. After several hours of inactivity I slept. My decisions over the next few days were remarkably imprudent and examining them now from the security of a humid Auckland summer Sunday afternoon I appreciate that they sound highly improbable. I even have to remind myself that it really did happen this way and I am not applying some kind of writer's license to the events. Perhaps I was suffering a form of temporary insanity at that time and I now vaguely wonder if there is a proper term for this particular madness and how many people fall prey to it given the right circumstances.

I decided to fake an abortion in order to protect the child inside me for a little longer. I did not contemplate what might happen when Vanith discovered this further duplicity. In fact I thought no further than protecting the child from the abortion I had promised to have before the following Friday, the day of his return.

It's all very well for whoever the present reader might be to pontificate about the obvious lack of good sense in this decision, to point out how irresponsible it was and how it was only going to lead me into further, deeper trouble, etc., etc. Even I can see all that now with him safely dead and scattered, and after a pleasing revenge has been exacted. At the time it was far from straightforward.

I bought the hare on Thursday evening from the game butcher in Upper Street and he was surprised when I asked him to include the entrails and told me they were not good to eat. I carried the newspaper-wrapped parcel home through the gathering dusk with the blood seeping from it. The flesh I prepared into one of Vanith's favourite meals, a nourishing stew with red wine somewhat akin to Clive's jugged variety, to be left to cool overnight and be reheated next day when the flavour would be more fully developed. It simmered away on the stove top and filled the whole flat with a comforting winter aroma.

I cleaned and tidied the flat slowly and methodically whilst listening to the recordings of Young Menuhin when he played so brilliantly, and then I slept again. And strangely I slept well, clearly not unduly concerned about the huge and irrational deception. I did not feel guilty or hesitant in any way or rethink the idea because it simply seemed to be the right thing to do. I have never been in the habit of making decisions in life on the basis on what is considered by the majority to be right or wrong but only ever on what feels like the right thing at the time. Generally I try not to do what feels wrong and I am therefore largely protected from the feelings of guilt or remorse that often plague others.

An hour or so before his return I distributed the hare entrails somewhat artistically across a towel on the bathroom floor, washed my hair, and ran a warm bath into which I added half a bottle of red food colouring. I got into the bath when I heard him on the stairs. And so that is how he came across me, looking I imagined, rather tragic and a little like The Lady of Shalott. I apologized faintly for the fact that I had not had time to clean up the mess and he assured me that he would do it himself, and he did so. And it was while he obligingly made a pot of coffee that I emerged from the bath and executed the most difficult part of the plan by slashing my genitals with a razor so that I could bleed convincingly through my white cotton nightgown and onto the bed. It did not hurt very much. He was clearly relieved to observe this further evidence of fetal destruction and at once solicitous, urging me to sleep and moving about the flat quietly in order that I might do so. So I did. I was suffused with feelings of triumph and relief and I slept for hours and whilst I did so he ate a great deal of the fetus-preserving hare.

When I woke late the following evening I was dazed and confused and fearful that in the interim he might have re-examined the recent events and begun to suspect some chicanery. But on the contrary, he was so cheerful that I almost abandoned my proposed second laceration with the razor to produce another convincing issue of blood. All most extreme behaviour but back then in early 1968 I was quite unaware that there would be children other than the one I was trying so desperately to preserve, and in any event I was still so besotted with Vanith Lefarge that then he was the only father I could have possibly considered. The extraordinary plan had worked and he was in no doubt that there had been an abortion and even commented on the size of the fetus judging it to be about eighteen weeks which served to convince me that mostly we see what we expect to see. I had saved myself a lot of pain and grief he told me and he would now lift the curse from me, he would do so that very day although lifting a bad spell was almost as strenuous as laying one and would be emotionally depleting for him. He would need to prepare himself mentally and physically. I reheated the remainder of the magical hare and together we ate it and drank a bottle of red wine. It felt symbolic.

I should have used the next couple of weeks to plan my escape because now he believed the child gone I was safe again for the time being. I could have left at any stage with impunity and could have even been seen by him as doing what was right and proper. Instead of leaving I stayed, and even began to hope once more that things would somehow change between us and we would be able to be happy. Once the baby was born, I rationalized, Vanith would begin to realise that like himself, this child was somehow meant to be. A miracle would take place allowing him to re-assess our relationship. If it was not now for the tangible evidence of Daniel himself it would be easy to reduce all of these events to simply the dark disturbance of my own imagination. Inevitably then of course it became too late for me to continue as controller of my own destiny and this was something that I should have realised would happen. That power was abruptly snatched from me when I reached the twenty-fourth week of my pregnancy, with things between us more settled and Vanith emphasizing daily that I had done a good thing to rid us of That Demon Fetus. It came about because the middle of the night excruciating pain began to re-visit me. So again we ended up at the hospital only this time with him importantly explaining that I had recently had a miscarriage. An hour later he was told a little caustically that I certainly still had some kind of pelvic mass. The short story regarding the nuclear blast that emanated from him over the next hours and days is that I tried to convince him that it was clear that I had conceived twins and had he not seen the destruction of the first one with his own eyes?

And then astonishingly he seemed to begin to accept the idea. The justification he gave to himself was that there had been some powerful magic afoot and that consequently the equilibrium of his world was now in grave danger. My faint hope that this might mean to him that the child, his child, was destined perhaps by divine providence to have life, was not even given the slightest consideration and he only concentrated on planning the complete destruction of what was Evil. In fact he quickly came to believe that the annihilation of the child was part of his own divine purpose. It was as if we then became prime players in some malevolent folk tale where we re-enacted processes set down in a dark history destined to be played and replayed over centuries. I was very, very afraid of him and could neither eat nor sleep over the following days. In my terror I sought help both from the Police and from the Catholic Church. My consultation with the Police was in the middle of the night anonymously from a telephone box outside Sadler's Wells Theatre. The theatre goers had long since disappeared and the theatre façade looked bleak and uninspiring.

999 responded unemotionally but efficiently when I said I wanted to speak with someone about a crime that was about to be committed. Within seconds it seemed I was connected to a strong, pleasant, fatherly voice. I explained that the father of my child wanted it aborted and that I was anxious to preserve its life. If I gave the relevant details was it possible for him to be arrested? How serious a crime was an abortion on an unwilling recipient? The fatherly male assured me that my call would continue to be treated confidentially and I did not have to give any further details if I did not want to do so. He kept me talking for another ten minutes until the kiosk door was wrenched open and two policemen demanded to know more. I told them I had made up the story for a joke and ran away through the warren of streets and alleys behind the theatre. They did not pursue me.

I confided in Vivien, an erstwhile friend who was also an ex nun and therefore treated with some caution by Vanith. She lived with a cat called Phryne above The Catholic Bookshop in The Strand and also worked in the shop. Her free time she devoted to the study of orthodox religion and the study of unorthodox beliefs such as Magic. Vivien listened attentively to my half-truths because of course I did not dare to reveal the complete story, especially the trickery with the hare's entrails. She gave me a bed for the night and said she would speak to someone at the Cathedral for advice. It was raining heavily when I returned a day or two later to be instructed that the following afternoon at four o'clock I should go to Westminster Cathedral, to a particular side door and ask for Canon Gonzelli who would advise and counsel me. I must tell the Canon the absolute truth Vivien urged, and if I did so he would do his best to find a pathway through the problem. Canon Gonzelli was an important and powerful man, she said, and he could cast out demons; he was an Exorcist. I imagined him to be a giant of a man.

In fact he turned out to be quite a small person, rather shorter than average, hunched over and with a wizened appearance though he was not an old man and in fact it was difficult to judge what age he might be. He had sparse gingery hair and eyelashes, and surprisingly pale blue eyes behind gold-rimmed spectacles. He opened the side door of the Cathedral himself and led me down a number of narrow corridors to a small, windowless and cell-like room where the walls were lined with dusty books that appeared to have remained unopened for years. He switched on an electric bar heater before sitting on one side of a vast wooden desk, motioning me to sit on the other side. He spoke perfect English with a faintly foreign accent.

'Tell me your story,' he said and I did so, leaving out nothing this time. The telling of the story took longer than I imagined it would and when I got to the present and told of Vanith's hatred of the Church and of the Demons he had summoned to plague and pester me and his promise that if I did not abort the child, these Demons would follow me for the rest of my life, he interrupted for the first time and told me that I had been playing a dangerous game. And then the tears began to spill down my face and drip onto the wooden floor, faster and faster, until I felt I would never be able to stop the flow. As I wept he emphasized the risks I had taken and told me that I had now placed myself in very real spiritual peril and that the Demons Vanith spoke of were not merely figments of his imagination but agents of Satan himself. Then, of course, I became ever more terrified until he assured me that he could help rid me and my child of their influence.

Canon Gonzelli took me back through narrow corridors until we finally found ourselves inside the Cathedral itself, huge and quiet but for the background murmur of a priest somewhere speaking with visitors. In a small side chapel he lit candles and placed his hands upon my head, reciting prayers as I knelt still in terror before him. Then slowly I began to feel calmer. Before I left he gave me newly blessed

Rosary Beads, small black beads with a simple silvery link chain.

'Hold them to your heart when you feel the Demons coming close to you – they have the power to protect you.'

The rain had stopped by the time I left his counsel and the reassuring safety and security of the Cathedral. I left via a different door and quickly found myself in Francis Street, heading in the general direction of Victoria Station where I knew I would be able to search for the familiar underground sign. The rain-drenched pavements glittered eerily and street lamps sent a procession of demonic dancers to accompany me as I hurried through home-going Londoners not daring to breathe too deeply for fear of pursuing spirits. I clutched the black beads hard inside the right-hand pocket of my rain jacket and said several Hail Marys and as I reached the entrance to the tube station and began to descend the escalator, the shimmering inky dancers were at last left behind, howling abuse in a language I could not understand. But the underground system, as everyone knows, is a perfect habitat for unfriendly apparitions and once on the platform I was again under attack as shadowy fiends played games of biting and pinching with my lower legs.

Vanith was sitting in the kitchen when I returned to the flat and when he asked where I had been I told him. He said that my fucking Virgin Mary would not be able to help me no matter how hard I prayed to her and her envoys would be of very little assistance and support against the demonic forces he had invoked to chase me. 'Don't even think of running away,' he said with a strange lack of acrimony. 'The time for escape is long gone because no matter how you try to flee they will always catch up with you. Wherever in the world you go they will always hunt you down, they will always discover your hiding place!'

My teeth were chattering with panic and I found it difficult to form sentences. I brought the Rosary Beads out of my pocket and placed them in front of me on the kitchen table. 'I have been given these for protection'.

He chuckled faintly and leaned forward, touching the beads with the forefinger of his right hand and it was as he did so that the silvery chain simply broke in three places. Both of us drew back and after a few seconds he said, though somewhat uncertainly, 'You see, they do not have the power to help you – I have shattered them.' Later Vivien told me that it was her opinion that the beads had in fact absorbed the demonic force, deflecting it from its target, and rendering it impotent. I was not nearly as sure and in any case I had already stepped downwards into terror once more. Vanith quickly realised this and swiftly turned it to his advantage. He expounded in some detail what my life was likely to be like if I did not now do as he bid. He advised that the simplest way forward was for him to kill the child. And so it was that Vanith Lefarge with a long bladed kitchen knife within reach should I change my mind, performed upon me the second abortion procedure of our six year relationship almost within the presence of the fractured Rosary Beads.

And yes of course I could have simply pretended to agree, and escaped down the stairs and headed for the nearest Police Station. But I did not do so because I felt defeated. Vanith was jubilant when just hours after the procedure intended to dislodge the infant Daniel from within me, the certain and obvious signs of a terminating pregnancy began. He first asked me to give him a cheque for the next month's expenses on the flat; rent, power, telephone, etc. and he thought that one hundred pounds would cover the basics and leave a little perhaps for cigarettes and petrol. This of course I did, though resentfully because by that stage I had very little money as general terror had consumed me for some weeks and that, among other things, had made it impossible for me to work productively in any capacity. Then with a kind of weary triumph he dropped me at the hospital without allowing the car engine to stop for a second. He said that if I told them the truth then he would unfortunately have to end my life and he managed to make this sound as if it would hurt him more than it would hurt me. So I did not tell them and they treated me for a threatening miscarriage and kept me there for several days. Somehow or other Daniel survived this further attempt on his life.

I asked the hospital staff not to give Vanith any information if and when he rang and because perhaps this all happened at the first glimmering of the dawn of patient rights they did not do so. So I left their care still pregnant and returned to the flat only to collect my belongings and went to stay with Stella, dazed and bruised and unable to make sense of recent events. And despite her warmth and support and constant reassurances that I had acted rightly and properly, I mourned the loss of all the wild hopes I had nurtured for several years. Oddly, it occurred to neither of us that his unlawful conduct should be brought to the attention of the police.

FIVE

So began my life without Vanith Lefarge. Although I greatly feared him and his power, after the first week when I simply sat motionless and sometimes crying, I found the new freedom quite extraordinary and was at a loss to know what to do with it. If I wanted to visit the nearby Portobello Market I no longer had to almost beg permission and calculate to the quarter hour when I would return. I could wander between the stalls for several hours if I so wished and this liberation began to feel exhilarating so I walked for hours. It could have been all the exercise that promoted the labour pains three weeks after my departure from Clerkenwell. Whichever way I tried to analyse it later, there was certainly a lengthy interval from the time of the final abortion attempt to the time of Daniel's premature birth. Stella was away with her latest boyfriend for the night and so I lay restlessly from eleven pm when the first niggle began, until five in the morning when the pains were regular and too invasive to ignore. I took myself to hospital by taxi and it was a grim place at that time of day filled with little light, muted voices and every part of the delivery suite was chilly. I then believed perhaps that the child had been killed after all, and planned wild reprisals. The fetal stethoscope was prodigiously uplifting though the rapidly thundering heartbeat caused me further anxiety. But the doctor who looked ill at ease and had beads of moisture trickling into his eyebrows said, 'That's normal'.

I tried not to sound distressed and failed when I asked if the baby might die. He did not answer.

Daniel was born at last just before seven pm, abruptly and after hours of searing pain and increasing agitation when those sporadically attending us muttered to each other about 'depressed breathing' and 'gestational development'. He was suddenly there, purple and screaming, and I pleaded that he should not be allowed to die.

'He sounds very lusty at the moment.' The sweaty doctor looked relieved, almost jovial. Job very nearly over. He asked for an incubator. One was found then frantic minutes went by while they wondered where to plug it in and finally one of them hurried off to find an extension cord. Later in the day, on the ward of newly-delivered mothers complete with their infants, the rather new-fangled notion sweeping through maternity wards at the time, I was visited by an earnest female doctor. She told me that my son had been taken to the premature baby unit at Fulham and that he was doing as well as could be expected. She talked about birth weight and breathing difficulties.

So completely saturated in euphoria was I that I heard little but the fact that he was doing well and the accompanying information went to the four corners of the ward and never for a moment penetrated my consciousness. It was some days before I quite realised that my son's birth at twenty-seven weeks gestation was, for the time, critically premature and his birth weight, at just under two pounds, very low.

There were two of us on that hospital ward minus our babies. The other was a fifteen-year-old called Mandy whose baby was to be adopted. Her parents visited her daily, her mother fussing constantly, propping pillows and assuring her that she was going to buy her a nice new swim suit just as soon as she came home, '...and you can put all this behind you and go swimming with your mates again...' Her father stood at the foot of the bed looking uncomfortable in a shiny suit and said nothing at all. Mandy and I drifted into a powerful though short-term friendship. She told me that her baby was to be called Kevin after his father, a singer with a pop band, who knew nothing of the pregnancy and was gorgeous. She cried a lot and said she wanted to keep Kevin and that her mother would let her but her father had forbidden it and said she had to go back to school and get her exams and become a Telex Operator. She thought I was lucky being able to keep Daniel. I thought I was lucky too and ventured nothing about my own circumstances.

A red-faced social worker with slight asthma came to the ward several times to speak to both of us, which she did with not a hint of privacy. The woman on my right who was American with a husband at the Embassy had a bouncing boy called Tom and she listened avidly to all that was being said to me, Tom constantly at one breast or the other. The woman on my left was English and pretended not to be listening as she read articles about initiating best breast-feeding practice.

'What have you decided about Baby's future?' puffed the red-faced one. I replied as impertinently as possible with something about it being far too early to put his name down for Eton and her puffing became a fraction more exaggerated. She told me that my attitude was irresponsible and that if I did not give some serious consideration to making sensible plans for Baby she would be forced to recommend he remain in the premature baby unit until I came to my senses.

'Then I might well decide to take him home as soon as I am out of here – perhaps even tomorrow,' I told her. 'I assume you don't actually have him under lock and key.' And I felt both pleased with myself and just a little bit fearful that she might actually have the power to decide Daniel's future without my input.

She told me that They needed to know what kind of home he would be going to and I asked her if she would feel compelled to ask such questions if I was actually married. At last she turned her attentions to poor Mandy who simply cried and so she comforted her and said she was 'doing the right thing'.

Mandy told me she thought I was ever so brave to stick up for myself but to be careful because her family had been in the clutches of social workers once before when her brother went off the rails and they could 'really stuff you up' if you were not chary of them. So I was then more than a little afraid but having established myself as the ward rebel it was rather difficult to backtrack and become reinvented as more compliant. A day or two later, Mandy was white faced and melancholy and said, 'Kevin goes today – he's off with his new Mum and Dad. I really hope they don't give him some awful new name.' Neither of her parents came that day and so we sat together in the newly established 'Smokers' Room' and I introduced her to nicotine which she assured me was helping her to keep calm.

I was then still living within a bubble of elation and whenever I thought about my newly-born son became totally consumed with exultation simply because he actually existed, and he was Vanith's flesh and blood and I was his mother. Never had I felt such passionate and all-consuming emotion. Nothing that had ever happened to me previously could compete with the feeling of ecstasy these truths generated and I sometimes feared that it was merely a dream from which I would awake to find myself back in the Clerkenwell flat amidst the aborted remains of my child with Vanith telling me to hasten my arrangements for leaving.

And now I find it hard to believe the story myself. It all seems highly improbable and my own part in it truly farcical. What kind of woman reacts to sadism with such an odd mixture of submissiveness and aggression? And although the aggression grew insidiously over the years until the desire for revenge became too hard to ignore, conversely I am also aware that had I known that the future was to hold other children and a husband who would truly love me, I might have made completely different decisions. Vanith had been correct to warn me of the perils of wishing too fervently for something. Getting what you wish for often comes hand in hand with sadness and frustration. Daniel's life was destined to be strewn with difficulties as he grew older.

However, in those weeks that followed his birth I was suffused with an extraordinary feeling of bliss and felt myself to be one of the world's luckiest women because I alone had become the mother of Vanith Lefarge's son and I contemplated with gladness how envious the luckless Christina would be if only she knew. The problem was that apart from Stella and myself and the hospital staff, few were aware of my wonderful news. With more than a little good sense I realised that once Vanith discovered that his termination attempt at twenty-four weeks had become a live birth at twenty-seven weeks he would be more than a little upset and that, more importantly, he might seek to rectify matters. This was too terrible for me to contemplate for only the infant's death would satisfy him and at that stage as I have explained, Daniel was still the vulnerable infant who was to grow into the greatly-loved little boy. Some years were yet to pass before life became in any way problematical for him. Often in those first months of my son's life, I mused upon the fairy tale aspects of his entry into the world and tried to determine if there was some way of convincing his father that this birth had been inevitable, that his existence had come about from good rather than evil and that Vanith had simply misread the signs as the main players in all the best fairy tales so often do. I tried to imagine a moment when he would abruptly realise that I was correct, that he had simply been misdirected in his thinking by a malign spirit, a moment when he would embrace both Daniel and myself and beg our forgiveness. No matter how many times this scene played deliciously across my imagination, however, it did so without conviction.

I also thought a great deal about the circumstances he had often spoken of concerning his own birth, of the abortion his mother supposedly underwent, and the subsequent problems between his parents. I imagined the three of us – Vanith, Daniel and myself – in the presence of some lofty Psychotherapist perhaps in the Tavistock Clinic – who would pontificate whilst we, especially Vanith, listened:

'Can't you see you are simply re-enacting your own father's behaviour by rejecting this child... you do to him what was done to you... for years you have been hurting... but true healing will come to you when you allow yourself to love your son.'

And Vanith bows his head a little, his shoulders sag, and tears spill as he softly asks if I would consider accepting him into the life I share with Daniel.

'Of course,' I tell him unhesitatingly. 'You are my child's father after all...'

At no stage did any part of this particular fantasy seem to have much substance but I allowed myself the occasional daydream. The path towards the most favourable fairy tale outcome still seemed to lie via misread omens and warnings leading to a fatally erroneous conclusion. A mischievous fairy perhaps ensured a signpost indicating the wrong path; maybe even that very same intergenerational sprite working harmful enchantment on both Vanith and his father. And in any case all this might very well have been an extraordinary though unlikely Truth because the behaviour of Lefarge the Elder was, within the parameters of the times in which it occurred, very similar to that later re-enacted by Lefarge the Younger.

Was there some tangible scientific explanation? Did the truth lie somehow within genetic memory? How can any of us truly untangle reality from fantasy or the psychological from the spiritual in such a vortex of emotion?

Now, in the second decade of the twenty-first century, I struggle to recall the details of what happened next, the order in which events took place for instance, but somehow or other Daniel battled through his first few months of life, put on weight, and finally was allowed to leave the hospital with only an asthmatic wheeze to show for it all. It was then that my desire to show him off to the world became overwhelming and I now think that this must be quite normal and even commonplace for new mothers – the displaying of their new child for all to admire. I was quite aware that I would be unable to show Daniel to anyone and be sure that the news of his existence would not trickle back to Vanith and so perhaps the time had come for him to be told the truth. The only alternative was to completely abandon my old life and all those I knew and start a new one which I was most reluctant to do. I cannot now recall quite how I started the ball rolling with this Revealing of the Truth but possibly I simply rang him and told him there was something we needed to discuss. What I do remember clearly is going one night to the flat in Clerkenwell to talk and feeling a little afraid in case he should physically attack me. I was walking up the stairs behind him when he casually mentioned that Christina was staying with him and then wanted to know just how personal the matters were that I wished to discuss.

My mind turned cartwheels in the ten seconds it took to reach the upper floor of the house but by the time he opened the door to the living room where Christina sat in the middle of the carpet looking wraithlike and otherworldly I was telling him loudly and cheerfully that nothing was too personal and I was happy for Christina to be present. I was interested in her reaction and in any case I reasoned she was going to find out at some stage and it would be fun to observe her discomfiture. She sprang lightly to her bare feet, her white muslin skirt brushing against her thin, pale legs and her untidy long blonde hair escaping its many slides and clips and tumbling about her shoulders. Though inelegant she looked composed and natural and aloof. My heart pounded and my hands were clammy because I disliked her so much and I had to force my face into a brighter than natural smile as I greeted her. I heard my own voice echoing back to me. 'How lovely to see you – what a lovely skirt... hasn't it been dreadfully cold lately? My place is like Siberia. It's great to see this old place looking just the same...' All this sounding very artificial but I babbled on, walked to the window and looked out onto the darkening square before turning to face them both again, taking my raincoat off as I did so and dropping it over a chair.

Christina said nothing at all except to offer coffee. I said I would simply love one and she went off to make it. I hoped she was not lacing it with cyanide and almost laughed at this absurdity before wondering briefly if she was capable of it. I tried to remember the names of the poisons I had read about that were tasteless and later almost impossible to trace in the body. Thalium seemed to ring a bell so I then wondered if she had any and wildly followed her to the kitchen to help. She was standing by the kettle, waiting for it to whistle. My whistling kettle – the very one I had made his morning coffee with for years. My kitchen was now her kitchen. Oh how I had loved this kitchen. It was me who adorned the walls with Moulin Rouge posters. The homely peg rug on the floor was mine, bought at a library craft fair because it reminded me of my childhood. I wondered what had made me abandon these possessions because it was certain that Vanith had never at any stage coveted them. Then that thought was shoved aside because already I wondered when I might return to this place to live in harmony with my son and his father. She asked if I wanted milk and I said I did so she left the top thirty per cent of one of my abandoned Denby mugs empty.

I stretched out my hand. 'Shall I give Vanith his?'

But sharply and decisively she said 'No!' and she deftly swung the mug out of my reach. Her pale blue eyes looked directly into my still stiffly smiling, terribly aching face. 'You really hate me don't you?' Well she was right there of course. I hated her all right, nothing was surer. I hated her for her composure, her willowy slenderness, for knowing Vanith in those years before I did, but more than any of those things I hated her for standing in my kitchen, opening my fridge, holding my mugs and looking so very much at home as she did so. She was seizing my life. Of course I hated her.

'Heavens... you mustn't think that Christina – I don't hate anyone. It's such a negative emotion isn't it?' and I led the way back to the living room where Vanith slouched on the couch idly looking at an old copy of The Times as if he was reading it, which he wasn't.

He looked at me once we were all seated. I noticed that she sat beside him on the couch, her hair snaking over my red and blue sequined Tibetan cushion that had cost so much in the Emporium in Kings Road. She sat fractionally too close to him. I dropped as nonchalantly as I could onto the floor in front of them both, sipped my coffee, then hugged my knees. I was wearing a short tweed pinafore dress and under it a black polo neck sweater, matching my tights. I knew I looked up to the minute 1968 stylish and, confidence mounting, even fancied that I looked just a little like Jean Shrimpton from the cover of the latest Vogue magazine. Not that Vanith concerned himself too much with fashion, however, I imagined that the effect would not be lost on Christina who most of the time managed to look quite dowdy. She looked remarkably undowdy this evening for once, probably because she thought she now had her man in her grasp once more. Regaining he whom she so coveted had made her bloom perhaps, the way pregnancy affects some women. And I abruptly remembered why I was actually there in the flat, at that time, drinking coffee from a Denby mug and sitting on the floor attempting to resemble a fashion model dawdling between photo shoots. I hesitated for only a further second or two before venturing: 'I came to talk about a most extraordinary thing that has happened – something that concerns you and me Vanith.' I swiveled slightly to face Christina who was sitting quite rigid, both hands clutching her coffee mug with white knuckles and little red spots high on her cheeks.

'Although it primarily concerns Vanith and me, it really doesn't matter if you stay and listen Christina because ultimately you will know anyway – and in any case, now that you are an important presence in Vanith's life I guess it actually does concern you as well.'

Neither of them said anything but both stared at me unflinchingly.

'Three weeks after I left this place I gave birth to a live child.'

He jerked upright. 'What do you mean?'

I felt like laughing but instead I repeated the sentence, slowly.

After a second or two he said, 'You had a termination, of that I am certain. I did it myself.' He was totally confused and speaking very quietly, shaking his head from side to side. 'I don't believe you.'

Christina put her hand on his arm and hissed, 'But you told me she had two terminations... one while you were out of London... another when you came back. Twins, you thought. How on earth...'

He nodded. 'Yes, yes, I know for sure she had the first one... I saw the evidence with my own eyes. The problem must have been a twin pregnancy, a most regrettable business, and somehow the second fetus remained ...which I aborted with my own hands later.'

She looked at me in horror. 'How could you possibly have given birth to a child three weeks after you left?'

I shrugged and tried to look melancholy. The urge to laugh was overwhelming. I ventured 'Triplets?'

She gasped a short inhalation and her eyes widened. 'That is quite impossible. I find I am unable to believe that.' Her voice was sharp, school-mistressy and the words bounced off the nicotine-stained once white walls until I almost fancied they echoed several times. Vanith said nothing at all so I said nothing further. Christina demanded to know what she called 'the truth of the matter'. That same truth of the matter was itself hidden deeply inside the convoluted events of the past months and having never thought much further than the moment of revealing Daniel's birth to a first surprised then ecstatic father I just sat vaguely noticing that my eyes began to fill with tears that toppled over and ran steadily onto the front of the increasingly damp tweed pinafore.

'What has happened to this live child?' Vanith asked at last. 'This third fetus.'

What indeed. I explained about the prematurity, the long months in hospital and the growth to robust good health of the enchanted triplet. Fairy tale babies are indeed blessed. He was very still, eyes fixed somewhere at the point of my knees.

Christina moved constantly, hands twisting together. 'I don't believe it,' she said several times. 'It's not possible.'

I congratulated myself for the inspired purchase and use of the hare, the flesh of which he had consumed so readily. It was satisfying to know that a hare could be purchased on that day in Upper Street. Had I been forced to settle for a mere rabbit some of the underlying symbolism might have been lost. I began to enjoy the fairy tale. But there were no flies on Christina because she did not believe it for a second. That she could overlook the strange repetition of events deep in his past now linked for all time with my own was irritating. And she wasn't allowing for destiny, for fate. She was not taking into consideration my relentless determination to hold on to the baby regardless of the outcome.

He was saying very quietly that neither did he believe that it could be possible and so I offered to show him Daniel.

Christina said wildly that a divine communication was telling her: 'It is not... it is not...' She got up to join us as Vanith led the way down the stairs and I was thrilled when he said she could not come with us, that he had to do this alone. We stepped a little deeper into the fairy tale.

That was how he came to see the baby, lying peacefully asleep in his makeshift cot in Ladbroke Grove, unaware how alert and cautious I was, how closely I observed his unwilling father, ready to tear his throat out if he made a wrong move.

But Vanith did nothing except look and murmur to himself, 'This thing is not human.'

Astonishingly it was almost as if he now almost feared the powerful supremacy he perceived in the tiny child and briefly I was victorious, enjoying that the tables had so deftly turned. Over the following days I experienced a great deal of relief because the fear of Vanith finding out about Daniel's existence was now removed. I was free to enjoy the baby, take him out and show him off to people who would for the most part be completely uninterested as people are when the baby belongs to someone else. I was filled with satisfaction when thinking about how poor Christina might be feeling and how she and he would attempt unsuccessfully to untangle the increasingly tightly woven web of deceit. The fantasy had now become so adhered to truth that I no longer could rely upon myself to know what was accurate and what was simply invention. The most important thing was that he had seemed to accept my rescue plan for Daniel and had willingly immersed himself into the fabric of the myth.

Some two or three weeks after this time of revelation, he rang and told me that he would like to meet up with me for a cup of coffee and a chat if I was willing. He had some mail to give to me and there was a matter he would like to discuss. Was I willing? I could barely get to the meeting point, Farringdon Tube Station, quickly enough. This might well be the moment when he asked me to go back to him. Should I perhaps hesitate and demand time to think? Probably not wise because Christina would still be lurking somewhere, ready to step in with coffee and words of wisdom if I did not simply seize the day.

I worried that it might take him some time to adjust to the presence of Daniel. He had of course had time to think through the many tangles I had constructed, albeit finally with his collusion, there had no doubt been a moment of realisation when he recognised with horror that he had completely misinterpreted those fabled omens but now at last he understood that his son was meant to be part of his life.

There was a kind of glow about the old Metropolitan line that afternoon as the equally elderly train rattled and rocked from Ladbroke Grove to Farringdon. Westbourne Park, Royal Oak and Paddington seemed bathed in golden sunlight and even Great Portland Street and Euston Square looked cheerful. Farringdon itself had an air of anticipation about it, waiting with bated breath for the outcome of this momentous meeting.

We met in a workmen's café of the kind that no longer exists. He sat with a mug of instant coffee in front of him. He always called it Ersatz Coffee and said in Germany during the war it had been made from chicory and dandelion roots. I idly wondered what the Camp Coffee of my childhood was made of then I turned my full attention to him with what I hoped was a genial half smile. He wanted me know that he had thought deeply about my pregnancy and he realised that the very fact that it had happened in the first place was because of some outside force working for evil.

'Or perhaps for ultimate good,' I suggested, whilst at the same time attempting to look diffident.

'You only think that because your very thinking process has been altered by the meddling of a dangerous spirit.' He shook his head gloomily, not looking like a man about to accept fatherhood.

I persisted. 'How do we know it is dangerous? It could be the very opposite. Perhaps we only think it is dangerous because this entity wants us to think that way.'

'I do think I am in a slightly better position than you are to interpret such matters,' he admonished. 'I have studied the power of magic for years and you are at this very moment within the clutches of something very nasty indeed. I tried to save you from it but you would not listen. If only you had heeded me earlier, this would never have come to pass.'

The former warmth and sunlight of my surroundings began to dim and I asked him to explain to me exactly what it was he referred to.

'If you had not hesitated in the first place to abort that pregnancy, you would not be facing the unpleasantness that sits before you today.'

Well that at least was true. Neither would I be the mother of his beautiful child.

He continued, 'I knew that the longer it went on the more difficult it would be for you. That is of course quite understandable. What I did not understand was that the thing inside you might have been endowed with three heads… and now you are in an unenviable position because in order now to rid us of this beast, you will have to have great courage. You will have to assume the mantle of a warrior woman.' He leaned forward and took my hand in his, looking directly into my eyes. The eyes of my baby son looked back at me and I ached with a thrashing love for both of them. He was saying, 'You will have to have the courage of Artemis, be as bold as Boudicca.'

My throat began to feel tight and my heart to thump very hard indeed. I asked him what I was to do because it was just possible it was achievable. If standing inside a circle of daggers reciting the Lord's Prayer backwards whilst being pierced by demons was going to win him over then I would certainly give it a go.

'I want you to rid us of that child. Neither of us can move forward with our lives whilst it lives. I do not want you to look upon it as human because it is not. It is as foul a creature as it is possible to be. It spews its filth into the lives of us both and it must die.' He went on to instruct me how to suffocate Daniel using a plastic bag and how and when to remove it from his face, how long to wait before dialling for an ambulance. He intimated that if I had the courage to carry out this act he would reassess his feelings for me because it would indicate an enormous strength of character.

The inside of my mouth now felt as if it was frozen. I heard myself ask whether he would prefer to carry out the act himself and he said he would not because I had given birth to the creature and therefore the correct thing was that I should rid the world of it.

We both drank what remained in our slightly chipped china mugs. I wondered idly what the café clientele of men in blue overalls would think if they knew I was being asked to murder a child with a plastic bag. And if they had known, what they would think of the situation.

We sat like that together for quite a long time. At last I got up, feeling stiff, all my muscles now ached as if I had been involved in a great deal of sudden exercise.

I said, 'I don't think I will be able to do it. I do not have that kind of courage.'

He told me he was very sorry to hear that. 'Because that disgusting fucking thing will now attempt to sit on my tail for the rest of my life.' His voice began to rise and then the blue-overalled men together with a woman whose hair was tied up in a red scarf looked at us in a half interested way.

He added, 'And I therefore will curse you both through this life and into the next. You will have no luck I will make sure of that.'

And then somehow we both walked out of the café, he in the direction of St. John's Road and me back into the station once more, where a Hammersmith-bound train thundered in almost immediately. In my despair I briefly thought of throwing myself under it but instead I nursed the misery closer and stepped inside the carriage.

SIX

So then the years began to intervene and needless to relate Vanith Lefarge did not abandon his life of sexual debauchery and uncover a paternal instinct within. Somehow or other he told his mother about the baby and, then in her mid-eighties and plagued with arthritis, she valiantly travelled from Munich to London and demanded to see the child. Vanith, always predictable, and this was indeed a contest he knew well, waited until she arrived before explaining to her in some detail that of course she could see Daniel, he would not dream of preventing her from doing so, but she must realise that if she did elect to do so then he would be totally unable to continue any kind of relationship with her himself for the remainder of her life. The choice was hers and hers alone. After some days of hesitation and argument she conceded that her relationship with her younger son was more important than that with an unknown grandson. However, she wrote to me saying that her one wish was to meet Daniel before she died and I vowed to keep the letter so that I could show it to him as he grew older but somehow or other it got lost, probably in the transition from London to Auckland.

And in the interim Daniel grew into the small child of my wildest dreams and beyond. Endearing, demanding yet engaging, eager to converse on almost any topic he would try valiantly to offer opinion on matters he was not yet capable of comprehending and although nothing he added to day-today debates ever made much sense, he managed to exude an excess of confidence and charm. I could not have envisaged a more perfect child but the time I speak of was when he was three and four years old and the older, more complicated Daniel belonged to the future and to a time when Persephone Faith, who had for so many years lain neglected and gathering dust in my memory, was resurrected along with the technological advances of 2000 and beyond. That is of course the way of the world.

Persephone Faith Callahan had, after all, made but a fleeting appearance across the periphery of my life and some would think it distinctly odd that I remembered her at all after so many years. It is possible she would have been totally forgotten had it not been for her association with Christina. 'I have begun to truly hate Persephone... I detest her so much I can smell the hatred.' If Christina had been so disturbed by the unknown Persephone then my feelings towards her were benevolent. She was certainly worthy of occupying a corner of a small store in my memory. It is not clear why all these emotions remained so powerful for so long. Something to do with the astonishing level of my own neediness probably, the length and breadth of my obsession coupled with the savagery of Vanith's own requirement to dominate and subjugate the women who came under his influence.

In essence he still remained much in control in those early days, so much so that when Daniel's birth was finally registered I was too fearful to name him as the father in case it should further inflame him. Accordingly Daniel was left with an embarrassing short form birth certificate such as was customary in those days and indicated an illegitimate child. I had won the battle of the mythical triplets but further influence over his psyche seemed to require greater persistence than I could muster. So from that time forth Vanith and I had little to do with each other. Mutual friends such as Miriam revealed that he grew ever more wary of me in those years, fearful that I indeed practiced some strange and powerful magic. This knowledge gave me a great deal of pleasure.

When Daniel was four years old I re-met a man I had known from the days when we had first lived in the Clerkenwell flat, a man who had somehow been invited to one of Clive's routine even mundane dinner parties in Campden Hill, a man I found myself seated next to. It had been a Christmastide event and we had talked at length that evening and over the next year or two he was in the habit of occasionally contacting me and patiently listening to my relationship problems. Then he returned to New Zealand to practice medicine and for the most part we lost touch. I knew him simply as Jack and it was not until the day before we were due to get married that I found he was not Jack Hillier at all but his real name was Graeme, a name he disliked. Madame Sandra had predicted a man with the initials GH and here he was! Coincidence, I decided.

It was initially intended that Daniel and I should go to New Zealand on holiday simply to see how we liked the place. Daniel was of course very, very enthusiastic. Years later he told me that he was ecstatic at the idea of living even short term with a man about the house, having a father in fact. And it was his totally unbridled enthusiasm for Jack that propelled us into marriage. We settled into cosy domesticity in an Auckland beach suburb and Daniel started school shortly after we arrived, becoming St. Joseph's newest pupil, where he importantly told everyone in some detail about his new father Jack and his old father who did not seem to want to live with us. In due course Jonah and Martha were born and at eight Daniel had become an ordinary Auckland schoolboy, still very much attached to his stepfather and even more so to his siblings. A few weeks before the birth of Martha we bought a house, still close to the city but with its own pocket of unspoiled native bush, a half-acre of adventure possibilities for the three children.

I had begun to live a different life and at times it was as if I had simply stepped outside my own skin and into someone else's. At times when his shadow fell across me it felt that Vanith Lefarge had existed only in my imagination as a badly orchestrated piece of fiction. As for Christina, during those busy child-rearing years I thought of her rarely and did not pause to wonder what might have become of her. And Persephone, known more widely as Faith Callahan, did not appear on the horizon of my awareness for decades. This was not unduly odd since her existence had always been spectral to me, existing as she did as a discernibly less substantial adjunct of Christina herself, a mere line or two in a long discarded note that pulsated with hatred. 'I detest her so much I can smell myself....'

During the time I knew him Vanith had done little to make Persephone any more substantial, mentioning her rarely and then only to explain that she had been Christina's friend. Only once he told me that the rivalry between the two women had been so fierce that it disintegrated their once close friendship. As he spoke I had noticed how the memory of the misery inculcated in each woman seemed gratifying to him.

Essentially, none of those peripheral to Vanith himself in this still festering drama occupied me to any degree at all for forty years, though I cannot honestly say the same of the man himself. There were times during those years when I would wake at some hour between two and four am and think about him, wonder if his life was happy and hope fervently that it was not. Occasionally I heard news of him through mutual long abandoned friends, some of whom were still too influenced by him to reveal a great deal to me. As Daniel grew older he attempted to make contact with his shadowy father through his Uncle

Rudy who was at first astonished because he had not been told of the existence of a nephew and had to first check the validity of the story. And then, when he did so, he politely rang back to say that Vanith had forbidden him to have anything to do with either of us and so in order to keep the family peace, such as it was, he had elected not to get involved. Daniel was pragmatic and employed the use of philosophy and appeared to react little to these setbacks.

Miriam remained in contact intermittently, even writing quite amusing letters about how her life was progressing though as time went on she said less and less about Vanith. On the few occasions I revisited London she and I would meet briefly and it seemed that she was more comfortable meeting with me away from her own flat and on one occasion explained that it was in case Vanith dropped by to visit because explaining my presence might be difficult and she could do without the extra stress in her life.

A year before her death she even toyed with the idea of making a life in New Zealand herself. She might open a flower shop she said because a relative had left her forty-five thousand pounds and she wondered what to do with it. She admitted that the only person she then saw on a regular basis was Vanith. However, she failed to make the momentous life changing decision and later died of lung cancer, which was not totally unexpected as she was still smoking forty cigarettes a day. I wondered whether she had had time to make arrangements for ensuring

Vanith received the bulk of her inheritance. I knew this was what she had wanted and she had even written as much to me in what was her final letter that documented how much she still valued his friendship. Then for some reason hard now to explain, I made efforts to speak with him about Miriam's money but he was reluctant to enter into any dialogue with me and put the phone down. And because my aim at that time had to all intents and purposes been philanthropic I was aggrieved at his animosity after so many years. Clearly we would never be able to speak together again on any matter at all. It seemed that his refusal to engage with me had deftly prevented any hope I had of exacting revenge upon him. But there I was quite wrong because then came The Internet.

SEVEN

The internet changed everything. Imperceptibly for me at first because it crept into my life on slippered feet, something shadowy in the background that fully occupied my teenage children. Then somehow or other it became the necessity that no home should be without and local doctors, dentists, plumbers and electricians began to direct clients to mysterious newly-built websites. Like the telephone before it, the internet became essential for instant communication with the added advantage of offering direct access into a frenetically disordered wealth of information.

I did not do a search of his name for many years, however, and when I did it was without much hope of an interesting outcome. So I was astonished when a number of slightly differing references burst onto the screen and I at once learned that he was available for translations of German to English or vice versa, that he had translated a number of volumes of Tibetan folk tales that were available for me to buy via the good offices of various on-line book depositories, and that he was searching for an old friend. That friend was none other than Persephone Faith Callahan.

'I am looking for Faith Callahan, sometimes known as Persephone Callahan who used to live with me in St. Mary's Mansions in 1958. I last saw her in 1968. I would love to catch up with her again. If you are there Faith, please get in touch .Vanith Lefarge.'

I could reach out and virtually touch him across the intervening years, abruptly, unexpectedly. I printed the message to better absorb it with growing astonishment. He had taken increasing care over decades to do nothing that might lead either Daniel or myself to him, had kept his number out of the London telephone directory, was never enrolled as a voter, and yet here he was, unable to resist the temptation of technology, like everyone else wanting a presence in cyberspace with a mini webpage and contact details for all the world to see. I wondered how often long-lost friends and relations were to be rediscovered via such online missives. The message stayed for months. I know that because I checked it on a regular basis.

It's hard to recall when the time seemed right to take the first step towards slipping beneath the skin of Faith Callahan, slithering inside her Persephone persona like a bad fairy, but on one ordinary Auckland morning it seemed that even though I knew little about her there was no doubt that I must now take control of her phantom being for a while. Although regrettably it might have been a little unprincipled, it seemed at the same time to be quite correct and proper. It all depended on how you looked at it and I was prepared to be somewhat cavalier in my overall scrutiny. Secure and impenetrable moral codes were for those who had never been subjected to the wants and wishes of Vanith Lefarge and his like. So it was with only the slightest hesitation that I set up an email account for poor unaware Persephone which, after consultation with Daniel upon procedure, was surprisingly straightforward. I was then able to remit my own enigmatic little message into the ether.

From: PersephoneFaith@highmail.com
To: Vanith@inthesky.co.uk
28th May
Who is this Vanith Lefarge person? I once knew someone of this name many years ago when I liked to be known as Persephone.

And within hours came a reply.

WHO AM I?
From: Vanith Lefarge (Vanith@inthesky.co.uk)
To: PersephoneFaith@highmail.com
29th May
This Vanith person is indeed me and I have been looking for you for such a long time. I am delighted to hear from you! How are you, where are you? I am in North London and looking forward to hearing from you again. Lots of love, Vanith.

The printer deposited it with a quiet purr, transferring him from the screen to the white A4 page in my hand at the touch of a button. A little surge of pleasure swelled within. It seemed he was no longer completely enlightened or if he was then that enlightenment did not extend to evaluating those who contacted him via the internet. What should my response to his message be? I thought about this for perhaps a day and even wondered briefly if it should be discussed with Daniel then dismissed the notion since his current preoccupation was with a Chinese student with the impossibly unrealistic name of Salome. Better by far to keep Vanith in the palm of one hand where I could observe him quietly and without intrusion. So I wrote that I was delighted to have re-discovered him and urged him to tell me something of his life. And obligingly he did so.

MY LIFE
From: Vanith Lefarge (Vanith@inthesky.co.uk)
To: PersephoneFaith@highmail.com
31st May
It must have been late in 1968 when you came to my flat in Clerkenwell and you had a son with you, who was little and slept in the studio upstairs all night. We sat up talking and in the morning you went off to Dublin to visit your parents.

I had a lot of problems at that time and had to leave my flat. I got a tiny office in Soho and slept on the floor there for a couple of years. I nearly went bankrupt but managed to sell all my studio equipment and in 1974 went to UCL and did a degree in mathematics. I then got a badly paid job with a firm of consultant engineers for a while. In the summer of 1978 my then girlfriend Milly and I decided to go off to see the world. We went East to Iran and then Afghanistan, through India, Sri Lanka, Nepal, Thailand, Malaysia to Singapore, where we got a flight to LA with stopovers in Jakarta, Sydney, Fiji and Tahiti. When we got to the States we travelled around for some months and finally in the summer 1980 we decided to settle in LA.

Milly's family were tax exiles in Jersey and she had inherited quite a lot of money already so luckily we had no financial worries. From the time we first met she repeatedly told me that if I ever left her she would die. However, we had been in the LA flat for only two weeks when she brought in my morning coffee and told me she had to leave me. She now had a calling to go alone to South India to find God. I have found it hard to forgive her because without her support I was forced to go back to England with little money and I could not find a job. So I became a night watchman. I then met a German girl called Brigitte. We had a very intense affair but the intensity was too strong and she left. I was very, very upset to lose her.

I first tried to find you again in 1984. I wrote a letter, but it was returned after a few weeks. In about 1995 I tried again but via the internet. I tried Friends Reunited but to no avail. Then, remembering how intuitive you are, I tried to send out thought waves, but you obviously did not receive them. Finally, about 3 years ago, I set up a webpage with a photo of me and my email address, and in the end that worked!

One so easily loses touch with old friends. Incidentally, Christina rang me up to meet for coffee in about 1969 and said she was going away and that it was unlikely that I would ever see her again in this life. So far I have not. In my flat I have a workshop with a guest-bed in it. I can make my outgoing telephone calls via Skype, which is very cheap. You could come and stay and if that is not possible for you at the moment we can speak for as long as we like.

Do write soon. Love Vanith.

What a wealth of information. I felt sorry for poor Milly whose financial reserves had clearly funded the extended world trip. I was keenly interested in what it was that finally made her see that she should part from him and applauded her decision to do so. It was even possible he might even have been forced to finance his own air ticket from LA back to London. I hoped so. I particularly enjoyed the idea of his suffering when the German girl left him.

I lost no time writing back to say that I had little memory of the night I stayed with him in Clerkenwell which was at least true. I talked a lot about Christina and because of my past animosity towards her, emphasised her possessiveness of him. As he had mentioned my powers of intuition and I wondered if he had ever managed to access Miriam's money I conjured up a prophetic dream about a dark haired woman leaving him a legacy and hoped he would respond well to the idea. And finally I told him that I had somehow heard that Christina had gone to Exmoor to practice as a witch. It seemed an appropriate place for her to be. I observed that life takes very strange turns.

It was immediately clear that Vanith had made writing to Persephone Faith Callahan a priority because a reply appeared with more speed than I had imagined was possible.

LIFE IS STRANGE
From: Vanith Lefarge (Vanith@inthesky.co.uk)
To: PersephoneFaith@highmail.com
1st June
Life takes strange turns indeed. Christina did indeed become possessive of me and believed that she and I were destined for one another, which caused a number of warning lights in my head to start flashing and so I left her. I then had a long affair with a girl called Bernadette, who I can only describe as an avatar of the Queen of the Night. She caused me a great deal of trouble although I think she also taught me a lot. I had the greatest difficulty freeing myself from her. Christina thought that when that affair was over, I would return to her, which I had no intention whatsoever of doing.

I very much wanted to get in touch with you in the eighties because it was then I first began to realise what an important influence you had been in my life and how much I owed to you. You were light years ahead of me in your spiritual development and it took me more than twenty years to realise what you were trying to convey to me and where you were trying to lead me. I eventually made that journey and learned a great deal. I have lived alone since Brigitte left in 1982. I always knew that I would have to spend some years alone meditating in order to progress spiritually. I have now finally managed to link physics with metaphysics and understand the relationship between mind and matter.

For a long time I felt forced to hide myself away and I am not in the phone book simply because of Bernadette, I have spent years trying to escape her though she has always managed to find me when she really wanted to. I cannot understand your prophetic dream. I will have to think about it. I am not a good writer, and it would be nice if we could speak properly soon.

Lots of love, V.

Naturally enough I was not quite as keen as he to actually talk and after some consideration of the problem, in her next communication Faith explained that a minor stroke some years before had left her with a speech problem. Speaking on the telephone was particularly difficult. If Vanith wanted to continue the contact it would have to be by email. She made mention of her partner Josef and the two teenage girls they cared for whose names were Tamzin and Larissa. She lived in Israel and her life was full because Josef suffered from Parkinsons Disease and needed a great deal of her attention. Faith's visionary ability to see into the lives of others became stronger and she again spoke of Christina. She asked if Vanith had ever had children and commented that the propagation of one's genes was an important matter and it would be a pity if his own splendid genes were not so proliferated. Finally she was confident he could manage to write because for her, contact by telephone was simply not possible. And he did not disappoint her, a response arriving rapidly.

MORE NEWS
From: Vanith Lefarge (Vanith@inthesky.co.uk)
To: PersephoneFaith@highmail.com
4th June
Dear Faith, I am sorry to hear of Josef's illness. It is a truly horrible condition.

Christina was a strange person and in some ways quite telepathic. When I was having an affair with her, I was being very careful as far as birth control was concerned and when I asked her after a little while whether and what precautions she was taking, she assured me that there was no need to worry, because she was able, psychically, to control her fertility and there was no chance of her getting pregnant. That is when the first warning lights came on and my trust in her dissolved somewhat. I shall always be grateful to her though for her practical help to me over the years.

With regard to having children: Bernadette had a child, which was probably mine, although she was a compulsive liar amongst other things. We separated while she was pregnant, and I warned her that if she carried on behaving in certain ways, I would never have anything to do with her again, or with her child. She refused to make the changes I asked for and I have therefore been forced to keep my word.

The propagation of one's genes is of course important. I think Darwin showed that fairly clearly, even before the discovery of DNA. I have myself been on a long and difficult, mainly spiritual path and I think I have rediscovered some things pertaining to procreation which were probably known in Babylon and Egypt long ago. But these things are difficult to talk about, and impossible to write about, because people invariably understand only a little of what one says. Take for example, fairy tales which are of course written in fairy language, which sadly very few people understand. Consequently the meaning of the stories is not grasped at all by the majority of readers. Lots of love, V.

It was disappointingly clear that he still harboured a great deal of antagonism towards me and was consequently as hostile as ever towards poor unaware Daniel. Absorbing this fact created a strange mixture of disappointment and distress. As for Faith, she spent the weekend wondering how best she should reply and in the interim ran a Google search on minor towns in Israel where she and Josef and the two girls might happily reside just in case he enquired. I determined that she had lived with Josef for eleven years and that he was now 87 years old and frail because of his illness. He had proved to be the most rewarding relationship of Faith's life. She had met him when she took the job as his housekeeper shortly after his wife Zena had died of cancer, sadly within a year of adopting the two little girls who were refugees.

Faith spoke further of Christina and agreed that she had been aware of the belief she held that she could psychically control her own fertility. And she asked questions about his child, what had become of it and the mother. The child would have benefitted from contact with its father and it was a pity that the situation was the way it appeared to be. Then she touched a little on the subject of fairy tales and fairy language, but just a very little because she and I had only the slightest grasp of the intended meaning of his remarks on this topic. She chided him further for continuing to hide himself away out of fear of Bernadette. This was not the Vanith she had known all those years ago. It was a nice long, newsy message which he should enjoy. And he did.

NEWS EXCHANGE
From: Vanith Lefarge (Vanith@inthesky.co.uk)
To: PersephoneFaith@highmail.com
6th June
Dear Faith, thank you for your long email. Well, I don't quite know where to start. It seems it might be difficult for us to meet in the near future, but I would very much like to talk to you. It would be so much easier than writing.

Christina was never that important to me and it was emotionally a one sided affair. So much so that I felt bad when I had to accept her help but when you are penniless it is difficult to refuse.

Like most of my girlfriends, Bernadette was somewhat of a fairy and had considerable powers, telepathy being one of them. She and I had a long and fierce battle, because she was in love with me and determined to possess me and I was equally determined to keep my freedom. For a long time I had not fought all that hard because I had seriously underestimated her. She was a nasty and ruthless adversary.

It took me a long time to overcome the bitterness she had left behind in me. She became determined to do me harm and actively tried and nearly succeeded at times over the years. I think she still would if she could. She last phoned me a few years ago, but I put the phone down. She gave birth to that child very much against my wishes. It was born after we parted much to my distress because I would not want any child of mine to be brought up by somebody like her. A few months later she married a New Zealand doctor and went to live with him there and had 3 or 4 more children.

Tell me about your daughters. Are Tamsin & Larissa Jewish or Palestinian? Why were they refugees? Where in Israel do you live? What is life like there? I assume your parents are both dead. Have you been back to Ireland? There is so much I want to know and so many questions I would like to ask.

You were extremely important in shaping the course of my life, but I don't know how much was intentional and how much of it you actually realised. I would love to talk to you, unhurried and at length.

Much love for today from Vanith.

As Bernadette, lingering inside Faith, I felt that he could have paid more attention to the time frame between Daniel's birth and the advent of his New Zealand stepfather. I was, however, vaguely flattered at having New Zealand children other than Jonah and Martha bestowed upon me and wondered if they were boys or girls and what I might have called them if indeed they had ever existed. He was exhibiting rather too much curiosity about Faith's life in Israel which would clearly necessitate more research. I began to wonder somewhat uneasily how adept he was in the matter of computers and whether, if he became suspicious of the details surrounding the sudden return of this old friend into his life, he would be able to investigate the matter with any likelihood of discovering the truth. So I began a careful reply and even as I tapped the keyboard another message arrived.

OLD TIMES AND STRANGE PLACES
From: Vanith Lefarge (Vanith@inthesky.co.uk)
To: PersephoneFaith@highmail.com
7th June
Dear Faith, I have been reading over our correspondence. When you tried all those years ago to lead me to the elusive place that is the territory of the Black Isis, I found it too terrifying to follow. Had I done so we could have had amazing experiences together. Did you ever go there with another? If so with whom? I feel that your relationships have not always been happy and successful, the present one excepted. I want

you to know that I certainly would have wanted to go to those psychic-sexual places with you if it had been possible. Love V.

It was as Bernadette that I read this several times whilst being more than impressed that Faith clearly understood, or was expected to understand, this rather incoherent rambling. Bernadette deliberated as to his meaning. Then she wondered how best to reply in order to convey complete understanding. It was not going to be as easy as she had originally imagined to simply don the mantle of Persephone Faith's long ago relationship with Vanith Lefarge. If he had searched for more than one old friend via the internet, it might have been easier to have entered the essence of Christina instead. However, given that Christina lived on Exmoor, and adding his present desire to catch up with the past into the mix, this may have thrown up even more problems keeping him at bay. The moor was just too close to North London for comfort. She consulted Google, and she put a great deal of energy into trying to understand the meaning of his message. A lengthy and laboured reply was called for, one that put Faith firmly beyond the reach of telephones whilst posing questions that needed answers as to the parameters of his technical ability.

She asked him how skilled he was as far as computers were concerned. She said she only had a hazy idea as to how Skype worked but imagined that her girls would be familiar with it. Most of their communications were sent and received by email these days because the range of mobile phones was unreliable where they lived. She admitted that they were Luddites, now living at Josef's summer house just north of Haifa and they would be moving further south soon depending upon his health. She admitted that life was full of upheavals for them. She spoke at length of her adopted daughters, their Palestinian mother and Jewish father, both murdered by neighbours in 1995. Then she moved cheerfully on to Darwin and natural selection before launching into communication misunderstandings, people only half understanding what is explained to them. She touched upon art and music and a little upon poetry, commenting how easy it was for a culture to be debased by praising bad works of art. She commiserated with him regarding the problems he had experienced with the dastardly Bernadette and emphasised how important it was for a child to have connection with both parents. There must have been extreme forces at work at the time that child came forth into the world. Then she likened Bernadette to the goddess Kali, a fearful and ferocious mother. She felt particularly satisfied with that observation. She wrote several pages, touching more than briefly upon his child and the sad situation that had developed. She spoke of how much Josef meant to her, how deeply she loved him. As he now seemed to be waking she would have to stop writing. She was pleased with the length of this letter and she knew he would appreciate it.

She did not make the mistake of sending it immediately, assessing it again with her first cup of coffee next morning. Her first waking thought had been that a sentence querying whether or not he had been required to give financial support for Bernadette's child should be deleted. But at eight fifteen when she re-read it, she found herself quite satisfied with the slightly admonishing tone. She thought her comments created just the right amount of preachiness in assuming that as a father, he would most certainly have been expected, if not required, to provide some kind of financial support even if he had decided to withdraw all vestiges of emotional sustenance.

She fervently hoped he would clarify how much technical skill he had and whether in fact he was a geriatric computer wizard. If he suddenly decided to attempt to trace where in the world her messages originated, their future relationship might be in some jeopardy. She pressed the send button decisively and wondered how long it would take to traverse the Earth and settle itself in his inbox. The rapid reply came in the late Auckland winter afternoon when rain hurled onto street surfaces in sudden short bursts and walkers hurried towards the beach with their dogs, shivering damply in light sweaters, wishing they had remembered to take umbrellas with them.

REPLY
From: Vanith Lefarge (Vanith@inthesky.co.uk)

To: PersephoneFaith@highmail.com

9th June

Dear Faith or do you prefer to be called Persephone I am wondering? When I first met you, you gave your name as Faith, and I think it suits you. Thank you for your long email which I got earlier on today. I am not sure how to answer systematically, and I shall try to go through it point by point.

As a mathematician, physicist and engineer I obviously understand how a computer's hardware works. As regards the practical technology, my understanding is limited, because I have never worked on modern design. In any case, I doubt that anybody understands everything thoroughly. An expert on the making of microchips would not necessarily know about networking systems. There is a big difference between being a first class car designer and being a first class driver, which is not necessarily the same as being a good racing driver, who might be a menace on a public road!

I have 'built' the computer I am writing on at the moment, but that simply means I have fitted the various components together. That requires no great technical knowledge, because it is little more than connecting a printer to a computer, and I would hardly call that building something.

When it comes to using the damn thing I find that is a completely different matter. I preferred the earlier operating systems like MS DOS. I hate Windows which I think was designed for people who do not understand computers. I am reasonably familiar with Word and

Photoshop, and I have used Excel a few times when I was doing translations, because some of the originals were written in it. I know nothing about website design.

Emails are indeed useful for communication, especially for people who like writing, but I am not one of them. However I am doing my best, which is sort of adequate. I was always reprimanded as a child for my writing.

To other matters: Intelligence is certainly a matter of natural selection. It just depends on whether intelligence is useful for survival. I think that for the people living in small pockets of Eurasia in the middle of the ice age it was a great help for survival. Hunting Woolly Mammoths is not simply a matter of physical strength. For survival in Africa, immunity to Malaria might be more important.

Completely hazardous for survival is the irrational philosophy of Christianity. If you suggested applying its principles of procreation to a dog or horse breeder they would think you mad. For centuries the best males have killed each other in battle while the priest made sure that the twenty children of the village idiot got fed and survived. In WW1 five million of the finest young men in Europe were killed and the dregs of the communities were left at home to make babies!

The temporal forms of Christianity (Communism, Socialism etc.) are even more deadly. In this country the average prison inmate has two or three times as many children as an average university professor. The level of intelligence and education in Europe has fallen steadily and dramatically in the last couple of centuries. There is not a university professor in this country or in the USA who would qualify for university entrance in Europe before 1950. Yet even an ordinary sea captain in the 18th or early 19th century soared above the so called educated elite of today. Captain Bligh of Mutiny on the Bounty fame could speak, read and write Latin and probably some Greek. He could navigate astronomically without a Nautical Almanac which requires a very considerable knowledge of higher mathematics. He could speak several modern languages, knew a bit about ship building, weather forecasting, etc. And he did not claim to be a scholar.

True knowledge is a wonderful thing, but whether such knowledge improves one's chances of survival Darwinistically is debatable. I fear our wonderful civilisation of the Age of Enlightenment is in decline. My parents' world ended to some extent in 1918 and according to a mathematical model I made in 1970 our entire civilisation will vanish around 2030. The Soviet Union collapsed in 1989 and with the many on-going financial crises I think the days of the capitalist world are numbered. But I doubt that world will roll over quietly. There will be catastrophe upon catastrophe.

The difficulty in making leaps in understanding is always the letting go of false notions. But the nonsense inherent in the so-called science of Economics nothing compared to the total rubbish people talk when it comes to spiritual matters. The belief in God is absurd and the belief that there is no God is probably even more stupid.

To return to the fairy language of myths & legends touched upon a few days back. It is noteworthy that Siegfried kills the dragon, then breaks Wotan's spear and then marries Brunnhilde, the daughter of the mother-goddess Erda. Oedipus meets and overcomes the sphinx, then kills his father and marries his mother. Odysseus encounters the one eyed Polyphem, wisely gives his name as No-One, then has an affair with Circe and subsequently has to visit the underworld. You find there are similar stories in both Hindu and Tibetan legends. They are all tales of spiritual journeys.

To Bernadette and her child: it was a boy. However I am not as you seem to think very concerned with her and now seldom think about her to any extent. The reason I had nothing to do with her or the child is because her behaviour was outrageous in every way. There were of course very powerful forces at work around me at the time of that child's birth, and for that matter to some extent for all my life. I have had endless and fruitless arguments and discussions about all this with my brother and my sister-in-law, and it has seriously damaged these relationships. As I am surrounded by unusually potent forces, I therefore have to live in accordance to different laws to other people. You too seem to imply that I have not thought about these things sufficiently, and you know better than me how I should behave. I can assure you that when I have tried to explain seriously what happened in the matter of this child's birth in the late 1960s no-one has ever believed me. The events as I relate them are quite impossible in their philosophy. They always think they know better. I have therefore long given up giving explanations.

To Music: Furtwangler was a great conductor, much heavier, and deeper than Toscanini, but to me that slow earnest depth tends to become boring. However Toscanini can be fast and almost superficial. Regarding the Beethoven symphonies, to me Toscanini is definitive. Lots of love from Vanith.

PS do you remember what you said (or whispered) to me on a London bus when we were living in Pimlico?

It was a great pity that he seemed so very much against explaining in detail the circumstances of Daniel's birth because Bernadette would certainly have listened attentively to his version of events. She was pleased that she seemed to have made a fairly good fist of holding her own in the strange debate regarding fairy lore. Maybe he simply paid little attention to what others wrote, being primarily concerned with himself and his own thoughts.

Overall it was reassuring to know that he was clearly not in a position to start tracking the source of messages though the cosmos with any degree of ease. As far as Skype was concerned, she had no intention of becoming involved in the obvious difficulties of prolonging the mythology of a stroke in lengthy traditional conversations. When she re-read the message later she regretted that she had no idea what had been whispered to him on a London Bus in Pimlico so many years ago. She wondered if Persephone herself would remember. She also wondered if Persephone was still alive somewhere, going about her daily business totally unaware that her identity had been borrowed for a while. She reflected how very odd it would be should she be found living in Israel, perhaps with an elderly and sick partner and two lively teenage daughters. But then possibly not completely unexpected since Bernadette was at least partially a fairy of some significance.

EIGHT

After giving frequent thought to his comments over the next day or two and re-reading them several times the fear of him realising he was being deceived abated and very nearly disappeared. He was clearly still far too egotistical to contemplate such an idea and possibly it was foolish of anyone who had ever been involved with him for any length of time to think otherwise. Should she feel guilty about the deception? On balance she thought not and it took no time at all to reach that happy conclusion. So she went about her daily tasks with a somewhat lighter step, attending to housework, shopping for meals, meeting a friend for coffee. Late at night fortified with a large glass of white wine she read his emails once again and slowly. Persephone Faith Callahan was clearly a woman who had shared a number of interests with Vanith Lefarge. She wondered what kind of psycho-erotic antics she had tried to inveigle him into that had him simply hovering on the brink of a dark but desirable abyss in the late 1950s. It was not like him to be half-hearted in any matters pertaining to sex but Faith seemed to have struck a chord of fear in his young narcissistic life.

He deserved a thought-provoking reply. She thanked all the Gods for Google as she slipped beneath Faith's skin once more.

From: PersephoneFaith@highmail.com

To: Vanith@inthesky.co.uk

12th June

My Dear Vanith, I am very happy to simply be Faith. I too would love to be able to speak to you properly, but it is so very difficult for me to do so. I know you will try to understand. But oh dear – I fear you are already a little displeased with me for my questions with regard to your son. However, one must always be prepared to take risks in relationships and perhaps even more especially within the folds of an old friendship. Would you agree? Anyhow, whatever you think, let me register now my sincere apology for urging you to rethink the matter of your child when it is now clear from what you say (or what you do not say) that I am not in possession of all the facts relating to this event. Possibly I would not have urged you so emphatically to rethink the matter if you had enlightened me more of the happenings leading to his birth – I mean those matters that your brother and sister in law find so difficult to accept. Perhaps there was indeed something very potent happening at that time and if it was something outside the realm of experience of your immediate family then of course they will be seeing an incomplete picture. You will find a more sympathetic listener in me I promise. But if I stray from what you find to be acceptable then you have to tell me… as I am not as psychic as either of us would like to believe!

You sent a message the other day asking about paths I might have been leading you down in the 1950s, about psycho-sexual explorations, etc. I had to think about what you had asked – I had to ponder a great deal in order to send you a sensible and honest reply. You must understand that I too was much younger, much less experienced and had only the brash enthusiasm of youth with which to arm myself. You are of course right – yes, I was trying to mould you into a form that I imagined at the time, to be magnificent. You had an enthusiasm and an ability to focus on mystical ideas that I had not come across in another before and it excited me. Perhaps those adventures were not for this life. I think I might, at least at times, have been having glimpses of what I yearned to be rather than what I was. Does that all sound terribly foolish? I have at times tried to initiate that voyage of discovery with others but never successfully. Always it seemed that the situation very rapidly descended into neurotic, compulsive, fixated attachment as far as my prospective partner was concerned and so, with that huge amorphous cloud of emotion between us the journey was then interrupted whilst we halted and examined our earthly relationship and where it was going, what the future held for us, etc., etc. I long ago realised with some regret that these matters have little to do with love and everything to do with an expansion of spirit and of perception of knowledge yet they are invariably confused with love.

You are correct when you say that my relationships have been largely unsuccessful (to say the least). My present situation with Josef is quite, quite different because in the first place I was unaware that it would develop into a relationship and therefore I did not bring to the situation any previous hurts or scars. I have been able to love him in a completely different way – it has been a wonderful experience and I am grateful to him for enriching my life in this way. My problem for the most part has been that at a human level I have been unable mostly to 'fall in love' in the accepted sense of the term.

As far as your own journey through four or five decades is concerned, how many 'important' relationships have you formed – and with whom? How long did they last? How did they compare – one to the other? At what stage did you realise that the Truth you had hoped for, even inadvisably spoken of perhaps, had twisted imperceptibly to become a trap? At least in those unenlightened days of the 1950s we could actually live with someone for a year or two and society merely murmured disapprovingly. These days we proclaim the unwary couple be married after 2 or 3 years (to all intents and purposes), without enquiring whether or not they want to find themselves in that happy state. In some ways therefore we had far more freedoms in the bad old days.

Now forward to issues relating to Isis. Some years ago I investigated the World Centre for Isis which is based, strangely, in a castle in County Wexford. However, it was disappointing. You can find them on Google. I think they still exist because I met someone quite recently claiming membership. On the bright side, although as you say, much of what is spoken of spiritual matters is errant foolishness, it has at least allowed for a certain freedom of expression that was simply not possible thirty or forty years ago. And it has also allowed more access to texts that were once forbidden. I found a copy of The Grimoires in a very ordinary book shop a few years ago and I have been surprised to see both the Egyptian and the Tibetan Books of the Dead for sale along with cookery books and gardening guides (in perhaps the Hobbies section). And of course you can find all these things very easily on line. In short we are now 'allowed' to have access to that which was not so long ago considered at best cranky and at worst dangerous in the same way as society now totally accepts the much despised Gay Rights and demands Gay Marriage. We live in an era of pseudo enlightenment and the spin-off for people like you and I is that it gives us freedoms that we would previously have thought impossible! We no longer need to whisper along telephone lines – we absolutely have the right to join a Coven, brew magic potions along with the family's soup and even advertise on the internet for a cannibal sex partner. Anything goes!

I meant to ask you about your family. I seem to remember that your father lived in Devon or Cornwall but can't recall where. Have you been back there in recent times? Is his house still standing? It's strange how we become much more interested in the lives of our parents and grandparents as we become older ourselves. Has your brother had children? I ask this because if he has not then possibly his attitude to your child is coloured by this fact. What of other relatives – are you in touch with other members of your family?

And with regard to health – you have told me nothing about your state of health. Are you fit and well – or as fit and well as the years allow? Finally, you ask me if I remember what I whispered to you on a bus... and sadly I do not. Enlighten me. I am enjoying your emails so very much. Love, Faith.

Again Persephone Faith determined not to send it impulsively. The lengthy typing exhausted her and she padded up to Bernadette's quiet kitchen, opened the refrigerator and refilled her wine glass. Jack was still outlined in the half darkness of the living room, watching a Sky History programme on the progress of submarine technology in the 1920s. He did not glance in her direction.

Overall the tone of the message satisfied her. She felt it conveyed just the right amount of offhand intellectual curiosity coupled with a sound knowledge of all things esoteric. Faith was clearly quite a formidable woman who had dealt with her various lovers in a commendable manner and she began to see what Vanith admired in her. It was close to one in the morning when she sent the email flying off through the Auckland winter sky towards Europe. And then she went happily to bed.

She slept very well indeed and next morning the instant coffee that usually tasted bitter and quite unpleasant, was almost palatable. She looked forward to his comments and hoped that he would talk about his health. She knew from the occasional contact Daniel had with Rudy and Angela over recent years that he was having ongoing problems with stomach pain. Rudy had said on more than one occasion that in his opinion it was guilt concerning Daniel that caused these pains. Apart from that she looked forward with some anticipation to any further scurrilous comments he might make about poor Bernadette. Faith had begun to feel quite disapproving about some aspects of Bernadette's behaviour.

When she went into the office she found to her enormous satisfaction that he had already replied. How astonishingly simple it was becoming to bend him to her will. How satisfying it felt.

DIFFICULT TO TALK.
From: Vanith Lefarge (Vanith@inthesky.co.uk)
To: PersephoneFaith@highmail.com
13th June
Dear Faith, Parting from Bernadette was a long and hard battle. For three-and-a-half years she lived with me against my will. How this was possible with blackmail and other nefarious means is in itself a very long story. The battle slowly became more and more desperate and bitter. Telling you in detail would involve writing a book the length of 'War and Peace' and I would not want to embark upon that, because it would be unpleasant and it has hardly been on my mind for years and therefore I have forgotten a lot of it all. Becoming pregnant was the last phase and equivalent to a nuclear attack! I am sure this explanation will not satisfy you, but more detail would only raise more questions and you would find the

answers incomprehensible. Also, and more seriously, it involved magic and that is still something best not talked about too openly. As I have said previously, Bernadette was a treacherous individual.

Our whole collective consciousness and thinking is built upon a fundamentally false system of Axioms except for physics of course. Our ideas about the human mind are totally absurd. The entire vocabulary of metaphysics or that of the virtually non-existent science of the mind is very dangerous to use because of the silly concepts associated with all the words. So whatever one says, unless one could re-define the words, the listener misunderstands.

There are some people who have an affiliation with or even a hotline to the kingdom of Oberon, or similar kingdoms. Such people have supernormal powers, which may, however, be of a very different nature. Compare yourself and me and Christina and Paganini and Alexander the Great and Hitler and Joan of Arc. All may have in common the fact that they are extraordinary people but they are very, very different one from another. The explanations of these differences are complex and when religious groups or occult societies pick up bits and pieces and attempt to fit them together, a web of inaccurate information emerges. There is no way the fundamental faults in our collective thinking can be repaired – that thinking must be discarded in its entirety and we need to start afresh but that is easier said than done. Letting go of deep-rooted ideas upon which our entire world has been constructed is painful and unpleasant. This is why it is invariably counterproductive to speak about matters magical.

I have only a human intelligence and therefore it took me about fifty years to understand these things, in spite of the fact that I had all conceivable advantages. I come from a family of occultists and started at the age of seven to perform mental exercises in order to acquire supernormal powers to defend myself against the very strong personality of my mother. I have practiced and studied experimental magic all my life. And it still took me a hell of a long time to absorb what I have learned.

To you and I: You Faith taught me an enormous amount all those years ago, but my understanding of these matters was not good enough for me to prosper from it. It is a great shame I was so slow to make progress, because we could have explored amazing and beautiful worlds together.

You put it all very well in your last email and I know you understand much of this perfectly. As to love, the ancient Greeks had three words for love and we only have one – and love itself comes in so many shapes and forms. I have led or tried to lead a number of women into these worlds that interest you and I but they are so far removed from the world around us, the normal everyday world that they invariably became frightened. When you find yourself in the 49th heaven (7x7) and suddenly look down, you often suffer from vertigo. This happened because I had not adequately prepared them.

You ask about my family. My father died in his house near Newton-Abbot. He was 88 years old. My mother died in Germany in 1976 also aged 88. My brother is nearly seven years older than me, and has made quite a name for himself by sailing 3 times around the world. He has written a dozen or so books and made quite a lot of films. He and his wife live in the house of his mother-in-law who is a very stupid woman. In 1999 she was very rude to me during an argument about that child of Bernadette's. Since then I have not been allowed to visit her house and so my brother and I have to meet from time to time under difficult circumstances. The on-going disharmony is all very disagreeable.

As for my health, unfortunately I have had stomach pains on and off for more than two years and no satisfactory diagnosis has been made yet. I am having further tests done soon and I think it could be a hiatus hernia and could be cured with a simple operation. It is a nuisance because these cramps at the stomach/diaphragm/oesophagus junction can be very painful and can last for just five minutes or several hours. I was so fed up and desperate six weeks ago, that I went to see, what should be a very good surgeon, privately which cost me £190. I am hoping he will be able to provide me with a solution.

I was sorry to hear about Joseph's illness. Watching him not getting better must be very hard for you. With love, Vanith.

PS I am sending an attachment – some music we used to listen to years ago.

I read it seated at my own kitchen table in eight am sunlight. It pleased me enormously that he had found the parting from Bernadette so difficult though I did not altogether accept that he had lived with her against his will for three-and-a-half years and I wondered what the details of the blackmail that kept them together were. Still, it was pleasing to find that he still believed the events to be steeped in magic so powerful that could not safely be spoken of.

Other things that could be spoken of were difficult to have any understanding of even after a refreshing night's sleep and I wondered not for the first time the exact nature of that which Faith had taught him, those matters in which he now pronounced so earth shattering. What should her reaction be? It was difficult to know how she would feel about it these days but the part of her that lingered inside me as the day went on was loth to simply ignore it. I sat trying to open the attachment he had sent which would not open for me no matter how hard I tried.

Later that day when Daniel, who lived as quietly as possible downstairs, and continued to be almost completely engrossed in his new relationship with the girl called Salome returned from an orchestra rehearsal, he opened it swiftly, easily and without curiosity. He began to attempt a discussion on his impossibly young beloved's latest university assignment mark before noticing my lack of interest and retracing his steps as the first Act of Verdi's 'La

Traviata' infiltrated the small room with the strangely mechanical and disconnected 1908 voice of Luisa Tretrazinni 'Follie! ... Sempre libera'. He came back and lingered a little in the doorway and commented on the strange beauty of the sound.

It was about the time of the Tetrazinni aria that I began to discuss the events of which I now write, with both Daniel and Jack. Daniel was at first intrigued, even excited, but lost enthusiasm as he began to read his father's letters because he could not understand them. Jack was rather more interested, commenting that for a man who found it so difficult to put pen to paper Vanith was doing extremely well. He wondered if he was a 'real' typist or a two finger one. I gave neither of the men in my life my own emails and for several reasons that I could not quite put my finger on. The most pressing was because I thought they made even less sense to the average reader than his to me and part of me was a little embarrassed by this obvious evidence of my own lack of perception and insight. There was also the question of the blatant deception made somehow more manifest by the existence of my responses printed out on A4 sheets for ease of reading, a duplicity that could be better ignored if they remained concealed behind a password in computer memory. Examining the situation from a purely ethical viewpoint it had to be quite wrong to impersonate another human being. It would certainly be illegal if it was done for pecuniary gain. But what if it was just for...a prank? For a caper? Just for larks?

Not illegal then surely but still unethical or at the very least unprincipled. But then how principled did I really have to be?

The following day I sat down and composed a reply. I asked a number of questions. Some because I had half-forgotten the answers he gave years ago. Some because I wanted to see if the answers he gave would differ substantially from what he had said in the past. Some were mischievous and I asked simply because it amused me to do so. Donning the mantle of Persephone Faith Callahan made me at once supreme and invincible and I no longer felt an urgent need to protect myself from discovery. It seemed somehow right to begin with a comment about the aria, the piece that had always been a favourite with me, allowing me to stand beside Verdi's tragic heroine.

From: PersephoneFaith@highmail.com
To: Vanith@inthesky.co.uk
15th June
Dear Vanith, It was lovely of you to send me that special aria. Perversely it would not open at all for me no matter how hard I tried but it opened just like magic for Larissa. And then of course I was transported back over decades and suddenly began to recall small details like the texture of grubby cushions (Pimlico?) and the greyness of the sky outside with little bitty clouds scudding across it. How effortlessly music can take us immediately into other times and spaces, other worlds. I remained attached to that particular piece throughout the following years and I will try to find a

version that I enjoy to send you (with the help of the younger generation of course).

I think I am beginning to realise with some regret that often we impulsively turn corners in life ...and yet if only we had hesitated, if only we had thought twice instead of once, things might have been so different for us. However, contemplating what might have been can only lead to despondency and so the focus for you and I should be 'upward and onward' and let us see where this correspondence takes us. I must comment now on how very impressed I am with your spelling and fluency of writing – I know that these were not your strengths all those years ago.

Thank you for explaining something of the problems with Bernadette. To live for three and a half years with someone against your will must have been horrendous. I cannot imagine it. Was that the entire period that you lived together – or was there a period when you were able to live in harmony? If so, then you were with her for a substantial period. Was it not possible to simply evict her? Or were you being too kind, too considerate perhaps? This begins to sound suspiciously like the Vanith I knew who was simply incapable of an unkindness to anyone.

With regard to your family - is your father's house still standing? What happened to the house after his death? Had he been parted long from your mother? Clearly there was something quite dysfunctional in your childhood if you felt at the tender age of seven years that you had to protect yourself from her.

I find it extraordinary that your brother is so completely and utterly of this world. Why do you think that is? What is it that so differentiates him from you?

I seem to remember you once telling me that your parents were much older than is usual when you were conceived and that there was something unusual about your birth (am I remembering correctly?). Perhaps you were born prematurely? Often very premature babies are so born for reasons the medical teams fail to understand. I now ask because as you of course will well know, often there are curious aspects and forces around the dawn, naissance, conception, birth of unusual beings who are to live in this physical world – if correct these things would have pre-determined a great deal of that which came later. Specific forces at times merge or coalesce in order to better avert, thwart and foil the earthly incidence even existence of certain souls. Is it possible that something like this might have happened in your case? I am pondering on these matters as I write.

I was distressed to hear of your health problem but thankfully it seems unlikely to be a major one –painful clearly but also it seems it can be overcome. if a simple operation can solve the problem then that would seem the way to proceed. I meant to ask you if you are still a smoker or not. Few of us smoke now. We are like missionaries in our zeal to stamp out even the memory of the cigarette!

You are right when you note that it must be hard to watch Josef simply not getting better from his illness. Sometimes at night I watch him as he sleeps and I try to imagine life without him – and fail to do so. He has disturbances of sleep and so has to use a breathing machine at night – it simply pushes air into his lungs so that he can in fact breathe regularly.

Enough of morbid thoughts! We must concentrate on the positive and right now the positive has to do with all the years since we last met, and the joy of catching up again. Write soon and tell me more of your family because I would truly love to refresh my memory on these matters. And tell me also how you spend your time. Do you stay at home a lot or do you visit friends the way you used to? What is the place like where you are living and have you been there long? What are the neighbours like? Do you still listen to a great deal of music I wonder. At the moment I am listening to Caruso – (Di quella pira, Il Trovatore) a recording from 1906, Nimbus Records. I am certain you know the collection. Much love, PF.

When Faith stopped typing she felt to some degree both concerned and compassionate towards her old friend, and affectionately attentive to his problems. It pleased her to visualise his delight as he opened her email, delight evidenced by his oh so speedy replies. She sensed that it was this same strength and compassion that enabled her to take care of Josef so diligently. She began to wonder what her relationships had been like with other more shadowy past men, those she had spoken to him of. She determined to think more upon this subject because it would be good to know the breadth of her womanly value.

Bernadette's appraisal was that Faith was indeed a virtuous woman whose worth was far above rubies. She searched her memory for the Biblical reference which she thought might be found somewhere in the Old Testament but she could not be altogether sure about this. Rising from the computer she wished she was wearing something more suitable, something Faith might wear. Tweed and cashmere perhaps with pearls.

As she gazed down at herself Faith slipped hurriedly away because Bernadette was quite unsuitably attired in a multi-coloured self-designed knitted jerkin and fashionably threadbare jeans and had adorned herself with loops of amber beads intended to look like a casually artistic addendum. This was not the usual garb of a woman featuring in the Book of Proverbs. Bernadette was trying hard to force back the years.

His reply came swiftly, as both women knew it would.

THIS WORLD AND OTHER WORLDS.
From: Vanith Lefarge (Vanith@inthesky.co.uk)
To: PersephoneFaith@highmail.com
15th June
Dearest Faith, At the moment there is a wonderful thunderstorm going on. I always feel especially excited, when the rain is coming down and the close tension is going and the air gets fresh and cool again.

The version of that aria I sent is one that you had on a 78 rpm record and played to me when we first met. It is wonderful how these old recordings can be cleaned up and the noise reduced. It is all done in the Fourier Transform Domain.

The Fourier Transform or sometimes known as the Fourier Integral is a very interesting mathematical device. It transforms equations relating to what is happening here in space and time into a kind of parallel universe, in which neither space nor time exist. This parallel universe is what the sages of old used to call Eternity. It does not actually mean everlasting. It simply describes a world without space and time. If you study the equation you can see immediately, that when you transform from eternity, everything becomes omnipresent in space and time. The study of the Fourier Transform has helped enormously in my understanding of some things. For instance I had known for many years that telepathy works. Our minds can work partially in the transform domain. That is why, if you pick something up telepathically it may be more or less a simultaneous event, but it could very easily be an event from the past or future. That is why telepathic people are liable to pick up events (or memories of events) that have taken place a long time ago. They then think that they remember a previous incarnation, which is of course not correct. The same applies to the future. It is impossible for me to know, whether any of this can make any sense to you. If it does not, do not worry. I tell you because I know you to be highly telepathic.

With regard to Bernadette. We began an affair a couple of years before we started living together. When I got a roof over my head again she wanted desperately to move in with me. I had doubts, but she promised that she would leave if things did not work out. We lived together for about a year with a lot of problems, and when I told her, after several warnings that her conduct must improve and finally when this did not happen, that we would now have to part, she refused to leave. I could not leave myself, because I had a business and my flat was in a friend's house and I paid him rent in cash so he was happy for me to carry on a business in what, strictly speaking, were residential premises. Bernadette was very good at convincing my landlord, and everybody else, that she was putting up with an ogre. It is astonishing how many people believed her. At first I treated her kindly but eventually she forced me to treat her more harshly. It all left me very hurt and bitter.

To move on to more pleasant memories, I don't actually know if my father's house in Dartmoor is still standing. I went to see the people who had bought the house in about 1960 but have not been back since then. Very briefly: my father was born in 1855. When he was a little boy, the older men had fought in and told stories about the Napoleonic wars. His father was an extremely rich German industrialist and in about 1850 he went to America, to see whether there would be a market for his silk in the USA. He decided that the time had not yet come for this trade but found instead a very attractive girl of Anglo-Irish aristocracy whose family had become totally impoverished, and who were desperately trying to sell her quickly on the marriage market. The deal was done and her later suicide attempt on the crossing was unsuccessful. She had been educated in Paris and introduced at the court of Napoleon the 3rd at the age of 14 or 15. She was Catholic and spoke fluent French and English. His marriage to this foreigner upset all the mothers for miles around his home village for they were all hoping he would settle for one of their own daughters. My grandfather loved and adored her and did everything to make her happy, including allowing their second son to take her family name. But he was away a lot of the time on business, often travelling to the Middle East to sell his wares. During his absences my grandmother amused herself in Paris and Brussels. On one of her trips to Paris, she met a man called Eliphas Levi, a Magician and became one of his chief disciples.

Later she became disenchanted with Levi and more impressed with Madame Blavatsky, the founder of the Theosophical Society. Helana Petrova Blavatsky (HPB) eventually became my father's spiritual teacher. She told him her earthly mission was to break the offensive materialism of Christianity and that he must acquire real wisdom – which under her guidance he did. He began a search for Truth and gathered around him his own disciples, one of whom was my mother.

After the death of her first husband on the honeymoon my mother became a voluntary nursing sister in the order of St. John. She was very religious in a primarily Christian way, but also interested in the occult. She felt that there was something lacking in accepted religion and this may have partly been because her Great grandfather had been an occultist and Freemason with his own Lodge. Her father was Lord Chamberlain to the last two Kings of Saxony and that was a most influential position. When she and my father met in 1915 she became very interested in his teachings and had an instinct for the real meaning of them though she told me years later that she never fully understood what he was trying to convey. She learned his teachings verbatim and taught them all to me when I was in my teens.

In 1916 or thereabouts when she and my father started having an affair this was quite outrageous for a woman of her background. In 1920 with birth control in its infancy she became pregnant and my father reluctantly married her in April 1921 and consequently my brother had to be born very prematurely indeed because they had been married less than three months. It was a difficult birth and her womb was torn and she got a thrombosis in her lung. She was told she would not be able to conceive again because of the severe scarring in her womb. However in 1927 when my father was 71 years old she became pregnant again. As I might have told you in the past, she went to Zurich to see Professor Waldhardt, a famous gynaecologist, for advice. He thought her chances of surviving childbirth were poor and in view of her husband's age and the fact that she already had a six-year-old son, she should have a termination. This abortion was performed by means of curettage. Eight or nine weeks later she still had not had a period and still felt pregnant. She went to Zurich to consult Waldhardt once more and of course he found her to be pregnant still.

I was born in February. In July that year my Grandfather committed suicide, because of the imminent bankruptcy of the family due to maniacal feuds within the family. My mother became very depressed for many months after this. When she recovered she became difficult and made life impossible for my father. In 1932 she decided to leave and went home to the family castle quite forgetting it had been sold. Of course this meant she had to find lodgings. She expected my father would beg her to return but he did not do so. She refused to return to Switzerland and he would not live in Germany under Hitler (and under her). In about 1937 or 1938 he moved to England and went to live at Selsdon Park Hotel in Surrey together with a Scottish Nurse-Companion. He then bought a house in Guildford. My mother at once revised her ideas about living in Switzerland and hired a large apartment in Geneva. We then went together with my brother, to Guildford to fetch my father but he did not want to leave. My mother and I then went to a Spa in Bohemia and left my brother in London with instructions to visit my father at weekends. War was about to break out and she decided to return to Geneva and we travelled through the night. She got out of the train at every station to ask for news. At six in the morning the train reached Switzerland and there we received word that German troops had entered Poland just one hour earlier. She sent a telegram to my brother to come to Geneva via Paris immediately. Rudy asked my father what he should do and was told that he was now eighteen years old and should make up his own mind – so he went to Germany and joined the army!

My brother as I have said previously is one hundred per cent a person of this world. I am not of this world at all. I am something else and both my parents realised this before I was born. On her deathbed my mother told me that when she conceived me she knew within half an hour that something extraordinary had taken place inside her and that she was harbouring an extremely powerful being.

That is why they called me Vanith. A strange and unusual name for a very unusual child. Either way it has not always been an easy life for me. My charisma has brought me good things of course – such as your love. All has not been bad. Please do not divulge these things to others because they would fail to understand.

On to other matters: I gave up smoking in 1983. It was very, very hard but I am glad I persevered. Tell me something about your own health. You said you had a car accident and a stroke. How are you now, How many times have you been married? Where is your son and how old is he now?

I hope I have answered some of your questions, at least partially. I shall leave it at that for today. Much love from Vanith.

Even before opening this particular message I had the distinct feeling that it would contain a lot of the information I had hoped for. Call it telepathy or simply put it down to Fourier Transform confusions, or what you will.

NINE

The various stories he had told me all those years ago began to filter to the forefront of memory. The tale of his mother's failed abortion being particularly poignant when I recalled too vividly for comfort the endless anxiety and trauma he had created for me and for Daniel. And reflecting once more on the depth of that misery he had forced upon me I allowed myself a pleasant little daydream where Daniel and I together broke into his North London flat whilst he was conveniently absent. In this fantasy we then arranged various items such as books and CDs in an alarming pentacle on the floor before secreting ourselves close to the ceiling in order to observe his agitation when he returned. It was while I nursed this particular piece of make-believe, reluctant to relinquish it and trying to imagine the precise layout of his North London home, that his PS, together with an attachment, popped into the in-box.

MY FLAT
From: Vanith Lefarge (Vanith@inthesky.co.uk)
To: PersephoneFaith@highmail.com
16th June
Dear Faith, I think you asked the other day about my flat. I attach a drawing of it, which, I hope your daughters will be able to open so then you will be able to see better what my place is like. I have lived here for 20 years now. It is a council flat and as such very nice,

because it is not one of those horrible modern boxes, but a converted Victorian house (1870). It is in Wood Green in North London but south of the North Circular Road and near Alexandra Palace. I have a large bedsitter, kitchen and bathroom and a workroom with lathe, milling machine and a complete electronic workshop. The workroom has a single bed in it so can be used as a guest room.

My stomach problems are currently absorbing a lot of energy, and if they can be solved, by means of surgery or otherwise, I would have more enthusiasm for other things. In the last year I have not even played the piano much because I am at times so consumed by the pain. My upstairs neighbour is absolutely wonderful. He is an alcoholic. When I was very ill last December, he looked after me, even gave up drinking when I was at my worst. He did all my shopping for me, and cared for me in general. His name is Steve. Downstairs is a man there who thinks he is God and when he found mice in his kitchen he fed them because the Lord loves all creatures. Before long he had several hundred mice, who had a lot of babies, who came as asylum-seekers into my flat and and also Steve's. Eventually he set fire to the house to teach Steve and myself a lesson for not having enough love for mice. I was asleep because it was five in the morning. Steve broke the door down and rescued me but I was in hospital for a week. This is just really a PS. Love from Vanith.

It was a very kind thought to attach a plan of his flat but again I battled to open it and was frustrated by not being able to do so for more than an hour until Daniel surfaced in the kitchen making tea. We were both pleased to note that he had even included details of where in the room the furniture was. For a city like London, the flat looked reasonably spacious and I was at once a little resentful. How was it that Vanith Lefarge, technically an alien, lived in a Council flat in London whilst I who was born there, lived in Auckland, New Zealand with no reasonable expectation of being accepted onto the Housing List of any London borough?

'We could break in,' I suggested, still immersed in the fantasy in which Vanith now stood transfixed in horror as the creeping realization of something magical afoot dawned on him. I had already decided that I would rather like him to realise immediately that Bernadette rather than Faith was responsible. It was pleasing to dwell upon his unease and confusion at the complexity of my particularly venomous style of gipsy magic.

'You mean to steal something?' Daniel looked puzzled, both hands spread around his large breakfast cup. I shook my head, 'No – just to frighten him a bit.'

Daniel wondered how many of the family items I had often described to him were still in his father's possession. The banqueting cloths and dozens of Irish linen table napkins, the hundreds of pieces of silver that came from his mother's side of the family. Did he still have the campaign table said to have been used by Napoleon? Or the huge desk with secret drawers? Or the travelling chess table together with its delightful ebony and ivory pieces? His son would have very much liked to own one of these pieces, perhaps simply because it would make him feel just a little bit closer to the family he had never known, even afford him a faint sense of rightful belonging. He wondered a little wistfully if we should break in and search the place and perhaps take the chess pieces, adding, 'That is if he still has them. Maybe he sold them years ago.' But I believed that hell would freeze over before he would sell such items and I said so but Daniel looked unconvinced. Then, being unable to lure me into a discussion about the current problems of Salome whom he now admitted was only eighteen years old, he went back into the lower regions of the house to send text messages for her to receive during her ten am audiology lecture.

It was tempting to compose an immediate reply to Vanith, but I resisted the urge because I knew my response deserved to be lengthy, and instead drove into the city to buy a toner cartridge and two reams of A4 copy paper. Once I returned Jack suggested a walk through the winter sunshine along the waterfront to Mission Bay and perhaps a pause for refreshment at the Belgium Beer Cellar. So it was late evening before I thought again of poor Vanith, checking his computer hourly for messages from Faith. It was probably time for her to reveal more of the events of her own life. She would couple this information with a certain amount of comment regarding the child so unwillingly fathered in 1968 by her old friend. Apart from all this, she might even once more demonstrate her telepathic power because as Bernadette had now come to realise, this gift of clairvoyance used as a weapon, was formidable and should never be underestimated.

She thanked him for the fascinating family history and made comment once more upon the more ordinary and conventional life and personality of his brother. She said she was beginning to understand some of his misgivings regarding the birth of the child and that her initial reaction had come out of an impulsive maternal instinct, the natural desire women have to protect the next generation. She emphasized that she had felt considerable alarm at the lack of connection between Vanith and his son. She added reassuringly that it was not her intention to raise more questions than answers and then noted once more and briefly the presence of Christina in the mix of the unfortunate narrative. She even wondered if under the circumstances it might have been more providential for all concerned if the intractable Bernadette had been persuaded that the life of the child should be terminated before it began. She even wondered ominously how much of his father's powerful genes the child might have inherited. The inner strength of such a person might be formidable. Then she paused to reflect with some pleasure upon his possible discomfort when he contemplated that thought. Rather more reluctantly she turned to the details of her own life and wrote of the death of her parents and commented briefly on the small son she had with her when she and Vanith last met but of course knowing little of what he might sensibly remember of that meeting there was not a great deal she could safely say. She turned her attention to her imagination's freshly created man called Toby whom she met in 1972 and married and lived with in a kibbutz where a second son had been born. She explained how sad it had been when that relationship failed to work and that eventually the boy had to be handed over to his father who had fought for him bitterly. She told him then of the next unhealthy relationship with Ralph that had ended in her returning to England for a while to a flat in Acton when she had tried so hard to rediscover Vanith who had seemed to have vanished from the very face of the earth.

She spoke more confidently of her two boys, now both middle-aged and married, the older one living in Tokyo and the younger in China, both more or less estranged from her. She shuddered when she thought that he might be interested enough to ask for photographs and thought perhaps a disastrous fire might have led to their destruction should he do so. She emphasized that her greatest joy as a parent had come from the nurturing of the two adopted girls, Tamzin and Larissa, and was anxious that he would requests photographs of them because two fires might ring alarm bells. She spoke half-heartedly of her health, her arthritis, her stroke and the bouts of pain that sometimes plagued her. Then she asked more questions about his family, his mother's first marriage and the sad death of the young husband, his own relationship with his father. She flattered him with references once again to his writing ability and wondered that he might write a family history because in his background clearly lay great universal truths. And then she mentioned music, the playing of Menuhin, the conducting of Toscanini. In a PS she revealed that Larissa had opened his drawing and printed it and that he was indeed fortunate because his flat in North London looked so cosy and inviting.

It was not an easy email to write because poor Faith had not had a completely stress free life and Bernadette had hesitated for some time before abandoning further failed relationships. Jacob and Mike and the pain they caused her were therefore deleted together with the intricate details that accompanied them. However, she knew by now that her alter-ego was nothing if not stoical and if anyone could cope well with misfortune then Persephone Faith Callahan could. Nevertheless, it was better by far not to overdo the trauma and consequently not have too many sordid details to commit to memory. She then carefully read what she had written and it gave her pleasure. She pressed the send button and went happily off to bed, falling immediately into a deep and dreamless sleep.

She woke next day to find two messages from him. The second was a postscript and had been sent about thirty minutes after the first. She knew at once they would enormously please her.

FAMILY HISTORY
From: Vanith Lefarge (Vanith@inthesky.co.uk)
To: PersephoneFaith@highmail.com
17th June
Dear Faith, Oh dear, you are still going on and on about Bernadette and also Christina. I will therefore try to explain further. Well about the time Bernadette got pregnant, she and I had an argument and I went to bed and refused to be drawn into an endless dispute. Thereupon she took my little poodle that I loved dearly (Puddles by name) and threw him against the opposite wall of the room. That did get a reaction from me and from David my landlord and the police got involved, and I lost a lot of sleep, which was not good for my business.

Knowing her as I did, I was quite certain that she would without doubt use a child in the same way and it was for this reason that I therefore insisted that she should leave at once or have an abortion or I would leave myself and let her have my business and all the equipment. She then made the choice to have an abortion. I had to leave to go to Germany on business for three days during which time I got almost no sleep at all. When I got back, Bernadette was in bed and told me that she had the actual abortion at about 5 o'clock that morning and apologised for the fact that she had not yet cleared up the mess. I used the bathroom and saw the mess on the floor, but was too tired to clean it up, because I had been driving non-stop for thirty hours. A little later Bernadette got up and cleaned the bathroom. The next day Christina phoned me and said she needed to see me urgently, because she had something very important to tell me. So I went to meet her somewhere for coffee and she said: did I know that Bernadette was pregnant. I assured her that she was wrong and that Bernadette was most definitely not pregnant. I emphasized that I was quite sure of that. Christina was confused and said that in that case she did not know what to say. Later it turned out that Bernadette was in fact still pregnant, and later still, I found out that the abortion I had seen with my own eyes consisted of some hare's entrails she had obtained from the butcher. She of course practiced black gypsy magic, which uncannily tended to work.

It is really not good to revive all this because it was all a long time ago and it is no longer relevant. But you are right, that Christina had a part in the saga. However she was always kind and good as far as I could make out, which is more than you could say about Bernadette.

With regard to my mother, when she was sixteen she fell in love with a man who was a suitable match but did not consider her seriously because of her age. She decided she would therefore sacrifice herself by marrying a man who was interested in her. He was a commoner and an industrialist. He came from the poor branch of the Hoesch family, who owned most of the German paper industry. The rich branch owned most of the German coal mines and steel production. My

Grandfather insisted that she must wait until she was 20. Of course the King did his best by ennobling that branch of the family, but new titles did not really count for very much in those days.

At her engagement party (or maybe it was even at the wedding?) the man she had originally loved asked her why she had done this to him because his heart was broken, but it was all too late. It was a great tragedy, and her husband, Alfred's death on the honeymoon would not have been all that terrible, by comparison. The man she loved had got married in the interim and that was the real tragedy.

My mother was born a girl and of course as such was a disappointment to her parents from the beginning. She had a brother George, a couple of years younger than her. She, being only a girl, was birched from an early age for bad behaviour. However George, being a boy was horse whipped and especially, when at the age of three or four he showed ominous tendencies, like playing with dolls and crying too much and being afraid of sitting on a horse. He grew to be an unhappy teenager and then joined the Household Cavalry. During the Great War he was ordered to teach the cowardly French a lesson by leading a sabre charge at them. Miraculously George survived though none of his friends did but he was certainly a bit shaken. In Gallipoli he got dysentery but again survived. After the war he married a beautiful Lithuanian aristocrat who treated him like a servant. He did have a very weak personality of course. In 1928 he inherited the family Castle but bankruptcy was on the horizon and in 1932 everything went under the hammer. George was penniless and so the wider family clubbed together and bought him a second hand car so he could be a taxi driver. He jogged along until WW2 and went back to the army. He was no longer young and sleeping in tents in Russia caused arthritis.

George always tried to do the right thing but he was unlucky. In 1944 he joined the 20th of July Falkenhausen plot to assassinate Hitler. With George in it, the plot of course failed and Falkenhausen and the nine so-called ring leaders were hanged on meat hooks. George was taken to Auschwitz, where the Gestapo had a special torture section. Maybe not quite as bad as Guantanamo Bay, but pretty bad all the same. Then in March 1945 he was suddenly discharged and sent back to his army unit; shortly afterwards he was taken prisoner by the Russians and made to work in a salt mine until his health was totally broken. He was then sent home and died a few months later. So don't ever believe that one's bad luck must change some time. His never did. His younger sister was a non-entity and the youngest brother Hans-Carl was schizoid with criminal tendencies.

That is a little background on my mother's family.

As far as music goes, I am not terribly into violinists though Master Menuhin was phenomenal. I do still play the piano, but I don't practise very seriously. Love from Vanith.

FAMILY HISTORY POSTSCRIPT
From: Vanith Lefarge (Vanith@inthesky.co.uk)

To: PersephoneFaith@highmail.com

17th June

I would add that as you can now see, without complete information and understanding, which is not always possible, you must invariably come to false conclusions. You thought initially that my mother's first husband dying on the honeymoon must have been absolutely terrible. But without knowing the other surrounding circumstances, you misjudged the situation. You could not do otherwise.

That is one of the reasons why I do not think that I should write a book. I have told you a great deal more than my brother knows about these family matters, because my mother never told him much of it. One does not normally tell everything to one's children. My brother is still very bitter about the way my mother seemed to favour me over him, and he therefore feels it necessary to write an autobiography, to tell the world, what a difficult childhood he had, and how bad my mother was. I think this is a pity.

In Germany at least, and in sailing circles throughout the world he is a famous man. How can I advise him in a way that will compel him to listen? He always wished to be famous and make a great deal of money and he has achieved this but he is not happy. He is under the thumb of his mother-in-law and to some extent lost his self-image through being famous. He sees himself through the eyes of the public and the media.

To matters esoteric once more. Most people believe that they have a soul of some sort and also free will. At any rate their individual mind is independent of others and their thoughts are their own. But all this is nonsense. Their mind is part of the collective consciousness (Alaya Vijnana - Sanskrit) and they cannot think independently.

It is now after nine o'clock and I must go out shopping, because the supermarket close at 10pm. Again, lots of love etc.

The version of events concerning the pregnancy as now related to Faith made me angry. So angry that I was for a while tempted to dial the number he had added to his very first email when he so much wanted her to speak with him in order to tell him in no uncertain terms that he was a liar. The idea of me throwing the dog across the room was preposterous. On the other hand I do not want the reader to get the wrong impression because there were times when I would have dearly loved to throw the wretched dog because I grew to hate it. However, I was far too terrified of Vanith to even speak harshly to the animal. I have made little mention of the dog thus far in this story. I had bought it in a pet shop in Camden Town one Christmas Eve, because it looked so sweet sitting in the window and I was inordinately fond of animals. I knew shortly after I got it back to the flat that it was a huge mistake. Vanith loved dogs but he did not extend that love to dogs belonging to someone else. If the animal remained mine it could not be tolerated. It had to be his and so after a day or two I gave it to him as a present. He then did a very good job of training it to obey him – and to mostly disobey and sometimes snarl at me. Often when travelling in the car, the dog occupied the front seat and I sat in the back because as Vanith pointed out, 'Puddles likes to be in the front.' At best I began to heartily dislike the dog and when he left on that three day trip to Germany and was not able to take it with him, I vowed to show it the mettle of the temporary new Boss! Strangely though, whilst he was away, Puddles wisely did not put a paw wrong. He was obedient and affectionate, going to his basket the moment he was asked and telling me how much he loved and admired me in a thousand different doggy ways. All that changed when Vanith returned.

This latest missive caused me to wonder at what stage and exactly how he had discovered the truth about the hare's entrails. I thought I had taken care not to reveal this to anyone so perhaps it had been a somewhat inspired guess. This was definitely disappointing. However, it was hugely reassuring to know that he was still wary of Bernadette's gypsy magic which had in the interim become decidedly black.

Although I read his comments on collective consciousness and independent thought carefully, and although I could clearly hear his voice lecturing on these matters as he so often had, I could make little more of these ideas now than I had been able to in the 1960s. I wondered how to respond because it was evident that Faith was someone whom he saw as on the same wave-length as himself and able to enter into powerful and protracted philosophical-psychical debate. Faith could be awkward like that. Daniel had a whole shelf of philosophy texts, however, and some even had titles like '*The Dumbest Person's Guide to Socrates* or *Kant* or *Einstein*' so just as long as Vanith did not currently own the same volumes, and just as long as he did not frequently consult them, I could probably manage. His detail of the family history was interesting for Daniel, and also for Jack who thought the story of George extremely amusing.

Faith's reply was sent a couple of days later and she determined to persevere with questions and so posed some regarding the family silver and the pieces of furniture he once owned. And although it would hurt to do so, she would show considerable concern about the wretched Puddles being hurled against a wall.

From: PersephoneFaith@highmail.com
To: Vanith@inthesky.co.uk
19th June
Dear Vanith – I have now studied the drawing you have sent me of your flat at length. You certainly seem to have all that you need there. The pieces of furniture you have detailed however, seem few. Have you decided to de-clutter in these past few years? I remember that when I visited you, you seemed to have far more items around you. Or did that furniture belong to your landlord perhaps? Did I ever meet him? – I can't really remember. Of course it's all a long time ago but I seem to remember a rather lovely table, a very unusual

rectangular one, maybe it was a trestle table, made of dark wood. Have I got that right? And there was a very large writing desk upstairs in your workroom that you told me had secret drawers. Do you remember any of this? You were sleeping on a bed you had commissioned someone to make specially and it was very good for the lower back! The funny things we remember. Years earlier you seem to have wandered through life with very few possessions and yet there in that Clerkenwell square you suddenly had acquired a great many solid pieces of furniture. And you had a great deal of silver which I must have admired because you told me a very funny story of how your mother got the family silver out of East Germany (over the wall when it still existed) with great ease. What a woman! I can't now remember if it actually was silver of course maybe it was the family jewels but it seems to me now that she would have had a great deal of trouble exiting the East with a table on her back. What wonderful family history you have sent me! Poor, poor George – and lucky Adolf that someone so inept was involved in the plot against him!

What an unfortunate series of events surrounding your mother's growing up. I can now see clearly that my first feelings regarding her life are based on presumption only – you are therefore right. But nevertheless, her first love asking her why she had deserted him on her engagement day/wedding day is the stuff of Grand Opera! Seriously though, your mother's story has some very tragic elements in it. Do you think that when she met your father she managed to express all that passion and emotion at last? Their relationship seemed stormy – but do you think it was based on love?

Your brother has of course got his heart's desire – I mean with fame and fortune. Despite this he has certainly lost freedom if he is under the thumb of his mother-in-law. How on earth could such a thing happen? Surely she must be a very old lady by now. You tell it all so well; you have turned into quite a writer over the years. How computers and the internet have changed us all. I am aware that writing is not your most favourite form of communication – however, it does have benefits because with a more traditional conversation, after the event, it is difficult when going back over it in one's mind, to recall all that was said and what might have been meant. Emails have the advantage of re-presenting themselves whenever the reader wants to be reminded of what a person said about a subject at a particular point in time. This does not mean of course that our words are set in concrete because all of us might say something one day that could be expressed differently on another day and so on.

With regard to your translation work, have you tried advertising for more work on your web page for example? At least it is work you can do in the comfort of your own home. I remember you once saying you wanted to write a volume on the spiritual exercises of St. Ignatious of Loyola. It comes to mind again because I have been recently reading something of his life along with the lives of other Christian mystics. His particular *brand of meditation seems to lead the unwary to more immediate results than most.*

I am sorry that you feel that I am going on and on about Christina and Bernadette – I can see you find them both tiresome. For my part, I am astonished that I have had (and recently) such strong feelings regarding Christina and the part she played in your life during the time when all this was going on. I am not terribly surprised that Bernadette's gypsy magic seemed to work. I have long accepted the fact that all kinds of elemental magic 'works' because there is generally speaking a great deal of intensity of wish, hope, thought involved in it... and all thoughts have a tendency to materialize to a greater or lesser extent. I was sickened to hear of her extreme violence with the dog and wonder how you could have kept control of your anger when it happened. Your fears for the child were well founded. A woman who cannot be trusted with an animal, can hardly be trusted with a child.

To mundane matters: I have become something of a cook over the years and I find myself wondering if you, also, cook for yourself? Or perhaps you have had a girlfriend or two who does this for you. You still have not told me much of your loves of the last 40 or 50 years and I cannot believe that most of the time you have led a monk-like existence. I realise now with regret that a week or so ago when you talked of the things we might have achieved together you were probably more than half serious. It's a great pity that the time for all this is past. But I believe that it may be no coincidence that we have rediscovered each other at this time and perhaps the reason will be revealed. I was very fond of you all those years ago and (sorry to mention her name again) Christina did not like me for it. Were you totally aware of all this dreadful interplay at the time I wonder?

No matter how much one yearns to explore other worlds, the reality is that we have to live physically in this world with all the problems that go with it. Of course it is sensible to totally ignore petty jealousies, etc. – but not always possible when one is younger. Much love, Faith.

Faith was beginning to find it quite difficult to maintain volume in her replies to him. If only he was not quite so prone to immediate and lengthy correspondence that could not simply be answered in ten minutes. However, she was resigned to the fact that in order to extract information that would satisfy Bernadette he would have to be provided with an interesting and amusing pen pal. He might even react to the query about cookery – who could tell? She fervently hoped for a delay in the progress of the communications so that she could better marshal her thoughts.

Bernadette was still showing his messages to both Daniel and Jack and had vaguely even discussed them with Jonah who lived mostly in China but had appeared on the doorstep one morning on a totally unexpected three week visit, and sometimes with Martha who lived in London and had a career in international banking law. Jonah showed remarkably little interest apart from being vaguely amused but Martha had been reasonably enthusiastic and attentive. Perhaps it was more a female thing. Though to be fair, Jack was enthusiastic too and read each of Vanith's letters carefully enough to comment upon them afterwards. Daniel showed the least interest and now that letters from his erstwhile father were commonplace, could scarcely be bothered to even glance at them. This was of some concern to Bernadette as was of course the continuing affair with the teenage Salome whose father, apparently, was only two or three years her son's senior. Fortunately her parents did not yet seem aware of the relationship.

In the matter of Vanith, Jack still warned her to be careful because he still felt it was only a matter of time before he realised he was being deceived but she had not the slightest intention of heeding this advice. She felt ever more invincible, with each emptying of the Inbox, each time wondering anew at the ease with which he allowed himself to be duped. And she thought back ten years to a time when the younger Daniel, unencumbered by a fascination with a teenage girl, anxiously sought a meeting with his father. He had travelled to Europe and after a great deal of debate had been allowed to stay with Uncle Rudy and his wife. It was Elsa the mother-in-law, a determined woman, who had led the charge in this particular plan. She was convinced that the unwilling father could be persuaded to come to a meeting with his son and so unsuspecting Vanith had been lured to

Germany with promises of visits to the opera. But of course he could not and would not, be persuaded to meet Daniel and finally left the lakeside house in a towering rage. Elsa wasted no time revealing which train and ferry his father would be taking, urging Daniel to follow and so meet him by stealth. And so he did so, finally catching up with him on the cross channel ferry and recognizing him at once as he sat alone playing Patience. He took at least a dozen photographs and finally approached him asking politely for the time of day. Then Vanith the all-knowing, being at least three-quarters along the way to Full Enlightenment, told his son it was twelve noon exactly, and went back to his game. Neither Bernadette nor Faith thought this was indicative of a man who could easily be persuaded that he had been tricked.

And so the stream of correspondence continued and in his next letter he spoke of Rona, as well as a number of other people totally unknown to Bernadette. But she had certainly met Rona because many years before, whilst Jonah and Martha were still very small, and Daniel about seven or eight, Rona had suddenly appeared at the door of their rented London holiday flat one early evening. She had been perhaps twenty years old, and in the throes of what was clearly a painful if not obsessive relationship, with Vanith. She had heard of Bernadette and wanted to meet her. She did not say how she had tracked her down but later it appeared that Miriam had facilitated the meeting. And very occasionally through the intervening years she had kept in touch, and since the dawn of email the contact had been on a twice or thrice basis annually. Rona became a nurse, had married an older man called Simon, and had a daughter who was now almost grown up. Despite keeping in touch she had not been terribly forthcoming over the years as far as news regarding Vanith was concerned because, like all his friends, she was under orders not to reveal information of any kind that might by default trickle back to Bernadette or Daniel. Though she had been asked on a number of occasions where he lived, what his contact details were, she had never wanted to provide them. Despite all that, Bernadette liked Rona and she was certainly a link to the past.

THIS AND THAT
From: Vanith Lefarge (Vanith@inthesky.co.uk)
To: PersephoneFaith@highmail.com
20th June
Dear Faith, The furniture I had in Clerkenwell was mainly from my mother. My business was going badly and about the time you visited and my landlord who had been influenced by the tales told to him by Bernadette before she left, wanted to double the rent or for me to leave. I was struggling to survive, and therefore my only option was to leave. Through a former girl-friend I got an offer of a small office in Neal Street, Covent Garden. It was maybe 11 x 14 feet. I had to get rid of virtually all my belongings, furniture, books etc. A couple of friends of mine were prepared to

store some of my most precious things. (Like the valuable portrait of an ancestor) The Neal Street office was just big enough to hold my studio equipment and there was a narrow walkway between the tape machines and the disk cutting equipment. That is where I slept on the floor with one blanket underneath me and two above. There was also one chair and a very small table on which I made coffee. There was a disgusting and virtually unusable toilet in the yard. Some girl-friends, in particular I recall Andrea (with whom I am still friendly) and Jenny (whom I have not seen for years) and Olivia (who died from a drug overdose) – came to sleep with me from time to time.

Bankruptcy was steadily coming closer, my debts were considerable. Luckily I then got the offer of contract work (disk-cutting) in another recording studio. It paid extremely well, and in about 7 months I repaid all my debts and then started to save. Next thing I was able to sell all my recording equipment at a reasonable price. I was sick and tired of running a business and in 1974 I was accepted as a maths student at UCL. At the same time Andrea's mother offered to let me a nice little flatlet in her house in Crouch End.

In 1976 my mother died and in 1977 I got my degree. During the 3 years at college I had an affair with a girl called Rona. We got on in bed like a house on fire, but did nothing but argue outside bed. She was incredibly stubborn and would refuse to speak to me at times. She had learned as a child that she could always get the better of her mother by refusing to speak. We broke up in 1977, but I had already met Milly through her. I think I told you about her. She and I went around the world together.

By the way, before I forget - you ask about the silver and I can tell you that all my family silver and other very valuable items were stolen by Bernadette before she left. As well as being a liar she was also a thief.

With further reference to my mother, I always believed that something was missing from stories of her life because there had been such a big change in her once her father died. At first my brother and I were told it was a heart attack but it turned out to be suicide of course and she never recovered from the shame. My father did not particularly want children and as explained previously he found my mother very difficult. From her point of view I think the fact that she had married a commoner created more guilt.

As for cooking - I do cook for myself and I think that might be at the root of my stomach problems. For a long time I lived on coffee and then I would occasionally eat some cheese or sausage. It was not a good diet. Now that I have serious stomach problems, I live on frozen mashed potatoes and boiled beef and avocados and rusks. But that is not a very good diet either.

I was pretty well aware of Christina's jealousy and interference, in my relationship with you. She was very prudish. You on the other hand wanted to be a priestess of Ishtar or Astarte or Aphrodite or whatever. You excited and delighted me because I knew what you wanted was a very difficult thing to achieve if you are *living in the Judeo-Christian world. And in the 1950's I certainly was not able to get out of it, let alone lead you out of it. I did not properly understand these things until the 1970's and 80's.*

I think I shall send this as it is. To-morrow I am visiting a friend in the country and Monday I am having a gastro-endoscopy. If I have any ideas I may write a little on Sunday. Love from Vanith.

Being told that I had stolen his family silver together with a number of other valuable items before leaving the flat in 1968 caused me considerable distress and even after forty years I could not make sense of why he made such claims. Though I knew only too well that people are prone to distortion of the truth, particularly in relationship break ups, I also knew that previously Vanith had taken pride in never telling lies. He had lectured me often on the matter of lying. He felt, for some reason that I never fully understood, that to tell even a small untruth was to completely halt progress on that challenging Path to Enlightenment. It was therefore something that at one time he would not be prepared to do under any circumstances. This was one of the reasons why he became disturbed if friends persisted in asking him questions he did not want to furnish answers to. He did not want to be cornered into telling a lie. Therefore I could only assume that he actually believed I had carried out the thefts. On the other hand perhaps he now lied deliberately and this behaviour that would once have been so uncharacteristic simply represented the extent of his rage towards me.

'Do you think I stole the silver?' I demanded of Daniel as he entered the house as quietly as possible, Salome half obscured by his body though she stretched and strained from that position, anxious to be seen and accepted and making a great fuss with the removal of her shoes. He did not move from the dim gloom of the hallway, shaking his head.

'No, because if you did, you would have done so for me, and you've never given it to me.'

To the same question Jack simply asked, 'Did you?' which increased my fury.

It was tempting to write immediately demanding to know why he thought poor Bernadette had stolen the silver, what evidence did he have, etc. but of course I restrained myself. Jack suggested that if he was as hard up as he claimed at the time, maybe he simply sold the items and then justified the sale by telling people there had been a theft. Either way, I felt disinclined to write a friendly reply immediately. Eventually I told him I was concerned to hear about the impending medical investigation and asked if it was being done privately or through the health service. I agreed that his diet of frozen mashed potato and boiled beef sounded poor but was probably adequate. I suggested making quantities of vegetable soup which would last for days. And knowing he was close to a Marks & Spencer I asked if he ventured into their food department, knowing it was probably too expensive for him to do so. I said it was a pity the interesting furniture had gone and that I was astounded to hear that Bernadette had stolen the silver and asked how he had explained the loss to his family. Had he called the police? I asked about his journey on the path to complete understanding and if he still maintained a 'No Lie Zone' because I understood how difficult this sometimes could be. I spoke more of personal integrity and having to make small adjustments because of living in society. I spoke vaguely of organized religion and in even more imprecise and ambiguous terms, of fairy language. I cut and pasted some interesting quotes on general philosophical life attitudes and pretended they were my own. Finally I wished him luck for the imminent medical investigation and fervently wished him ill.

Then I went to bed still feeling angry and quite forgetting to listen for the sound of Salome's departure from the house though she must have gone home at some stage because next morning her red patent leather shoes no longer lay on the pale tiles by the front door.

TEN

In no time whatsoever his next letter to Faith sat all alone without spam or other unwelcome missives encircling it. And although it rambled from topic to topic, it was informative.

CABBAGES AND KINGS
From: Vanith Lefarge (Vanith@inthesky.co.uk)
To: PersephoneFaith@highmail.com
21st June
Dear Faith, I went to see a Mr. McDowell privately. I told him, that I could not afford private treatment. This is commonly done here - you only pay one private consultation fee, and then you are likely to get slightly better and faster treatment, than if you are referred on by a GP. He arranged for a gastro-endoscopy to be done tomorrow, and also a CT scan.

Referring to cooking, I do sometimes make soups and freeze them, but I am not into cooking and do it somewhat reluctantly.

With regard to music: I think that great music is never cobbled together by composers. It comes from the Muses. Beethoven sometimes did a bit of cobbling to make money. Sonatas and chamber music used to sell quite well I believe. But the piano sonata Op. 31 in D min (The Storm) was certainly not cobbled.

Fairy language which we have spoken of before is a huge topic. It is coded and written largely in the Fourier Transform Domain and is to some extent like differential equations. Differential equations have infinite or many solutions. The moment you try to interpret a fairy tale, even if the interpretation is correct, you limit it, because it has many more simultaneous meanings. What Hans Christian Andersen wrote are not fairy tales in the proper sense. Wagner's libretti, especially The Ring, used fairy language. My father was very curious as to whether Wagner actually understood the language and went to great lengths to meet him. He came to the conclusion that the Muses merely dictated to him.

As for lies: Telling lies is destructive to oneself. You are quite right, that at one time I tried to tell the truth and nothing but the truth. Politeness however always requires a degree of dishonesty.

Concerning religion: As far as I am concerned Jesus and Yahweh and all their cohorts are very nasty and dangerous demons, doing great harm to humankind. However that idea is quite incomprehensible to most people and consequently arguments about the subject are generally futile. I could try to explain to you if you are interested, but it is quite a lengthy subject. The very concept of mono-theism is a form of megalomania that borders on insanity. Yahweh of the Old Testament was the tribal tutelary deity of the Jews created largely by Moses. He instructs that no other gods but himself should be worshipped but he does not say that there are no other gods! Judaism only identified the God of Genesis with Yahweh around the time of the early Christians. There is very little in the Old Testament about life after death – that only came in with

Christianity, taken from Egyptian initiation rites via Plato. When the Christians learned that the Muslims had everlasting life they certainly did not want to be left out.

Concerning our western world: We are obsessed with sex and violence and the preservation of human life regardless of cost or quality of life. Dishonesty is regarded as a lesser misdemeanour. I think sex and violence should be largely decriminalized and dishonesty made a capital offence. As for sexuality, that is another whole subject. We have a male god only which produces an imbalance immediately. The Christians have the Mother of God, but she is a terribly mutilated two dimensional creature. Mary is not even a proper virgin or a proper mother, and she has been completely stripped of sex, magic and wisdom.

Monogamy is a very foolish idea and appeals mainly to women. It is not natural and it does not work. There may be cases where two people stay faithfully together for a lifetime and are happy, but they are exceptions. Take our marriage vows. We are meant to swear that we will love a person for the rest of our lives, a totally irresponsible oath. I can promise not to sleep with other women (and that might prove difficult) but I cannot promise not to desire other women, because that is certainly not under my control.

Finally to health: I hope that my stomach problems will get sorted out at least at a practical level. The demons in my life all claim to be totally good, but that is of course part of their disguise. Atheists are extremely foolish, when they say that God, or these demons don't exist. They are in fact very powerful forces within the collective consciousness – like a hurricane in the atmosphere. Lots of love, from Vanith.

Faith, in her wisdom, should be able to make a much better fist of processing this discourse than I was and he seemed to believe her capable of it whereas I shuddered to think what he would make of poor Bernadette's capacity to do so. But like it or not it was Bernadette who would be required to manage some reply guidelines that Faith would be instructed to adhere to. Bernadette, via Faith, might even engender a frisson of fear into his life. That was the optimistic hope though they were in no great hurry to respond. So, for a day or two he was placed to languish in the 'too hard' basket and largely ignored along with the power bill and notes to remember to buy new batteries for the computer mouse.

From: PersephoneFaith@highmail.com
To: Vanith@inthesky.co.uk
25th June
Dear Vanith, I have been having email problems for a day or two but they seem to have resolved now so here I am again. I wonder how your appointment with the hospital went and whether you have any news yet as to the outcome.
I very much enjoyed what you have told me of your feelings regarding music and I quite agree with you that great music comes from the Muses. Some time we will speak of Chopin - and yes we will indeed speak

more of music at some later stage – and of great writing too I hope because I feel that also comes from the Muses. At a basic, reachable level some of the writing of Dylan Thomas or Wilfred Owen – or even John Betjeman can almost stop my breathing, as if I cannot bear to move on from the moment – and hurtles me the next moment to tears.

As for lying I have found it quite impossible to keep to the strict path you once (probably quite unwittingly) inspired me to follow. I have tried hard not to lie – I do not think I have ever told a blatant lie such as accusing someone of an act they did not commit for instance.

For the moment I want to speak with you more of fairy language. At some level in all fairy tales there seems to be a tantalizing higher layer of understanding that remains stubbornly undiscerned. The Brothers Grimm seem hypnotized by the expectation that '…all good (or perhaps bad) things would come in threes…' and that significant events surrounding birth, death, fate, etc. good or bad will repeat themselves through generations – the seventh daughter of a seventh daughter shall have special powers, etc. - but it does not seem to me that they are in any way cognizant of how to lift the final layer in order to become enlightened about the 'whole'. Therefore the language is only understood at the primary stage. Over the years expanded interpretations to stories such as 'The Golden Goose' or 'Hansel and Gretel' or 'The Clever Little Tailor' are added and at times one wonders if they have come to some great conclusion – but perhaps these additions are simply a manipulative device. What are your thoughts?

We see the same progression of understandings at differing levels in the world's religions. You are much more savage in your feelings regarding the human interaction with and understanding of these matters than I am. My feelings remain semi ambivalent. I see the young woman entering a religious life as often simply a person seeking to understand the things that you and I also seek to understand.

I think you have had a definite head start on the rest of us (and I know you can only concur with me here). You had the advantage of growing up with a certain amount of cultural affluence – and you were fortunate to be very well educated.

As I have said before, I do accept that despite the head start described above, none of this could have been in any way easy for you. You tell me that you felt compelled to arm yourself with the use of enchantment against the power of your mother when you were only seven years old. This was very unusual behaviour for a young child. Probably her mistake was that she gave you far too much information when you were too intellectually immature to understand the implications. How old were you for example when she revealed the quite startling story of your conception …the termination that did not work… and your eventual entry into the world? This would have been a frightening story. The child who hears he has been attacked in the womb becomes a vigilant child, perceptive and intuitive and will employ weapons in order to defend himself – most especially against the parent whom he finds responsible for the attack. The human child feels acute distress that his own parent sought to destroy him.

I was struck when working with maladjusted young adults some years ago, by several cases where children whose parents had determined to abort them at some stage of the pregnancy, harbour serious anger and resentment and in the worst cases will attempt to enact a terrible revenge once adult upon whoever they understand the destructive parent to be. Usually it is boys against fathers rather than boys against mothers presumably because it is so often the fathers who wish to destroy the child.

With regard to our past and those things you and I shared: What I find somewhat disturbing now, all these years later, is that I seem to have come to an intuitive understanding about those years and yet I have no real idea why this should be especially after so much time has elapsed. I am disturbed that I understand very little of what lies beneath our present communion. When we first began this communication I had the strongest feeling that Christina had been a force greatly involved in the latter part of your life with a woman you had been almost inextricably involved with. You have in some ways confirmed this. Much love, Faith

PS Vanith – are you absolutely certain that the abortion you saw on the bathroom floor all those years ago was merely hare's entrails? It seems a quite extraordinary deception and for what reason?

Overall, we were both satisfied with the above Faith and I, and we lingered particularly over his possible reaction to the idea of the enraged boys who sought to avenge themselves upon their would-be destroyers. We wondered if that thought would inspire a shiver of fear within him, ...or if he would only half absorb the notion, dismissing it immediately as not worthy of further consideration. And then we pondered briefly on the advisability of making that particular sentence or two just a little stronger and more menacing. Should we perhaps mention the strange predisposition existing in some families where behaviours and events curiously repeated through generations?

'In point of fact,' I said to Faith as persuasively as I could, 'We are almost not even inventing that – not when you consider his father's pursuit of his mother, then his own constant pursuing of young girls.'

She ignored me and so I developed my theme further, 'Then there's Daniel and that child Salome. He says she's eighteen but she looks fifteen at the most.'

'The problem there is that you don't like her because she's Chinese,' she spoke at last and triumphantly. Persephone Faith Callahan could be exceedingly irritating at times and there were moments when I looked forward to the time when I might finally dispense with her services and dismiss her from my life. After further half-hearted debate we finally agreed that there would be no additional elaboration of the message and vied with each other to push 'send'. Off it went, hurtling towards North London. Shortly thereafter his reply came equally rapidly back.

ANSWERS TO SOME QUESTIONS
From: Vanith Lefarge (Vanith@inthesky.co.uk)
To: PersephoneFaith@highmail.com
25th June
Dear Faith. Thank you for your email. First, the gastro-endoscopy on Monday showed that the mild gastritis I had at the bottom end of my stomach has healed up completely and there is nothing abnormal to be seen. That is of course very good to hear, but it does not explain why I get the awful cramps.

With regard to literacy, I have always had problems with reading and writing. When I was a child the head teacher called my mother in to see him and told her I was mentally subnormal and recommended a special school. While my mother was wondering what to do about this I had the skull fracture and Prof. Vogt (a very eminent man) said that my problems would last six to seven years, and that I was not to go to school or try to read or write during that time. I was very happy about this development.

I actually did read a lot during the next few years, mostly of the classics - Greek, Roman, German and I also read all of Shakespeare, Plutarch and Herodotus. I am not keen on novels. I have never read Dylan Thomas and the other two authors you mentioned. I prefer textbooks and books that have something concrete to say. Novels I find tedious. Dostoyevsky's description of what is going on in Raskolnikov's head is interesting, but I am not sure that it is really worth the time and effort of reading such a long work. Creative writing may have something to do with the Muses, but they would have to be Muses of a lower order than those previously discussed.

To return to telling lies - I did think at one time that one could avoid all lies but now realise that good manners too frequently prevents that.

Now to come to fairy language once again: Some of the Brothers Grimm tales are indeed in fairy language but I am certain the brothers did not understand anything of what perhaps could be called the language of the gods. The pre-occupation with all good (or bad) things coming in three's is simply a superstition, and superstitions are nonsense.

My father had a limited understanding of all this, and he wrote a book about it. It was published in 1940 and called 'The Tradition of Silence'. I doubt that you would be able to get a copy now. It is quite badly written and did not sell well. If you like reading and you want to understand something of fairy language, read 'Monkey' by Wu Cheng'en, and 'The Superhuman Life of Gesar of Ling' by Alexandra David-Neel. These works may very well allow you more understanding.

With regard to religions: They are almost always demonic. These demons like human sacrifice. By becoming a nun, the girl sacrifices her life to Jesus. That makes him strong, fat and powerful.

As far as my own life is concerned, I certainly have had great advantages. I was not brought up as a

Christian, although I had to grow up in a Christian world. The biggest advantage is that I had an early and thorough grounding in occultism coupled with the opportunity to study mathematical physics.

My mother told me the story of the abortion that did not work when I was quite young. Other things she said about my destiny, my ability, I think I put down to the tendency of mothers to overestimate their children. The exact details of what she felt at the time of my conception she only told me on her death bed, because over the years we had had terrible battles, she trying to force me to be obedient. When she was dying, we talked about these battles and I remonstrated with her. I asked her who she thought she was dealing with, when she tried to force ME into doing what she thought was right against my will.

I now realise that I stand on the shoulders of a number of giants. They include people like Galileo and Newton, Plank and Einstein, Blavatsky, David-Neel, my father and C.G. Jung, amongst others. Apart from that I have been helped spiritually by a number of good fairies who came to assist me on my way, guide me, and show me directions.

And now to you my own dearest Faith: You may wonder why I speak with you on these matters. And the answer is that I know you to be a special entity and of utmost importance to me. That is why I wanted to contact you and talk to you and thank you, and it is why I have told you more than I have told virtually anybody else throughout my life. I would count you amongst the most important of those who have led me to the correct paths. I would never have revealed to you all these things or spoken with you on such spiritual matters if I was not quite, quite sure of this. You may, however, still be quite unaware of the fact that you are indeed a magnificent and powerful Fairy. And quite apart from these considerations you occupy a special place in my heart. You have always done so. You always will.

You are still overestimating the importance of Christina in my life because overall she meant little. Bernadette on the other hand was quite another matter, because she also was a fairy in her own right. Unwittingly I had called for her spiritually and I got exactly what I asked for, for she came to me. I learned a great deal from her the hard way. In particular, I learned that in war you cannot afford to be half-hearted, or kind or gentle.

As a scientist I would be very reluctant to state categorically what is or what is not possible. At one time physicists found it almost impossible to believe that Newton was not absolutely correct after all... But I am certain that Bernadette's bathroom floor abortion was entrails of hare. She has even admitted as much herself in conversation with some people but in the end that does not mean much because as I have said previously she was incapable of truth. I am absolutely sure that she was still pregnant when she left, and also reasonably sure that she eventually had a live healthy baby. But I have never been completely confident as to how this all came about. What I do know is that she was an adept practitioner of gypsy magic and a highly dangerous person.

A couple of months after the birth she showed me a psychiatric report on her, which she had stolen out of her medical file. After the delivery of the child she was a little confused and started talking about a person called Vanith and his effect on her life. The gynecologists present were very alarmed and called in a psychiatrist, who concluded from what she said that this monster Vanith that she was raving about could not possibly exist, and was evidently a figment of her imagination as she had become disturbed through pregnancy. The psychiatrist hoped that she would recover her sanity in due course and I think she did. I would love to have a copy of this report but did not ask her at the time. Fortunately she had revealed only a part of the story otherwise they would have locked her up there and then.

I must tell you that I put simply enormous pressure on her, emotionally, physically and spiritually and I could not understand how it was that she could withstand it – but withstand it she did! Even when I knew she was quite terrified, she still did not break, she merely bent a little more. Her strength was clearly something not of this world.

Anyone I related the story to in the immediate aftermath thought I was raving mad. For more than a year I sat dumbstruck in an armchair and thought about little else! Did these things really happen? What part of the saga could I be absolutely certain of? Did I see this or that with my own eyes?

If you want to ask more do not hesitate. Lots of love, Vanith.

Some of it was sheer fantasy. At no stage was there a psychiatric report to steal, though undoubtedly had there been one I would have done my best to purloin a copy, especially if it was as salacious as he seemed to suggest. Knowing the way hospitals work then and now, it would be most unlikely that a gynaecologist would have a psychiatrist on hand to call in following a premature birth whether or not he or she thought it necessary. I was both flattered and offended at the level of hostility he still exhibited towards me and astonished at the potency of his belief in the gypsy magic. And I was also just a little bit peeved that it was Faith who had ultimately become the official receiver of his innermost confidence. Why Faith who was simply a bulked-out figment of my own imagination? How had this female creation become so substantial? When did she attain such prominence?

But at last there was in black and white: the long awaited admission concerning the level of pressure placed upon me during that those nightmare weeks prior to Daniel's birth. That time that is still steeped in fear and darkness where what actually happened mingles with hallucination. How was it I managed to withstand the pressure?

I turned my attention to his account of his own 'specialness'. It was not totally unexpected and certainly not the first time I had heard this particular discourse regarding how unique he was, that his mother had always known that he was a very special little boy and destined for greatness, that only Newton and Einstein were superior in their analytical thinking, etc., but it was the first time I had seen it written down in such detail, against a duck egg blue computer screen, small black lettering in Arial 12 font, unambiguous evidence of his narcissism. As such it was shocking and I wondered that he could write such things and send them off into the great unknown optimistically towards Fairy Tale Faith in Israel but ultimately to the dishonest and devious, conniving and cunning, tricky and treacherous Bernadette in New Zealand. Was it Faith or Bernadette who then experienced the first real shiver of guilt?

ELEVEN

Bernadette began to find it more and more difficult to write him considered and intelligent responses. She so desperately wanted to relentlessly harangue him for gross exaggeration and blatant lies, castigate him for his puffed up paragraphs of unremitting self-importance. Did it not occur to him that even staunch and dependable Faith might begin to doubt his mental stability? In fact she wondered what the real Faith's thoughts would be if it was possible to tap into her physical reality. Whilst reflecting upon all this she typed quickly, efficiently, answering most of his questions and dwelling once again on the ubiquitous matter of fairy language, that simply did not want to go away, fervently wishing as she tapped away, that she had a firmer grasp of what it was he was trying to convey. Her priority, as always, being to force his attention back to herself, his son and the intervening wasteland of festering anger that he had created. Indeed a harder edge of that anger now began to encircle her.

And so, on 27th June she wrote at some length and told him that she was beginning to have a greater insight into all the matters he spoke of. She elaborated on her life with Josef and the two girls and the happiness they had found together. She spoke of her speech problems and assured him that she continued her slow improvement and that at some stage she was sure she would be able to have a sensible conversation with him. In the interim should he write to her of sensitive matters she would delete their correspondence. She said she felt privileged that he trusted her confidence. She told him that he carried a heavy burden of responsibility as did all who achieved a state of Enlightenment or Greatness and that she fervently hoped he was not too lonely in this earthly life. She wrote a little about education and how important it was for highly able boys with writing problems to perhaps be shown other ways to communicate effectively. She pointed out that today's gifted children were more fortunate and were being taught at a young age how to use keyboards. She briefly commented that she did not altogether agree with his thoughts on Lesser Muses and she was remarkably restrained when pointing out that Dylan Thomas, John Betjeman and Wilfrid Owen were considered noteworthy for their poetry, not for writing novels as he suggested and that she was just a little surprised that he was not aware of that.

And then, because she could almost see his face light up with pleasure, she returned to fairy language and discussed how it could become enmeshed in superstitions that curled themselves around Great Truths like unruly vines. She mentioned Voltaire's comments on staking the boundaries of superstition and did not of course tell him that she had come across them in a very recent Google search. She was in fact able to write several satisfying paragraphs on Voltaire. She went on to speak of medieval times when the bulk of European communities lived side by side with superstition, the humble peasant and the learned scholar. Sceptics were far fewer than today and even the most learned questioned only the more extravagant of the general beliefs. She pointed out that nowadays in the so called 'civilised' world witches and fairies were largely relegated to children's story books, that devils had been almost wholly banished and that weird beasts survived only on family coats of arms. However in some remote parts of the world such beliefs remained very much alive and men and women could die if the bone was pointed at them. Yet the eager young scientist would insist that such an idea is demonstrably false and merely superstition. She then turned her attention yet again and resolutely back to Christina and pointed out that although not of great emotional significance to him she had at the same time been involved in a disordered, even treacherous labyrinth of deceit and duplicity in the final months of his relationship with Bernadette. She had not been a mere innocent bystander in the pregnancy drama. She took a deep breath and gently reminded him that he had invited her to ask for more clarification of some things if needs be. She wondered therefore if they could examine together several puzzling questions.

He had claimed that Christina rang and told him Bernadette was pregnant. How did she know that? Did these two women know each other well enough to discuss such things?

He had claimed that Bernadette admitted the hare's entrails termination. A strange admission. Could she have been lying in order to mislead him?

Could someone else also have also become pregnant with his child during that time?

She explained that she asked for clarification on these points specifically because she had a most powerful feeling that there was more than one termination attempt, perhaps even a dual pregnancy of some kind. She told him that she was not surprised to hear of Bernadette's mental instability after the birth of her child. She could now see quite clearly that there had been a powerful set of psychic forces engulfing this young woman. She then stopped writing because Josef needed her to make him a glass of lemon tea.

Bernadette was satisfied with this email. His casual invitation to ask more questions had allowed her to draw him back to the events of the late 1960s with a certain ease and as a reward she had written extensively on matters she knew he was attracted to. And poetry had also been defended. She had been most displeased with his casual dismissal of Wilfred Owen, Dylan Thomas and John Betjeman almost to the ranks of writers of Mills & Boon romances.

CONTINUATION
From: Vanith Lefarge (Vanith@inthesky.co.uk)
To: PersephoneFaith@highmail.com
28th June

It is Saturday night, and I have just come home from visiting Paula, a very dear friend of mine. I lived with her for nearly a year in about 1970. She is one of few girl-friends I have ever had, who is largely human.

Let me explain what I mean when I say that Paula is from the human world, or that you are not. I use the oriental system for classifying Beings. One might almost consider it a psychological system. There are generally considered to be six locas (planes). The world of Gods, the world of Giants, the world of Fairies, the Human world, the world of Pretas (unhappy spirits) and the world of Demons. Beings are from any or all of these planes and are divided into Incarnate Beings, Disincarnate Beings, Beings with form and Beings without form. God the Father and Father Christmas are examples of Disincarnate Beings (or Entities) with form - human form. Influenza is an Incarnate Entity without form. You my dearest Faith are an Incarnate Entity with form. I would describe you as belonging both to the world of humans and the world of Fairies or the Kingdom of Oberon. These are all figures of speech of course.

The concepts of gods and fairies are interchangeable to a greater or lesser extent. The chief and essential characteristic of demons is stupidity and ignorance. Some demons are cannibalistic (they feed their own egos by destroying the egos of others) and some are malicious. There is no law that requires demons to be black, but they like that colour and find it becoming. It is therefore not a complete coincidence that the SS, priests, orthodox Jews, lawyers, a lot of business men, all wore or wear black. The Victorians were also fond of black. As far as colour is concerned, of course the Pope often wears white and Cardinals wear red. That does not mean that they are not demonic.

I would tend to have very little in common with people who are entirely from the human world. A Tibetan Grand Lama once officially declared Alexandra David-Neel to be an Incarnate Fairy. He was correct of course in one sense. In Tibet the people are as foolish as anywhere else in the world, and if you are a fairy, they treat you with great respect and expect you to perform absurd miracles. One group of student magicians even tried to kill her, believing that you can acquire supernormal powers by eating the flesh of a genuine fairy or divine incarnation. Just like the Christians think that they can acquire life everlasting and be cleansed by eating the flesh and drinking the blood of Jesus.

I would generally be inclined to regard all such beliefs as superstitions. However if somebody ill-wishes you or curses you or points a bone at you it is not likely to bring you luck. Thousands of witch doctors, juju-men, yogins, fakirs, medicine men etc have from time to time put curses on the white man. The white man largely regarded this as delusory nonsense. But perhaps it is not as you only have to look at what is happening to the white races now suffering as they do from a kind of cancer of the collective soul.

Fairies like you have special powers but they vary enormously. Some are good at telepathy as you are and as Bernadette was and others have healing hands, but *none can spin straw into gold. That is irrational nonsense.*

When you talk of the pain I have had, I assume you are talking about my stomach pain? I am certainly prepared to believe that these pains are caused by demonic forces. I was surprised, that even my brother asked me whether I had considered the possibility that my stomach problems might be of psychological or psychic origin. In fact I have little doubt that they are.

Now to our correspondence and the sensitive nature of it: I wish you to treat the matters we write of confidentially. Twenty years ago I would have been more reluctant to speak about these matters at all, but I am old now and if somebody reads this at some stage and finds it amusing or thinks we are deluded I would be more pragmatic.

As I have already explained to you, Galileo suffered in many ways just as I do. He was a very lonely man, because he was the only person at that time who knew that the Church was wrong and that the earth rotates around the sun. Consequently he lived to a great extent, in a different world from other people. He could not share his knowledge because apart from the possible consequences of facing the Inquisition, almost all of his contemporaries would have considered his ideas quite absurd.

A lot of the knowledge that I myself have acquired is more fundamental and important to shaping the world we live in than the Copernican system. I cannot discuss it because it is contrary to conventional thinking and impossible for others to understand because they lack the required basic knowledge of Raja Yoga, Psychology and Theoretical Physics - all of which are necessary to even begin. This is quite different from the Ptolemaic system versus the Copernican, which is a relatively simple idea. What I have discovered concerns the entire manner in which the human mind functions together with its relationship to the collective mind – and the relationship between mind and matter. This knowledge means that I live in a lonely place.

My problem is similar to that of a lunatic, who lives in a world of his own. When they first meet me most people realise intuitively that I am not mad, but they cannot enter my world and I only vaguely remember theirs.

I am tired now but I shall write soon. If you tell me what you do or don't understand and how exactly you understand it, it makes it much easier for me to explain. I can't explain if I don't know where you exactly are on your own progression towards wisdom. Lots of love for today from Vanith.

Infuriatingly he had chosen not to answer the three questions she had posed and instead seemed more concerned with recognizing an emerging disciple. She raided Daniel's bookshelf and took 'A Guide to Plato and Socrates' to bed with her and the next day exchanged them for something a little lighter, 'The Beginner's Guide to Newton' and 'Bluff Your Way Through Kant'. It was a start at least. She sent off a brief note to North London emphasizing that she was most anxious to help him with the pain and to steer him away from the emerging Master-Pupil relationship she said she was finding it suddenly very easy to tap into events in his life; they appeared before her like parts of a jigsaw puzzle, quite haphazardly. She was quite sure he would not be able to resist asking questions about them so she sat back and waited for him to nuzzle the bait. Disappointingly he did not quite do so but sent instead a short note saying he had been given a proton pump inhibitor for his pain but help of an occult nature though welcome, would first require lengthy explanations of the forces involved.

It was possible that Faith herself might be over the moon at that prospect but Bernadette certainly was not. She sent nothing further, focused on Plato once more, challenging though it was proving to be, and within a very short space of time he finished the conversation they had already begun.

FOLLOW UP
From: Vanith Lefarge (Vanith@inthesky.co.uk)
To: PersephoneFaith@highmail.com
29th June
Dear Faith, To continue: You are absolutely right in that Bernadette and Christina knew of one another and fiercely hated each other and that there was a lot of psychic linkage between them. They only actually met once and that was a strange and peculiar meeting where I was present. I could sort of tell you, but not now. However, they were both fairies and highly

telepathic, especially in respect to each other and to me. It was all most uncanny at the time.

Do you remember the astrologer, Ernest Page? I at times consulted him and spoke with him of these matters. He was a strange homosexual hunchback, who used to hang out in all night coffee bars in Soho and sleep in the daytime on the Circle line in the winter and in a deckchair in St. James' Park in summer. He was not very good at maths and the charts he set up were very often wrong. Furthermore his way of interpreting charts was weird and eclectic to put it mildly. However his predictions were nearly always correct. When I suggested as politely as possible, that he had a gift, he was furious because he saw his predictions as strictly scientific and he was insulted to be considered a mere fortune teller.

The link between Christina and Bernadette was quite amazing and once I was aware of it I did not like it. After Bernadette left, I sat motionless for many months pondering on what was true and what was not, what was trickery and might have been genuine magic. I am fairly certain that abortion of hers was a hare's guts trick and that there was probably just one pregnancy. I have examined and re-examined these things very thoroughly. But I would never be categorical regarding anything that happened at that time with Bernadette or with Christina or the three of us together. In answer to your question, when Christina told me that Bernadette was pregnant, it was something she perceived telepathically and she also thought that it was important and urgent that she *should tell me. Of course this could have been a lie on the part of Christina but she was generally truthful. Bernadette on the other hand was a habitual and compulsive liar, but I am fairly satisfied that when she admitted to the hare's guts, she was, quite exceptionally for her, actually telling the truth.*

She was not exactly unstable after the delivery of the child but as I have said, I had put the most enormous psychological and spiritual pressure upon her and at one stage I thought she might even perish with fear. Because of the terrifying ordeal she had been through I believe that in a weak moment she inadvisedly spoke of these events to a young doctor. Everything she subsequently said to the psychiatrist in that report I told you of was absolutely true but in a calmer state she would not have spoken to anyone in the first place. She was only too aware of the possible appalling consequences of doing so.

Generally speaking, the things you are 'picking up' on are quite correct or have lot of truth in them, but you then often make errors when putting the bits together. Nevertheless, your ability to focus on these events astonishes me more and more because I know absolutely that you had no prior knowledge whatsoever of these matters.

I spoke to you of my war with the Demons. This conflict has been proceeding for many years. I have thrown gloves at them and forced them to fight, and they have willingly done so. I am well aware that certain things that have happened in my life under the guise of fate have actually been their work. They often masquerade as good fairies so I am constantly on my guard.

My war with the main proponents of Christianity - Jesus, Yahweh & Co has been depleting. I have already explained to you that it is a terrible burden that I am forced to bear. I think you understand that very well.

I do hope to hear from you again soon. I don't want to be too inquisitive but I am of course interested in your present life and circumstances as well as in the history of what happened in the years that separated us. By the way, I have only one picture of you, of both of us, taken by a Dublin street photographer and it is not very good. Have you any pictures of yourself from the Dublin or London days or maybe more recent ones? I am sure one of your girls would know how to scan it and attach it to an email. For now more love and good wishes. From Vanith.

So there was to be some respite in that he was now anxious to hear more of the mundane details of life in Israel which could in actual fact fill more than one page if necessary. Bernadette began to wonder about Faith, how she lived, what her girls were really like, how sick poor Josef was and how to fill pale screen space with fascinating domestic details. And whilst Faith was talking about herself and her family, deliberately making all sound as ordinary and mundane as possible so as not to provoke further inquiry, how best could one or two questions be slipped between the paragraphs to elicit information that she, Bernadette, was determined to know for both herself and for Daniel. Questions that it was hoped would immediately catch his attention. Regrettably Daniel now expressed only the slightest degree of curiosity in these matters and gave almost his entire attention to Salome who was now a regular visitor to the house, irritatingly and persistently establishing herself as a guest of some importance with gifts of chocolates and wine and determinedly addressing both Jack and herself by first names.

She turned her attention back to North London. She was keen to hear more particulars of his father's time in America, how the family money had been distributed and how lack of forthcoming funds had eventually affected Vanith on an ongoing basis. She wished, not for the first time, that she had paid more attention all those years ago when he told her the stories. And of course she was still curious as to what his precise understanding of events was of the time around Daniel's birth. Her anger towards him for the cruelty he had shown in the past had been further fuelled by his casual admittance of the enormous pressure he placed her under all those years ago and had become a bubbling culvert of loathing. She pondered on how she could make him see a preordained correlation between his own pre-birth experience and his son's whilst ensuring that Faith maintained her position as an intellectual middle weight and was not propelled further along the dangerous path of the disciple. Inconveniently his frantic spiritualistic claims could not be totally ignored because the Persephone part of Faith was acutely concerned and therefore attentive to such information, more than prepared to be engrossed, fast becoming entranced.

Bernadette concluded that it was definitely time for Faith to declare her telepathic powers more vigorously to focus his attention. This was easier said than done since she had very little real information about what was actually going on in his present life, and indeed his present life was not where she wanted the focus to be. Annoyingly she had even less information about the moments Vanith had shared with Faith in the past. She only knew that she came from Dublin, at one time wrote children's stories adopting the name Persephone, had become a friend of Christina who grew to detest her and that all three had lived together in London. Not much to build a satisfyingly lengthy letter upon, one he could read more than once and ponder upon for hours.

Bernadette stared at the computer screen, waiting for inspiration which was slow to emerge. 'We could talk about his father's book,' she suggested to Faith. 'The book he said was probably unobtainable now...the book about fairy tales.' She and Faith were both aware that Daniel had found three copies via the internet and bought each one of them. He had even read it. Bernadette had tried to do so but found it fairly incomprehensible. Faith urged her to try again and she promised she would. The ongoing duplicity was becoming more time-consuming but they both knew the email had to be written and it had to be long and newsy enough to preoccupy him whilst posing questions Bernadette was determined to hurl before him. At last with grim determination and with Faith on her shoulder she typed unwaveringly for more than an hour.

She said she had searched for photos and found none. She reminded him of days in Dublin when they sat in Robert Roberts café together and listened to string quartets. She remembered that she might even have read a little of his father's book and thought perhaps at one stage he had possessed a copy. She told him a great deal more about her life with Josef and the girls. She spoke of Madame Blavatsky and the odd letters that were found always heralded by the sound of tinkling bells beneath the skirts of this powerful mystic. And she revisited the situation with Christina and the birth of Bernadette's child and said again that the sense of more than one attack upon the fetus was stronger than ever and that she failed to make sense of these feelings. She begged for his input.

Though it had been difficult to construct the response in order to make it convey just the right amount of interest in every facet of the increasingly complex relationship, having crept beneath the skin of Persephone Faith Callahan with ease once more, Bernadette relaxed because she was satisfied with it, almost jauntily confident. Vanith was also satisfied because predictably his reply flew across the eighteen thousand kilometres of separation with more speed than might ordinarily be expected from a three finger typist.

ANSWERS TO DIFFICULT QUESTIONS
From: Vanith Lefarge (Vanith@inthesky.co.uk)
To: PersephoneFaith@highmail.com
1st July
Dear Faith, Thank you for looking for photographs.
I did not want you to go to great trouble though. I was interested in what you tell me about your daily life. Mine is also not very exciting. It is, as you gathered, taken up visiting or being visited by friends, talking on the phone, doing shopping and housework.

To Dublin. Of course I remember Roberts' café. How could I ever forget it? Your memory for what I told you in the past is remarkably good. I told you something about my father's parents in a previous email. Mary was Irish and an aristocrat. Gustav was a largely self-made man of Victorian nouveau-riche background. She was more fairy than human. He was ninety eight percent human. She brought her sons up to be gentlemen and to despise anything to do with trade or commerce. When Franz, the eldest did not want to get involved in the business there were problems, but my grandfather accepted it. However when my father said he did not want to go into the business it was quite another matter. My grandfather tried to put his foot down by sending him to a silk weaving school. Nothing, however, could convince my father to work in the business.

My grandfather was a very important man, highly revered and held the title of Commercial Councillor which is one step below a Privy Councillor and there was no way he could accept the situation lying down.

He decided to send him to America In those days aristocrats who had done unacceptable things were usually given the option of committing suicide (and the more honourable ones would have chosen to do so) or to take a ticket to the United States. My father was given a ticket to America and a sufficient allowance to live there as a gentleman to the extent that was possible in a country like the USA at that time.

None of my poor Grandfather's sons wanted to take over the business and so it was left to nephews on his side of the family. However his fortune was so vast, that there was still enough money left over to leave each of his children enough to live on for the rest of their lives. A lot of money was, however, lost through bad investments, followed by the Great War then inflation. My father became so poor, that he had to travel without a man-servant and sometimes even second class on the railway.

My mother had been a rich and merry widow, because her father had a castle with thousands of acres of forestland, a manor house with a lot of valuable farming land and he had been second in command personal advisor to two absolute monarchs. Then when her first husband died she inherited a substantial fortune on top of it. However, by the time I was born, my parents could afford only four maids, a nanny and a cook but no menservants. Things deteriorated further and when I was four there was only a single maid. By the time I was eight or nine we had no maid and only a charlady coming twice a week. When I was 13 my mother and I were penniless refugees. Nevertheless, when I was ten I knew exactly whom one could challenge to a duel, how to find seconds, referees and a doctor etc. When I was 13 or 14 I asked my mother what to do in the event that I was insulted by someone not capable of giving satisfaction in a duel (i.e. a person of lower rank) and she told me that the correct thing to do in such an unlikely situation was to strike them with the blunt side of my sabre. So you can see by this that I was brought up in a peculiar sort of a time capsule. My life was arrested somewhere in the middle of the eighteenth century.

To return to my father and his problems: He realised that he was not good at handling money and the problems of business. He had a friend known to me as Uncle Ewald, more than 30 years his junior. In the 1930s some kind of arrangement was made between them and he financially assisted Uncle Ewald in the setting up of a steel parts business and in return Rudy, my mother and I would be looked after appropriately should this become necessary. However he had not foreseen the possibility that Uncle Ewald might die before him which he did of a heart attack at the age of only 50. When my father died himself in 1944 Ewald's wife travelled to Devon and took many of his possessions including a portrait of Master Morian, a great spiritual master. The Theosophical Society are most anxious to get hold of that picture even after all these years.

Aunt Ava became filthy rich. To some extent she honoured the promise to my father and when we were starving after the war she sent us a CARE food parcel every month. CARE was linked to the International Red Cross. It actually kept us alive. When my brother was finally discharged from his prisoner of war camp where he had nearly starved to death, she also sent a CARE parcel each month to him. Later she sent money to me when I had managed to starve myself out of the German army – by means of a forty-day hunger strike. Then later still she sent money to Dublin for a while.

Then there came some very unfortunate circumstances. They are so complicated that I have to simplify them a great deal or the story would become too long. When I first went to Trinity I went to study physics which I was very good at. However, because of a great deal of in-fighting between university departments and because as a foreigner I did not understand the various nuances, I became caught up in it. The outcome was that I decided to abandon physics and study medicine. Later I abandoned medicine and studied music instead. When I wrote to Aunt Ava to tell her these things she decided that as I had not been working hard and now seemed to simply be wasting my time I should go home to Germany. She refused to send me more money until I did so. Of course my mother heartily supported this stance.

These were the circumstances that left me penniless in Dublin at the time when you and I first met. I have never forgiven either Aunt Ava or my mother for their part in my suffering and I had no intention of returning to Germany despite their joint urging for me to do so.

Now to Madame Blavatsky (HPB): That is another long story. But I will try to throw some light on her place in things. The Society for Psychic Research reported on her once and said that they regarded her neither as the mouthpiece of the Hidden Seers nor as a mere vulgar imposter. They thought she had achieved a title to permanent remembrance as one of the most accomplished, ingenious and interesting charlatans in history. I read this report long, long ago at a time when I had already concluded much the same but I do not know how she managed to convince so many intelligent and educated people of her power and her absurd miracles. Most of the miracles would appear to be fakes and the Masters she spoke so volubly of were her invention. The letters she received were her not very good forgeries. However, having said all that, she did have considerable supernormal powers. If you or I tried to deceive people with such miracles we would never get away with it; you need very special powers to do so as successfully as she did. Furthermore, to create, or give birth to gods is something quite outstanding. She alone created the Masters and they are there for all time. My mother never quite understood the deception behind all of this. To her, either the miracles were genuine or HPB. was a trickster. But neither is true. My mother would ask my father and he would assure her that HPB. was not a trickster – she was genuine. But like me he did not like to tell lies either so he never actually told her that the tinkling bells or the letters were genuine.

In short, HPB was a very important figure in an enormous spiritual operation the purpose of which was to destroy the demons of Christianity, etc. And she explained to my father that it was completely necessary for her to perform gross miracles to encourage the materialistic people of the Victorian age to listen and take heed. I will try to explain further: You already know that it was Moses who created Yahveh and brought forth the tablets listing the Ten Commandments. I would describe Moses as a demonic incarnation that created a horrendous demonic deity. But I would not call him a trickster, or claim that the tablets were forgeries. Moses was a powerful magician, even perhaps a black one.

HPB created the Masters deliberately and with extreme care. She fashioned them and then blew the breath of life into them. That is quite advanced magic. But ordinary people cannot see that. And she did it in the materialistic monotheistic world of the 19th century. And when in about 1890 Mathers claimed to have met one of her Masters, who had materialised before him in a London coffee house and told him the occult secrets upon which the Golden Dawn was based, HPB and my father would have quietly opened a bottle of champagne and drunk to the health of the Masters. Mathers and the Golden Dawn and Alistair Crowley were fakes and deceivers, HPB was not. She understood very well how Christianity with its original sin and so on and so forth deprives man of all dignity and makes him a miserable sinner. The Masters were intended to be human and to restore some dignity to the human race.

Sadly, the foolish men of the Society for Psychic Research cannot see this either. In fact very few people can. Thinkers from Copernicus to La Place have attacked the Church on the basis of physics and astronomy but HPB was the first to strike on a spiritual level, and the Church to this day is not fully aware of the power of what she achieved. The whole hippy movement of the 1960s with tens of thousands going to India to look for wisdom was directly as a result of her work. They were to some extent looking for the Masters. And they found the Maharishi Mahesh Yogin of Beatles fame. He is of course an avatar or incarnation. An avatar (in Tibetan Tulku) is an incarnation or embodiment. He embodied the idea of a sage. If you ask a football supporter to describe to you a sage, he would tell you that a sage has a long white beard and smiles and is always kind and blesses people. The Maharishi is all that. He is also a bit of a fool and a conman. But his appearance in itself embodies the sage idea extremely well.

Now to that child: I am very well aware of the fact that Christina was much involved in the whole business. You are also right when you say that there was more than one attack upon that child before it was born and yet it still survived. There was much talk of a multiple pregnancy and for a while I considered this but I have no hard facts to guide me. Finally, I suspect strongly that my brother has some ongoing association with the child and that is why I regard him with suspicion. He of course denies it absolutely.

To conclude: I must say to you that I think that most of what Freud said was foolish but that does not alter the fact that he was a great man and introduced the idea of an unconscious part of our minds. That was something incredible to the people of his time. Whether you can help me at present with my problems is something I don't know. As I have told you I am fighting a number of nasty and powerful Entities. Or if you prefer I am deluding myself that I am. I think I have wounded them mortally but they are by no means dead yet and so I am under constant attack. But for now I will stop. It is three o'clock in the morning. I think it is time to go to bed. Please let me know what you make of all this. Much love from Vanith

Bernadette was exhausted when she finished reading this. Faith was also weary. Her outline grew faint and her voice even fainter.

'What am I to make of all this?' she whispered before she quietly disappeared.

TWELVE

His responses were coming much faster than I had ever anticipated they might. This convinced me of his loneliness and hence his need to reach back into the past to a time when he was young and had influence over the women in his life and perhaps even to a time when women were still hovering, waiting patiently to be groomed and influenced. And for someone who claimed to be less than proficient as far as typing was concerned, with the help of a spell checker and the promise of a loving woman in Israel, he rose magnificently to the occasion. Even Jack was impressed and certainly enjoyed reading the letters, commenting again and again how entertaining he was. Though he still advised caution as to the manner in which he should be approached.

'He might not continue to be as easily fooled as you imagine,' he said. 'After all he clearly suspects his brother of deceiving him'.

I daydreamed delightfully on how his suspicions of Rudy would dramatically increase if he ever found out about the visit he and Angela made to Auckland some years previously on a Pacific cruise vessel as an on-board lecturers. I even wondered if Faith should have some sudden insight into this visit and mystically happen upon one of the many photographs we took of us all together, lunching at Mission Bay for example, to scan and forward to him. Or would that stretch the parameters of even Vanith's unusual gullibility?

'Isn't that just the tiniest bit like the Masters' letters conjured up by Madame Blavatsky?' Faith reproved when I suggested the notion a few hours later, and so for the time being at least the idea was shelved.

But I was nevertheless entirely convinced that he was hooked and so was happy to forsake caution to some extent which was perhaps unwise. I wanted to know in his own words the story of how he starved himself out of the German Army. I knew it well because he had told it with monotonous regularity in the past, but it would amuse Jack and possibly even remove Daniel for a while from the inordinate amount of time he spent contemplating Salome and the progress of her university studies. So I persuaded Faith to sit at the keyboard and write.

Vanith was thanked effusively for his lovely long letter which had filled in all the gaps regarding his father's time in America and his own penniless state in Dublin. He was told how fascinating the discourse on HPB had been because Faith and I had harboured doubts about her power. The tales of paranormal experiences in her presence were so numerous, there had been so many ghostly visions, poltergeists and haunted houses. We toyed a little with superstition, the fact that there are people who do not like having thirteen guests at a party, hotels that do without a thirteenth floor. Faith pointed out rather unnecessarily that the gypsy magic employed by

Bernadette all those years ago would have fallen into the same category. Did she touch wood for good luck? Throw salt over her shoulder? Not let a black cat cross her path? We bestowed an entire paragraph to his stomach pain and the demons causing or not causing it. Did he regret past behaviour? Had he ever done something so intrinsically wrong that he himself felt he should be punished for it? Then Rudy's possible association with his son was raised because Faith was sure that some years ago he might have even visited New Zealand and perhaps actually met with the family. And as she typed I urged Faith to look upon the plethora of photos taken at that very meeting – Rudy with Bernadette, Rudy with Daniel, Jack with Angela, then all of them together lunching in high spirits on fish and white wine. And furthermore, Faith could sense some relative in North America (In Nova Scotia to be more precise but best to be just a little vague - one who was also in connection with Daniel and his family.

'I don't think he will like it,' said Faith anxiously, 'I think we ought to tone it down'. But I was not in the mood to take advice and told her she was talking nonsense.

'That's my opinion anyway,' she added and flicked her tweed skirt for non-existent crumbs. But I folded her away without even answering.

His response came like a speeding bullet, and with devastating venom and accuracy. Strangely enough I was not quite expecting so much acrimony and accordingly whilst reading, I could only be amazed because it was vintage Vanith. He who tried so valiantly and with so much love and patience to assist the fools around him, to help them see that their abject folly would only lead them to grief. Yet they were incapable of doing as they were bid, bringing misfortune upon themselves when it could so easily be avoided.

BERNADETTE AND BABY
From: Vanith Lefarge (Vanith@inthesky.co.uk)
To: PersephoneFaith@highmail.com
2nd July
Dear Faith, Whether my brother is in contact with Bernadette's child or not is not of great relevance to me. Such contact as he has had already has pretty much destroyed our relationship as far as I am concerned. He probably does not realise it but he has forced me to treat him with great caution.

Like him you unfortunately persist in continuing to become more and more spiritually involved with the bloody Bernadette and baby business and thereby you are damaging our relationship. I have tried to warn you, but you have not listened. Therefore I am beginning to trust you less and I will treat you with more and more suspicion from now on. My warnings were clear enough. Why on earth do you not heed them?

If you got in touch with Rudy, he could probably give you an address in New Zealand where you could visit, maybe go with Christina who would also no doubt love to get involved, and make friends with both Bernadette and her son and all the fucking family.

I thought I explained to you right at the beginning of our correspondence, that I do not wish to have any contact with that child, mentally or physically, directly or via intermediaries. Women in particular are always curious about this situation and they all think they know better than I. You are no different and maybe you should try to think seriously about it all because you are damaging the possibility of a serious and close bond being established between us. And when our relationship is fractured and I am no longer in your life, you will be one hundred per cent to blame – simply because you refused to listen to my patient warnings.

Bernadette and her wretched child have destroyed a number of otherwise close and important relationships for me. Some of my former friends have become obsessed with it. It has meant they have lost me as a friend. By locking into that awful business telepathically you too are blocking any fruitful contact with me and so in this sense she is still doing me harm and therefore I curse her afresh! People like you and my brother unwittingly become her tools. Why don't you realise that?

As to my fight with the demons, I don't think it is something you could understand. Your development of thought in this area is not advanced sufficiently and I cannot be bothered to help you with this. So in order to avoid misunderstandings, it is best to say nothing.

You should know that I still bear a great deal of love for you because of the past, but you are making our on-going link extremely difficult. I would strongly advise you to think on this. Vanith.

This I read and re-read a number of times over the following days and each time my reaction hovered between pleasure at his fury, and anger at his indignation towards those who dared to ignore his advice. When Jack read it he simply said that he'd told me so and that I had gone too far and furthermore if I wanted to get more information out of him this was clearly not the way to go about it. And he added that he was surprised that I had not realised this myself as after all I had lived with the man long enough and should have been totally aware of his possible reactions. To which I think I advised that he should mind his own bloody business and if he was going to insult me I would stop showing him the letters. Jack turned his attention back to the morning paper and said nothing further.

Persephone Faith hugged her arms close to her body and rocked back and forth and said she knew no good would come of constantly re-visiting that same topic and now look what I'd done – I'd made him very angry. Not for the first time I wondered what the real Faith's reaction be if she could be made aware of this odd and unsavoury little puddle of enchantment lurking in an Auckland beach suburb? Her thoughts on the matter would undoubtedly depend upon the exact nature and balance of the relationship she had with him all those years ago and that was still much of a mystery to me. Vanith seemed to be more than a little bit in love with Faith, even through all the intervening years. Or was he merely harking back to a time when he was young and inexperienced in the ways and wiles of the opposite sex, when Faith had appeared to him to be a woman of the world, experienced in all matters and particularly sexual ones. Had she really been as he described her? On one hand it was hard to believe that she and Christina had lived together with him and shared him between themselves at first amicably and then as they each demanded the bigger share of him, found their friendship shattering to the point where it was impossible to repair it. That tended to imply that both fell hopelessly in love and yet although I knew that to be the case as far as Christina was concerned, it did not quite fit with the Faith I had come to know. My Faith had more strength and inner fortitude, of that I was certain.

It was a handicap to know so little about her so that even the most basic facts had to be guessed at; for example was she the same age as him – or older? Good sense told me that she was older because even allowing for exaggeration she could hardly have presented as the sexual siren of his memory as a mere teenager. Therefore she might be in her mid-eighties now. I began to feel pity for her with all the encumbrances I had heaped upon her in the form of sick Josef and the two somewhat wilful teenage girls. Quite apart from all that, it could not be easy living in Israel as she did, often out of cellphone range with the rest of the world, not to mention coping with the after effects of a stroke.

I Googled her in frantic attempt to find out more and was surprised to find a Persephone Faith Callahan featured on Facebook though she appeared to be fourteen years old. There were at least forty-five Faith Callahans in the white pages in the United States. I could find none at all in Israel. What did all this mean for the real Faith? She could simply have died. She might have been dead for years. Or she could be living in obscurity in Liverpool or London, or even back in Dublin trying to manage on a pension and finding it difficult. Hopefully if that was so she did not have an email account or even basic computer skills. And what, oh what indeed, if the real Faith Callahan actually suddenly turned up out of the blue?

It was Daniel I think who first said, 'What happens if the real Faith suddenly comes out of the woodwork?' I think I told him not to be so silly. But then Jack asked the same question and Daniel looked from one to the other of us in an interested and irritating manner. I said I would accuse her of being an imposter and they both looked unconvinced. However, I felt quite secure in the fact that Vanith at least totally accepted my Faith as the real Faith, and in any case he was for the most part more interested in explaining more and more aspects of himself than delving too deeply into facts pertaining to her. It would be a different matter if they were communicating by telephone because then Faith would have to think on her feet more, stroke or no stroke.

'If she did turn up,' I told them, 'I think he might well believe that she had totally lost her memory, that she was confused – after all she's elderly, she has a lot of responsibility in her life... she's entitled to become sick herself.'

We, that is my Faith and I, allowed more than two weeks to elapse before re-establishing contact with him and during that time she said more than once, 'I don't like the way this is going.'

From: PersephoneFaith@highmail.com
To: Vanith@inthesky.co.uk
19th July
My Dear Vanith, I decided not to respond quickly to your last message. My reasons were twofold. First of all I thought it better to allow your justifiable anger to subside somewhat so we two could examine more sensibly what has occurred. Also I was quite angry once I read what you had written – and extremely wounded because my intentions have at all times been to care for you and keep you from harm. You must realise that I have lived for many years now without concerning myself with Christina at all and of course I knew nothing at all of Bernadette and her shenanigans. Secondly and more pragmatically any intention or resolve I had upon hearing from you was overtaken by the fact that almost immediately Josef became more sick and has needed more care and attention than usual. He is lying nearby on the daybed as I write and

sleeping a little from time to time with very heavy and disturbed breathing. It causes me of course a great deal of continuing stress.

You are quite correct when you say you tried to tell me nicely not to meddle but it appeared to go in one ear and out of the other, etc. In fact I understood very well what you were asking of me but to my distress I continued to receive information that directly concerned you; I had no-one else with whom to share it and indeed I felt it was my duty to disclose these things to you. I did not want to treat you like a child from whom some matters must be withheld or only a sanitized version revealed. I can see in retrospect, however, that an alternative decision from me would have been more pertinent; hindsight is wonderful. Thank you for telling me of the love you have for me. Faith.

'He was not in the habit of telling me he loved me all those years ago,' Faith observed just a little wistfully as she sent the message off. Faith's feelings had been deeply hurt which was understandable and she was quite proud of her response to him She had, after all, only his best interests at heart and being the receiver of telepathic information was not always an easy position to occupy. What the hell was she supposed to do with it? Josef and the girls would have been totally uninterested and as for Bernadette, well she knew all these things already. He was fortunate to be given a second chance with her and he would do well to ponder on that himself, she began to think.

I pointed out to her a little curtly that in all the years we had spent together he had not at any stage mentioned the word 'love' to me except in general terms or as part of a philosophical discussion.

'You mean a bit like Prince Charles when he got engaged to Diana?' she said.

'Yes,' I told her. 'Love, "whatever love means".'

She smiled faintly, because she was already fading from the room so I felt a little bit like Alice with the Cheshire Cat. For the first time I began to see why it was that Christina had disliked her so much.

Somewhat fortuitously, Rudy had sent a message to Daniel during the two weeks of estrangement, saying that he was going to have another attempt at persuading his brother to examine his ongoing unacceptable behaviour as far as Daniel was concerned. As for Vanith himself, he was busy replying to Faith.

LET SLEEPING DOGS LIE
From: Vanith Lefarge (Vanith@inthesky.co.uk)
To: PersephoneFaith@highmail.com
19th July
My Dear Faith, I was so very pleased to hear from you again. I was very afraid you would not want to continue our correspondence relationship, such as it is. My rage was (or is) a rage against Bernadette, which was very violent indeed and I was angry that by telepathically tuning into the matter, you had managed to revive the affair. Indeed my brother also suddenly brought the business up again and asked me

if I could try once more to 'explain these things to his wife', who still blames him for failing to talk sense into me regarding that child. Such is Bernadette's power even now, do you now see that? You also moved the lid, which I had put over that rage and it is of course no fun for me to have to relive that all again. In other words that nasty business was coming to life again in all corners, and I had to deal with it magically, as well as coping with my anger against Bernadette, and I really did not want to do that, if I could help it. You simply became caught up in it all.

I appreciate that you want to help me, but it all happened 41 years ago, and I think it is probably best left alone. I did ring my sister-in-law twice because I had told my brother I would do my best to explain to her, but she has no time at the moment to talk about this on the telephone, and she wants me to explain it all in an email. This is yet another deceit because I know she wants me to write down these things in order that she can forward it on to Bernadette and her son.

I have had another gastro-endoscopy which showed that the inflammation in my stomach has healed. I have also had a CT scan. The surgeon who arranged it all is on holiday at present but his secretary told me that it had not revealed any abnormality. I am of course delighted to know that there nothing really wrong with me. However, the pain when it comes is real.

I may not be able to write much for a while as I am having a visitor from Canada come to stay with me. Edna is the ex-wife of a good friend of mine.

To-morrow I have to try to find some garage prepared to try to get a new (second hand) windscreen wiper for my 20 year old Fiat Panda. Fiat does not make them anymore. With a visitor arriving, I shall need my car more than usual, and driving in the rain without a windscreen wiper is illegal and dangerous. Lots of love for today from Vanith.

Faith was jubilant because he seemed to have forgiven her. More cautiously so was I, particularly so because the advent of a house guest for a week or so would no doubt curtail the frenzied stream of correspondence which meant that both Faith and I could not only have a well-earned rest, but we would be able to plan our next letter with less haste.

'If we have time to think about what we write,' I advised her, 'we are much less likely to upset him.' And she enthusiastically agreed.

THIRTEEN

The questions I had regarding Miriam's inheritance continued to niggle away in the background. I very much wanted to know if Vanith had ever received any portion of her money because there was no doubt that she would have desperately wanted this to happen. I liked to think my primary concern was for Miriam and her wishes. It had proved predictably difficult to pin him down to definitive answers to some questions, and not just those about that black topic that was no longer to be mentioned. He would so much prefer to wax lyrical for page after page on matters of spirituality, demons, bad luck and his own brilliance. Faith was infinitely more willing than I to listen patiently whilst he harangued his family, his neighbours, Jesus Christ, and all the Saints of the Roman Catholic Church. She was also more receptive of his self-assessment and all that it entailed.

'He is undoubtedly a rather special human being,' she told me softly. 'If you are really honest with yourself you will surely have to admit that.' It was just possible that her devotion to him had once upon a time been greater than my own, surprising though that thought was.

From: PersephoneFaith@highmail.com
To: Vanith@inthesky.co.uk
25th July

Dear Vanith, this will not be a long email because I know you must still be busy playing host to your friend. First I must tell you that I am glad we are able to communicate again without rancour. I will try not to make mention of matters concerning Bernadette and your son in future, unless you bring the subject up or unless something compelling happens where I think that your spiritual safety might be compromised. In the interim I must tell you that again I have had messages concerning a dark haired woman with a name beginning with M (Mary, Marion, Miriam?) who says she has left you a large sum of money. She seems agitated. What do you make of this, if anything? Faith

And predictably his reply was almost immediate.

MIRIAM
From: Vanith Lefarge (Vanith@inthesky.co.uk)
To: PersephoneFaith@highmail.com
26th July
Dear Faith, I am desperately tired because Edna likes to get up about 6am and go to bed at 10. Normally I go to bed after midnight and get to sleep at 2 or 3 am, and I wake up between 11am and 1pm. She is lovely company, but we are both suffering from lack of sleep.

Your telepathic powers are quite astonishing. You are speaking of Miriam: Unbeknown to me she inherited about £35,000 just two or three weeks before she died of cancer. Five days before she died she went into hospital, and gave me the keys to her flat and I was running forward and backward getting her things she needed, etc. In hospital she said she wanted to see a solicitor to make a Will and I would become a richer man and I thought she was going mad. She then told the nurses she would like to go home and the nurses said they would try to arrange that. Then Miriam said she would wait and make the Will when she got back home. I did not have the heart to tell her that she had only a few days to live, and that there was no question of her ever getting back to her flat. .

She died and I was the only person at her funeral. When I went through her things to wind up the flat I found £3,000 in cash, which I took, but I could not draw the rest of the money from her account. The Official Solicitor or whatever he is called said that next of kin would have to be searched for and in the end, after some months passed, a distant cousin who did not know her got the money.

I first met Miriam when she was a teenager and I had recently arrived in London. I remained friends with her and we kept contact over the years. I never had an affair with her but I was well aware that she thought the world of me. Much love for today, Vanith.

So there seemed no doubt that Miriam had only told him about her inheritance shortly before she died and I vaguely wondered why that was because she had told me a year beforehand when she had half made plans to leave London altogether.

To further extend the time between our letters Faith helpfully suggested that she and Josef should decide to go on a visit to an old friend who had a vineyard several hundred kilometres away. Whilst there Faith would have no access whatsoever to modern technology and they would be away for more than a month and this happily coincided with a forthcoming visit Jack and I were making to London.

To give Vanith something meaty to dwell upon during our absence Faith told him that Miriam had definitely inherited the money many months before she died. And because I still felt sore that he had put the phone down on me when I had originally tried to give him this good news, she added that a mutual friend who was hazy and obscured (almost as if Vanith did not really regard her as a friend), had contacted him at some stage after the death to tell him that Miriam wanted him to have the money. In fact she would have been able to ease the process of inheritance as she seemed to have documentation to this effect, we lied cheerfully, signed by Miriam herself. Strangely, however, and rather sadly, he had for some reason refused to speak with her, even put the phone down when she rang him. Could he throw any light on this odd happening? Then upon further urging, Faith was persuaded to pop in a reference to his cousin Arabella in North America of whom he should be wary as it appeared she might actually be communicating with those he considered his enemies.

'She's one of the cousins who has been putting pressure on him for years to recognise Daniel', I softly confided. 'She sometimes rings us. She's even asked us to visit her in Canada.'

Faith looked impressed and typed harder. With prompting she added a reference to Rudy and wondered if they were full brothers or half-brothers. They were very different after all. Then, as I thought I might drop by whilst we were in London to view the place where he now lived she asked if he was able to park his car nearby or if parking was difficult in North London. Thus further emboldened I suggested she should ask for the registration number but she looked incredulous and refused. She demanded why I needed to know such a detail and I confessed that I might feel driven to leave a note on the windscreen or even slash tyres should I feel particularly vindictive at the time. Faith did as she was bid whilst muttering, 'That's not a very good idea.'

I knew that Jack would think these references mischievous to say the least, and possibly even Daniel would agree so I wisely decided not to make any mention to either of them and warned Faith that she should say nothing either if she hovered above our heads as she sometimes did in the evenings whilst we ate dinner or watched television. The reaction came within an hour or two, just a couple of lines,

'...I had erased that treacherous bitch Arabella from my memory. Yes, she is in close contact with that child. I am more and more astonished at your telepathic ability...'

'Well he seems to know of whom we speak,' said Faith. I could only agree. And just a few hours later he wrote again and was solicitous with regard to Faith's family. We both thought that was very nice of him.

ANSWERS TO QUESTIONS
From: Vanith Lefarge (Vanith@inthesky.co.uk)
To: PersephoneFaith@highmail.com
7th August
Dear Faith, Edna's visit went wonderfully well. I could talk to her better than many people I have spoken with over years. As usual I did most of the talking, and I am not sure how much she understood, but I had the impression that she broadly followed me and was very interested.

I explained that I think I have made major advances in metaphysics by standing on the shoulders of Madame Blavatsky, Alexandra David-Neel, my father, C.G. Jung and others, and what is more I have had the advantage over them all as I have also studied mathematics and physics. I now understand how telepathy etc. works, and I have even succeeded in linking the science of the non-material world, the world of the mind, with modern physics. I explained to Edna that I am very lonely, because my discoveries are important and fundamental and yet I cannot discuss them with anybody. I had the feeling she appreciated my terrible position but of course she could not help me.

With regard to Miriam. She only inherited that money quite unexpectedly about three or four weeks before her death. That is absolutely for sure! She most certainly would have told me if this was not so and of that I have no doubt. Miriam held me in very great regard and she would never, ever keep such a thing from me. She was no longer able to profit from her inheritance in any way whatsoever. She was much too weak and ill from cancer. Furthermore she had no friends or contacts, at all. I would have known about them because she confided in me totally.

Most of the £3000 in cash that I recovered from her flat went into buying an electronic piano and a good quality carpet, thus making my home a much nicer place to live in. I also got a better second hand car. It made a huge difference to my life. I did not think that Miriam was all that close to me in an emotional sense nor I to her or that her death would affect me in any great way. However, shortly after she died I developed severe alopecia which lasted two or three years and looked very peculiar. So she had meant much more to me than I had consciously realised.

I have owned this present car of mine for about five years, and it is a very good and reliable vehicle. (Fiat Panda 1989). It is the best second hand car I have ever owned. It is generally safe and sound and reliable. I got a second hand wiper-system over the internet in the end. The resident's parking permit for Wood Green costs only about £40 a year and most of the time I can usually park just opposite the house.

I have been to see Paula today. I spoke of her to you previously. She lives in Essex just north of Dartford in Kent. There is now a tunnel, which is part of the M25, the orbital motorway, which goes right around London. Although it is quite a distance from here *(about 30 miles) it takes less than an hour to get there. She was enormously pleased to see me.*

About my brother. He and I are not just from different planets, we are from different Galaxies. We are light years apart! When he was born my mother handed him to my father and asked him what he sensed psychically about the child. My father said he was not sure but he might have had more than one incarnation. When I was born, my mother gave me to my father and asked the same question and my father said with great certainty and conviction: 'This is an extraordinarily special Being. He is not from the world of men at all. He comes straight from Devakhan, the abode of the Gods.'

When we were children there was always fierce rivalry between us and it is still alive in Rudy's head. He has always chased fame and to a large extent got it or it got him. I was closer to my mother and the circumstances of my birth made my parents' attitude to me different. My mother's belief that she had given birth to a divine avatar may have been complete nonsense, but it would inevitably result in me becoming irrevocably different. It would be a self-fulfilling prophecy.

Whether I hear from you before you leave or not, have a lovely holiday if that is at all possible. You know, in the oddest way I feel very, very close to you and it is as if we share something very important together and always have. Vanith

So safe in the knowledge that Vanith felt closer to Faith and to myself than I would have ever imagined was possible, I packed in preparation for our trip to London. We were to stay, as usual, with our good friend Norris who had often stayed in Auckland with us over the years, and who was the proud and lucky owner of a house ideally situated a few moments' walk from Marble Arch and the delights of the Marks & Spencer flagship store.

We were to be a few days in London before heading for our rented cottage in Kent and as soon as we arrived our daughter Martha sent a text demanding to know when we would be free to meet with her. Between the delights of Marks & Spencer, The British Museum, The City of London Wren Churches, London Walks and meetings with Martha it was more difficult than I had expected it would be to find half a day in which to explore North London to stake out Vanith's flat. But when I did it gave me a wonderful opportunity to make the most of my travel pass and renew my love affair with the London Underground system. I descended in childlike bliss into the depths of Marble Arch station, travelling in ecstasy to Holborn to change onto the Piccadilly line. Russell Square, Kings Cross, St. Pancras, even Caledonian Road, Holloway Road were safely familiar enough but then we entered the middle reaches of the Piccadilly line through Arsenal, Finsbury Park and Manor House where familiarity ended and all became a little strange and almost alien and by the time we flashed through Turnpike Lane and on to Wood Green we were in a foreign country. But emerging out of Wood Green station into bright sunlight turned the adventure through a parallel existence back into ordinary everyday life once more and it was with predictable difficulty that I managed to execute the final ten minutes of the journey to the house where he lived, making several wrong turns along the way.

But all at once I stood nervously before the house in which he lived and from whose depths he had sat laboriously typing message after message to send with increasing love across thousands of miles to Faith and to me. It was as he had described, a very ordinary late Victorian terraced house with no basement, simply a ground, first and top floor with a tiny attic window in the roof. The ground floor window at the front was of the bay variety and as I stood there I wondered if that meant the building was Edwardian rather than Victorian and could not make up my mind. Was he in fact inside, possibly still sleeping as it was only eleven am? Should I knock on the door and demand to see him. Perhaps tell him that Faith had told me where to find him and when his jaw dropped and he gasped, 'How do you know Persephone Faith Callahan?' simply smile and calmly inform him that Faith and I had been close associates for months now. Would now be an opportune time to reveal the vast parameters of the deception?

Directly across the road was his little car, pale blue, newly rain washed with piles of newspapers, plastic cartons and books on the back seat. I walked back and forth past it, keeping the front door under observation, and wondered if I was really courageous enough to do damage to it. But I had nothing with which to slash tyres so finally I abandoned that idea, though reluctantly, and returned, this time more directly, to the station and descended into its thrilling abyss once again.

Then it was uneventfully back to Marble Arch through home-going office workers and to dinner with Martha and her partner Lucas. The men discussed wine growing and whilst they did so I managed to explain to Martha a little of what Faith and I had been up to in the ether. She did not know quite what to make of the economical truth I revealed and it was clear that she only half believed me and would have liked to check the more sensational details out with Jack but there was no opportunity to do so.

Next day we went on to our cottage in the countryside. And so our weeks in England were spent in a delightful companionship of exploration of those things that interested us both.

Once back in New Zealand some considerable time went by before I applied myself, or nagged Faith to apply herself to the serious business of reviving our contact with Vanith Lefarge. The holiday had made us both slothful and yet we knew he deserved a reasonably lengthy and flattering communication, one that would prepare him emotionally for an unexpected attack in the form of a question or two that he would find unwelcome.

From: PersephoneFaith@highmail.com
To: Vanith@inthesky.co.uk
26th September

Vanith, It seems so long ago that we communicated so you must forgive me if I overlook some of the matters you spoke of and the questions you raised. I do know that you asked me what I might make of the matters you discussed with me. When I actually try hard to receive information telepathically it never works very well but I have applied myself perhaps somewhat over-diligently to things concerning your family over the past twelve hours and a number of details have come to me. It seems somehow that it is not 'too late' for this information. Don't ask me to explain what that 'too late' actually means because I do not know – I am human. I only know that when some matters reveal themselves it is in fact too late for them to be of any consequence to our lives as human beings. These concerning us presently do not come into that category.

It is as if your mother experienced some profound transformation – even metamorphosis of spirit around the time of your conception. She does not appear to be a woman consumed by sexual energy – it is almost as if this momentous incident simply happened upon her somewhat capriciously. It was absent at the conception of your brother. I do not want to seem indelicate in this very complex and personal family situation but it might appear that your father, though perhaps initially profoundly affected by the birth of a son from some almost celestial space, was unprepared for the human aspect of actually nurturing such a child. I have felt the following: Your father was not young... he had taken more kindly to the first baby... he found the second vastly different and difficult in the extreme... your mother on many occasions felt she was being pressured to choose between you and he... she always chose you.

There can never be any common ground between your brother and yourself. He does not have within himself anything that is necessary to begin to understand your situation – if you wanted to meet him halfway in any matter it would be up to you to take the necessary steps toward him because he cannot even begin to understand in which direction to walk.

These are the bones of the results of my cogitations over past hours – make of them what you will. I realise you may say to me that this is nonsense because possibly it is. As I have said to you before, our current relationship is or should be strong enough to take some bruises. There is of course more but perhaps it is better left to another time.

You said that you had been in conversation with your brother. What is it that he wants of you currently? If it is not too onerous for you perhaps it would give you breathing space if you simply were able to accommodate him. Or perhaps you could invite him to visit with you if the matter is more complex so that you two can speak together. I mean speak together quite alone – without the presence of the women on the periphery who are so anxious to force decisions. He wants to please – this conflict with you distresses him greatly and he sees you as totally unreasonable. But then I feel his attitude is that you have always been his totally unreasonable younger brother – the brother who forced a split between his parents perhaps. He still sees you as the small boy who was inclined to have tantrums that forced the adults to give way to you. He is of the opinion that you are attempting to manipulate him and make him say, do and even think things that he does not want to say, do and think. He feels thwarted in his relationship with you – he sees himself as being the one who is dictated to and he bitterly resents that. At the same time his love for you as his only brother draws him towards you and urges him to make sacrifices and simply do your bidding in order to retain that love.

A lot of the above is repetitive I realise. You are surrounded by people who want the best for you and that goodwill towards you emanates from places where you would least expect it to. Even those from the past whom you see as perhaps directly or indirectly responsible for problems in your life do not wish you ill. But in every corner of relationships concerning your blood family – those who went before you, those responsible for your birth, those who go forward after you, there is cloud after cloud of confusion and bewilderment.

You said that you feel somewhat close to me – I want you to understand that the feeling is certainly reciprocated. Much love, Faith.

Well at least some of what was written was based on fact. It was Rudy who had told us years ago during his Auckland visit, that his beloved father had left the family, in his opinion at least, because Vanith had been a tyrannical pre-schooler who remained largely undisciplined by his devoted mother. That was the way he saw the situation many years later.

AFTER YOUR HOLIDAY
From: Vanith Lefarge (Vanith@inthesky.co.uk)
To: PersephoneFaith@highmail.com
27th September
Dear Faith, Before I go into a long discourse, I have to know a bit more about where you stand in the matters that form the base our discussions. As I have said, I have advanced metaphysics (call it parapsychology or magic or anything you like) considerably and made it into something quite scientific. The reason people can't understand is because the fundamental axiomatic is up the creek. The reason Newton had great problems understanding the principle of inertia was not because inertia is a particularly difficult concept, but because it ran diametrically opposite to the fundamental axiom of medieval and pre-medieval physics that there can be no motion without force. Furthermore the concepts of force and energy were not clearly defined. The first problem East and West have is the belief in a soul or self or jiva or whatever you may call it. The Buddha taught again and again that all phenomena are transient and that all aggregates are impermanent and that there is no such thing as a jiva or soul. This does not stop Buddhists from believing in re-

241

incarnation or the transmigration of souls. The idea of a permanent or immortal soul is a pleasant one and people like it. The alternative does not appeal so much. Secondly Buddhists as well as Hindus have no less of a problem with the Alaya Vijnana than the Europeans have with Jung's Collective Consciousness. Again it is not gratifying to man who likes to think that his mind is his own and therefore quite separate from the rest of the universe.

Next, in Europe we still tend to believe in Descartian dualism, i.e. that man consists of a mortal body and an immortal soul and that at the moment of death the two separate. Without having a clear and similar understanding of these concepts, talking about gods, fairies, incarnate or disincarnate, avatars, tulkus and tulpas would lead to very serious misunderstandings. I would therefore ask you to tell me a little about your beliefs regarding these matters.

In the meantime I shall make comment on your letter.

My father did not really want children, and explained to my mother that he was too old to play the role of a father, regarding my brother and even more so regarding me. He would give her help and advice, but he never interfered and left the upbringing of the two of us entirely to my mother. When she found herself pregnant with my brother, he was not pleased and said that he was not prepared to get married, especially not in a church. When she was six months pregnant and explained for the hundredth time that it was simply not possible for the daughter of a Lord

Chamberlain to have an illegitimate baby he gave in, most reluctantly

As far as Rudy is concerned, you are quite correct when you say that he cannot understand who I am or where I come from. He very much wants to see me, because I think he feels that he may not live that much longer and in fact a meeting is arranged between us for October. He wants to take me either on a cruise down the Danube, or stay with me in a luxury hotel near Garmisch-Partenkirchen, a German resort. He insists on the luxury and he can afford it. He was 88 last month. Both my parents died just before their 89th birthdays. He has a standing invitation to stay with me here, but is below his standards and beneath his dignity. You are quite right that he wants to speak to me alone. I am looking forward to that, because mostly when I see him I do not get more than an hour or two alone with him.

I am so glad you are back from your holiday and we are able to converse once again. I have missed you so very, very much. Vanith.

'We are getting into very deep water,' Faith murmured but I ignored her as I tried to make some sense of the opening paragraphs. What would the real Faith make of it all? There was no doubt at all that Vanith was prone to demanding extensive discourse on very difficult topics. I had little idea of the meaning of the opening paragraphs and wished I was more truly telepathic and able to tap into the more helpful thought processes of others. I feared that Google would be of limited assistance. And so inevitably our response was difficult to construct and It took a great deal of time to do worthwhile internet searches on the base beliefs of the Buddhists and the Hindus and also to discover something of the dualism a la Rene Descartes. A great deal of cutting and pasting took place. And to deflect the focus and reinforce the more whimsical I hastily followed this with a telepathic incident involving our mutual friend, Rona. Was she by any chance requesting him to solve maths problems for her? Did she have a teenage daughter with a name beginning with S? and possibly also an inept husband?

I was reasonably confident that this would stop him in his tracks as very recently in London Rona and I had met for coffee and a catch up chat in Hampstead and she had mentioned that she would be seeing him soon for the above described mathematics tuition, and I was of course fully aware of her daughter and her husband, together with their names and various aspects of their characters. Furthermore since she had long been forbidden to have contact with me I was more than confident that she would be most unlikely to reveal any details of our meeting. Then to explain any aberration of attention on Faith's part, I had poor Josef experience a small infarct. Faith did not like that at all for she had grown fond of her mythical partner. 'Oh do we have to do that?' she asked.

CATCHING UP

From: Vanith Lefarge (Vanith@inthesky.co.uk)

To: PersephoneFaith@highmail.com

28th September

Dear Faith, Thank you for your email. A heart infarct is not such a bad thing but I do hope poor Joseph improves soon. My own health is reasonable at present. My gastritis has now healed up completely and I can eat more or less normally. However, I get out of breath easily with subsequent chest pain if I exert myself like vacuum cleaning or making beds. I finally saw a cardiologist a couple of days ago and he is going to have an MRI done on my heart. But in a funny way I feel that I have had a mystery illness for the last two years peaking around last Christmas and that the gastritis and angina have been in a way secondary phenomena. I certainly have been getting better over the last few months so much so I am now wondering if you are in fact helping me.

I am supposed to meet my brother in the second half of October and with luck it will still come off. There have been predictable problems with the arrangements and the cruise has been changed to a stay in a hotel.

Your telepathy continues to amaze me. Rona is a nurse and would like to go on to become a doctor. She had to do a kind of entrance exam for her course last Friday and she came to me on the previous Tuesday for a mathematics and physics lesson which lasted 9 hours. I was shattered in the end. She has a daughter called Saffy, who is seventeen years old. She also has a very inept husband, who is a dreadful liar and a bit of an alcoholic. She is not happy with him, but this is largely her own fault because I warned her not to marry him.

I have created a word (doc) file, which contains all our correspondence in date order. Would you like a copy? It is 60,000 words, which is a small paperback. I am astonished at how much we have written to each other.

I am very tired and will stop but do write soon and I will endeavour to answer any of your questions. Lots of love for today from Vanith.

A rather disappointingly prosaic little missive. Faith was impressed that her long distance healing methods were working, and to be honest so was I.

'He really does want answers to his questions about your understanding of soul, of self...' she said reprovingly 'His questions are not just going to go away you know...you can't go on ignoring them'

'He's asking you, not me,' I snapped but I knew she was right and we could not go on producing mini emergencies in the hope of diverting his attention for a while.

'He's not being exactly unreasonable,' Faith chided, 'and if you want him to answer your own endless questions about that pregnancy and that child and how he sees that situation after all these years, then you just have to bite the bullet and give him something of what he wants.'

Warming to her theme she even added, 'After all it was you who started all this – not him!'

Well of course she was right and if any progress was to be made, we had to stop flying by the seat of our dual pants and actually give him what he wanted. It was something that Faith had to direct really. I generously suggested that she should have a go at it and I would type whilst she dictated.

From: PersephoneFaith@highmail.com
To: Vanith@inthesky.co.uk
1st October
My Dear Vanith, Your message greatly reassured me – regarding Josef I mean. The infarct was of enormous concern but underneath it all I do realise that there are worse things – far worse! And I was also reassured that your own health is now more stable; long distance healing has been of benefit.

I am also pleased that my meditations --telepathy if you will have proved once more to be close to accurate. Often exasperatingly it will NOT work as I would have it work and I am quite unable to perform at will. Also, if someone tells me that I am wrong about a point that to me appeared to be relevant (such as me telling you Miriam had received her money long before you were aware of it) – then I am plagued with repeat performances of the original information that often grow more intense. Once a wire has become crossed in fact it simply seems to stay crossed. Sometimes I wonder if it is my own personality being as stubborn as a mule and not accepting that a particular aspect of something is in fact reality. What I absolutely do not understand is how and why it happens – for example why Rona? I do not know her, am unlikely ever to meet her, etc. The only flicker of human interest or concern I have regarding her is that I wonder how truly she is your friend – and I feel you should treat her with some caution other than at a surface level. You should also perhaps treat your relatives with similar caution – not that I think they bear any ill-will towards you but because your world is not their world. All this you are very well aware of. I am disturbed at the level of animosity you have towards the woman Arabella in North America. I don't think she is as dangerous as you believe. There is obviously some history here that I am not aware of. How is she related to you? Does she actually see your brother or do they communicate only by telephone and letter? He seems to like her and trust her. Again, it would appear on the surface at least that she simply would like to do what is right or what she currently sees as that which is right. He on the other hand continues to be nervous and is becoming pressed into a tighter and tighter corner. She must have a strong character because she has some influence over him - unless of course he has an especially weak character and is easily influenced.

To return to one of our previous conversations, with regard to metaphysics, parapsychology and so-forth: you ask where I stand. That is a question almost impossible to answer because I hardly know myself. I cannot see any logical explanation or answers to the most fundamental questions. To go immediately to perhaps the most basic question we are prone to ask ourselves at some stage of our lives: What Is The

Purpose Of Life? My response would be – well, don't ask me! In fact to be more honest I shudder whenever such a question is posed. What most people mean by that is simply that they wonder about their own prospects for ultimate and long term survival. They hope that God whom they see as just and merciful, will not permit such a travesty as their short time on this earth should be the end of things for them. And that is all very well if you can find in yourself the least inclination to believe in God. Does God exist? If so where? Does the question actually mean the same thing to you as it does to me or to my children or to the man in the shop down the road? There are many perceptions of immortality, of survival past the grave, which all seem to make good sense. Therefore it is not the possibility but the probability that must be doubted. Take your choice. Christians believe in life, with a body, in some hereafter – the details of which vary of course from sect to sect. The old Greek idea of the body as a prison from which we escape at death- so that we have a continued life without it – is not a bad one. On the other hand simply to survive by merging with 'being', plants taking root in one's remains cannot be totally dismissed just because it happens to be at the other end of that spectrum – and possibly I am enough of an ecologist to be a little comforted. But at a grass roots level (no pun intended) I feel that survival must offer comforts of a different sort, the comforts of anticipation, of looking forward to tomorrow, to be able to experience, see, touch, smell, think and reason and remember…to be ME. Or to be related to me in such a way that it is correct for me to anticipate and look forward to those future experiences. I must relate to the new me in such a way that it will be right to remember what I have thought and done, to feel remorse for what I have done wrong and take pride in what I have done right. The only relation that supports anticipation and memory in this way is simply identity. I cannot anticipate what will happen to someone else in the same way. In any event I don't want to be sold the idea of merging with nature as surviving or being – I don't want to be convinced that my identity will then still exist because that is clearly nonsense. I want to be convinced that survival of identity is probable – not that it is merely possible. It must be real survival not some up to date ersatz survival which simply amounts to what any ordinary person would call totally ceasing to exist. I am of course happy to accept that this body I inhabit will not accompany me but will be buried and rot away. In the hereafter if it exists on any level at all, the correlation between bodies and souls as found on earth will not exist and that's OK. Principles found to work in one circumstance may not be assumed to work in vastly altered circumstances. January and snow go together at times in London and one would be a fool to expect otherwise – but the principle does not apply in Southern California. I certainly at a personal level cannot accept as the soul, what is generally offered to us for acceptance. Does it much matter what we call it? Perhaps the next leap should be to somewhat cautiously accept that what we term as the soul and what we know as the mind are one and the same thing and that it is they that are responsible for character, memory, belief. These are aspects of mind just as height, weight and appearance are aspects of body. Can this soul-mind, once it has emerged into existence, actually cease to exist? Does it amount to personal identity? Sameness of body does not necessarily mean sameness of person – and sameness of psychological characteristics do not necessarily mean sameness of person. From my present position in this world I can accept that for every person now on earth as well as those who have already come and gone, that the general principle 'one body – one soul' is in effect. This does not seem an insurmountable obstacle to further analysis and since there is nothing particularly special about me, I can assume that this arrangement applies universally until I am given some reason to believe otherwise. From time to time I give some consideration to the idea that my soul might not consist of one single soul that has been consistently connected with my body. Consider the possibilities...one of which is that a single soul, one and the same, has been with this body I call mine, since the moment of my birth... another is that one soul was with it until ten years ago and then another, psychologically similar, inheriting all the old memories and beliefs took over. A third hypothesis is that every ten years or so a new soul takes over....or again, every few hours a new soul takes over. The most radical is that there is a constant flow of souls through this body, each psychologically similar to the preceding, just as there is a constant flow of water down the Thames.

I think I should stop before you become totally bored – but you must understand Vanith, that although I have turned my energies over some years towards attempting to make sense of a great deal of what we have discussed – not simply recently, but in the past also, I have yet to reach a level of understanding that satisfies me.

You write about compiling an extraordinary file of our correspondence - I would truly love a copy, but perhaps you should wait a while before sending it because we have not (I hope) finished corresponding yet. Have we really written so much? Extraordinary. Much love, Faith.

'Wow!' I stopped typing. I was impressed. 'What does it all mean?'

Faith looked exasperated and hovered slightly above the keyboard in an agitated manner. 'If you don't understand then I can't explain it to you.'

'I suppose that would only lead to further misunderstandings,' I agreed quietly and she looked at me strangely before fading silently from the room.

It was a sad fact that this relationship between the three of us was not becoming easier.

PHILOSOPHY
From: Vanith Lefarge (Vanith@inthesky.co.uk)
To: PersephoneFaith@highmail.com
2nd October
Dear Faith, Thank you for your lovely long email. My brother as part of his need for self-importance has

re-scheduled our meeting once more. At the moment it is due to take place around the end of October or beginning of November. We shall see.

You say you have no logical answer to the most fundamental questions. You think that the most important question is 'what is the purpose of life'. Well I think the idea of purpose is a very human one. Life just IS. And if there is a purpose for man, it would be the breeding of a superior man. What makes a man superior as such is invariably seen as a controversial question. I would again say: higher intelligence or higher consciousness. I have a personal hypothetical scenario, in which the people living in Eurasia were almost wiped out by the last ice age, and that the ice age provided an environment in which intelligence and the quality of foresight gave a considerable advantage for survival. Thus the white and possibly also the yellow races evolved. When, at the end of the ice age, they managed to get south (first to Mesopotamia) they developed agriculture and animal husbandry. I think they learned, what every dog or horse-breeder today knows, and that they applied these principals to themselves. This led to a very highly evolved type of man, who could manage to out-psyche the common people. Just like a girl of eight can look after geese, which are creatures that can get quite nasty and I would not like to try anything funny with them. Unfortunately, these men eventually held or owned a great many slaves, who came voluntarily to them and the more highly evolved men intermarried with them. It says in the Bible (I think Genesis II) that the sons of *the gods found the daughters of men beautiful and married them.*

However all was reasonably well as long as man had predators and as long as the stronger of two men was likely to kill the weaker one and then make babies. With the advent of iron, men (in particular the Greeks) invented the phalanx and now a well-disciplined bunch of slaves had the best chance of survival. However, more recently things have deteriorated. In the wars of the twentieth century so many of the finest young men slaughtered each other. That is something no species can afford to do as I have pointed out previously.

However, the trouble really started with Christianity. Now we have Socialism of course which is far worse than Christianity and preaches racial equality and all that nonsense. If we had proper predators, they would eat the idiots, but the most advanced men go out of their way to create an environment where the average Negro is much fitter for survival in a welfare state than an educated white man. The latter are dying out rapidly and in fact I can count those that I know personally on the fingers of one hand. So we are heading towards an almighty catastrophe and who, if anybody will survive is anybody's guess. The catastrophe is unavoidable, because the planet is now grossly overpopulated with primitive people armed with a science and technology, invented by a type of man who is dying out.

The teachings of all the great world religions are largely nonsense but attractive to stupid slaves, because they find these teachings gratifying and ego-

boosting. Intelligent people use their brains. Kind and foolish people think with their hearts. Stupid slaves have gut-feelings. The belief that an almighty but fundamentally 'good' God made this so often 'not so good' world but that he needs the help of the unpleasant creatures he created in order to have his wishes fulfilled is quite absurd.

The idea of an eternal soul surviving death is also absurd and nobody in the Greek or Roman world believed in it. The Buddha denied the existence of a Self or Soul or Jiva, but that does not alter the basic Buddhist beliefs which encompass such ideas.

The idea of sinning against that great and good God is a kind of colossal megalomania. And Almighty God giving you the gift of free will is utterly stupid because it is a contradiction in terms. If he could give you free will, it would put an end to his almightiness.

All minds: human, animal, plant, virus, crystal etc. are linked (or networked to use computer language) and form a collective consciousness. Our minds are coupled to this consciousness and it is a very difficult concept to come to terms with. All oriental sages – Buddhist, Hindu, Tantric, etc. have problems with it. None of us is quite the individual we thought we were. Not many of us like this idea. I don't like the idea either as it so happens,

I would postulate that mind is a fundamental property of matter (and vice versa). I think the two are manifestations of one and the same thing, just as photon and wave are two different ways in which radiation can manifest. What radiation is as such we do not know.

The idea of a constant something, the jewel in the lotus that never changes and lives on forever is quite foolish. You have a sense of continuity because of your memory, but you are not the same person you were 5 minutes ago. Your DNA combination may be unique, but your identical twin is not in fact identical to you. Apart from that, DNA itself undergoes changes.

This is an abbreviated summary of what I call my beliefs and as far as I am concerned, they add up to a valid scientific theory. To produce all the necessary evidence would take a long time, and require the seeker of knowledge to have a considerable practical understanding and experience of various forms of yoga and other psycho-physical systems and above all, knowledge of modern physics and mathematics to a fairly high level.

It is this networking of all minds that enables the phenomenon we call telepathy. As we have discussed before, this telepathy works to a large extent in what mathematicians call the Fourier Transform Domain. If you understand this transform, it is quite easy to see that time is liable to get lost or shifted. There is nothing very mysterious about it.

As for a belief in God, of course I believe in God, just as I believe that there is a Father Christmas. They are both powerful ideas in the collective consciousness. But they are also in fact man made. Gods in general are forces within the collective, which have power over the individual mind. Priapus, Venus, Fear and Mars are examples of what we might call 'instincts'. The collective spirit of a regiment is another type of deity, physically represented by the regimental colours. There are many deities but the ideas of what constitutes them can vary enormously.

I am getting tired now and I will stop. If you ask questions it makes things much easier for me. You say you would like a copy of my complete file. I shall send it as an attachment, but in a separate email. For today, lots of love from Vanith.

There was no question about his utter belief in his latest disciple and I concluded that even if he should be handed irrefutable proof that Persephone Faith Callahan was actually the more than devious and scheming Bernadette, entangling him within a complex and cruel hoax, he would simply fail to believe it. The real Faith may be contentedly pursuing her day-to-day tasks in Dublin, Liverpool or London blissfully unaware that her identity had been stolen from under her, or she may be long since deceased. She may or may not remember with any clarity or warmth the young Vanith Lefarge on whom she made such an impression long ago. Whatever her present circumstances were, she now had another, altered existence and it might even be possible that she was in some strange way half aware of it. Did she have odd dreams perhaps from time to time in which, strangely, she swept floors and baked cakes and looked after two teenage girls in Israel?

With some unease I considered the fact that I had now progressed to a stage where I felt not a single shred of guilt as to the deception but only exasperation that his replies still arrived almost at the speed of light, and that some of the things he wrote seemed vaguely interesting and I wished I understood just a little better. And Faith who was clearly more capable of processing his ideas, preferred to keep a large part of her own understanding to herself and so she slid wordlessly away from the computer keyboard as quickly as she could.

FOURTEEN

On the fifth of October I insisted that Faith sit down and write a considered reply to him though she was almost as unenthusiastic as I was myself and this reluctance was somewhat exasperating. She thanked him for the file of correspondence which had of course arrived promptly just as he had promised, she went on to talk vaguely of relationships and the difficulties they posed, then told him she now understood telepathy much better than previously and thanked him for helping her with this new insight. She took the opportunity, with a great deal of prompting from me, to return to the subject of Miriam. She said she was quite certain that the legacy had come to her long, long before she revealed as much to Vanith. She added that she was also still convinced that some mutual friend, who held written confirmation of the fact, had tried to tell him. The written confirmation was of course a gross exaggeration if not a downright lie on my part. She went further and even seemed to see him angrily refusing to discuss it before putting the phone down.

Now she whispered anxiously, 'we're going too far and he'll start to suspect...' But I insisted and so she typed on, completing the accusatory paragraph. She then left the topic and went on to talk about the Darwinian theory which she assured him she accepted until such time as she should come across a better one. She spoke of the nature of intelligence noting that all too often highly academic people who ended up as Professors of Mathematics or Law, seem not to entertain a single intellectual thought during their entire lifetimes. She commented that although she liked his idea of the people in Eurasia disappearing in the last Ice Age, she rather wondered what strata of that society would actually be wiped out. She postulated that it might have been the fatter ones who were left to procreate and if that was so what might have become of them had the thinner and more physically active survived instead. She also argued the fact that it might not have necessarily been the best of the bunch who perished in twentieth century wars such as WW1, as he had noted more than once. Maybe a cluster of cringing cowards were left because they were as a sub group more intellectually advanced and some of them at least, more courageous as it would have taken more than cowardice to refuse to follow Kitchener or his German equivalent in the prevailing social climate.

In point of fact she tried to mildly disagree with more than one of his recent ideas, admonishing him a little and pointing out that you cannot have a functioning society top-heavy with intellectuals. Only a handful of Beethovens and Einsteins are actually needed and the rest are surplus to requirements. She thought that any meaningful development of culture, even folk music, is invariably created and advanced at the top and resonates to the bottom, never vice versa. As far as Eugenics was concerned she expressed disquiet and said she thought there was great difficulty in making the decision as to which particular group might be removed from society. Should the important decision be made simply by race? Or by intelligence? How about by physical fitness?

She talked of the transmigration of souls and assured him she was, after consideration, quite at ease with the idea that a soul might hop from body to body, residing first in one, then another; in fact, she told him, airing her somewhat new knowledge, the idea appeared in various forms in tribal cultures including Australian Aborigines who strangely seem quite familiar with and totally accepting of metempsychosis. This information had been gleaned via Google by Faith herself and I was impressed because you had to admit that she was by no means stupid.

It was a long letter. Well it had to be really. She obediently asked him questions such as: When did the doctrine of transmigration first appear in Hindu scriptures? Was it evident before the Upunishads to any extent? She spoke at length about Karma and admitted that she found the Buddhist position extremely complex and hoped he would be able to help her understand it better. She admitted that she worried that she might at some stage be punished for some of the things she had done in her life because she had not always been as good and decent a human being as she should have been. And this comment was because of the occasional moments of apprehension I had about my own part in the current twisting of truth. Willing participant though he was occasionally I wondered about Karma and then because I could not remember any of his own views on this subject, I urged Faith to broach it as a discussion topic. Did he ever have concerns about Karma? Had he at times behaved so badly that he felt he should ultimately be visited by some punishment?

'He should be totally terrified,' I said to Faith, 'considering the way he has behaved towards me and Daniel.' She nodded absently as she typed, but said nothing.

She spoke to him of Jung at length, saying she found him too enigmatic to be easily understood though she thought he did introduce crucial questions regarding religion and the soul that Freud seemed happy enough to neglect. She added that Jung was now seen as a quasi-religious individual, sage-like, probably because of the vast and endless following of ageing Hippies. She felt he should be seen more properly as what he was – a scientist, or a scholar. She said she was a little suspicious of his methods when dealing with mental instability and that in her opinion psycho-analysis pandered to those who were attention seeking and wished to sensationalize their mundane lives. She was particularly scathing about hypnosis and queried his own experience with it – knowing perfectly well how in years past he so loved to 'hypnotise' the woman of the moment and was easily persuaded into accepting any nonsense she cared to relate whilst in that make believe state. Even Faith recalled participation in such games.

Yes, a nice long letter, a tiring one to compose, but necessary if we were to lead him successfully towards further exposure of the kind of information that I at least was determined to uncover. She concluded by saying that she very much hoped he now trusted her again. To give them a modicum of breathing space, she said not to rush a reply to her as she would be out of email communication for a while. She was to help supervise a school camp for one of her teenage daughters.

Nevertheless on 7th October his reply arrived causing us both to sigh and exchange exasperated glances.

QUESTIONS AND ANSWERS
From: Vanith Lefarge (Vanith@inthesky.co.uk)
To: PersephoneFaith@highmail.com
7th October
Dear Faith, Thank you for your lovely long email. I was not very well last week. I had gastro-enteritis but the main thing is that I am more or less all right again.

You speak of relationships: In relationships, the mind is always by far the most important aspect. This is true in general and particularly so in love-making. It took me a while to discover that fully. When Humpty Dumpty uses a word, it means exactly what he wants it to mean. The dictionary meaning is irrelevant. In the same way a caress in love making should make the recipient feel exactly what you intend it to make them feel. Relationships are very complex. For a start there is a sexual and a non-sexual side to them. I think in a long term relationship, the most important thing is respect. Anything else can be mended or improved, but if you have lost respect for the other person, there is not much you can do.

You seem confused as to why some people are better at telepathy than others. It is the same as with intelligence, musical talent etc. but when you come to supernormal powers the differences are even more vast. Some radios are better than others and bring in a shortwave station much more clearly - but most do not have a shortwave band at all. In the sixties, I had one of the first car radio-telephones. The range was quite short but on one occasion due to freak atmospheric conditions I could hear cab drivers in New York!

I am no good at telepathy and have only experienced it on one or two occasions in my life. I am more of a Magician than a Seer in any event. Highly gifted and advanced individuals such as I am myself have differing abilities in any case. For example Hitler was able to enthuse millions of people with his speeches and Joan of Arc could make an army invincible. Paganini's violin playing was supernormal and unlike performer-composers such as Liszt and Chopin, he did not have to practice all that hard. People like this are Avatars (or Tulkus in Tibetan) or Special Incarnations or whatever you would like to call them. Napoleon was no ordinary person but not an Avatar - but Alexander was in a different league altogether. Do you begin to see what I mean?

An Avatar is a person motivated by special forces whereas ordinary people are motivated by the principal forces or ideas currently in the collective consciousness. Of course you can develop such talents deliberately. I myself have a considerable musical talent, but no amount of training or development would have made a Chopin or Liszt out of me and I would be better off trying to train as a heavy weight boxer.

An Avatar embodies special ideas. Alexander embodied the Greek idea of an Invincible Hero. He was an embodiment of Achilles. But he was not a re-incarnation of Achilles, although he believed himself to be so. Whether Achilles ever existed does not matter because he embodied, or incarnated the idea of himself in the Greek collective consciousness. The Maharishi Mahesh Yogi whom we have spoken of previously, is also an Avatar. But he embodies the collective Hippy or half-wit idea of a great Sage. He has a long white beard, he always smiles and tells everyone who comes near him, and many that do not, that they are on the first rung of the ladder to heaven.

Now to come to Miriam, I took everything she said with a pinch of salt, although I think that she was by and large quite honest with me. But I am absolutely certain that she only came by her inheritance just a little time before her death. I think you are quite, quite wrong about this.

What I have said about WW1 is of course a sweeping statement with hundreds and thousands of exceptions. But I think overall it is at least statistically true. What I mean is this: It is undisputable that Americans are taller and less intelligent than Europeans. But that refers to the statistical mean, not to individuals. There is a slight inverse correlation between height and intelligence. In most fairy tales giants are stupid and dwarfs are clever. But the fact that somebody is tall in no way implies that they are stupid (or vice versa).

Now to reincarnation: The idea is certainly very old, but the Upanishads are of course much older. However, this reincarnation idea is quite absurd, especially in the light of modern science. There can be no soul or consciousness without a brain because mind and matter are inseparable. I am quite sure of that.

Karma is the law of cause and effect. The simplified laws of Karma for the physical world are summed up in Newton's three axioms and the law of gravitation. Without causality it would not be possible to predict the future. (such as foretelling lunar eclipses in a hundred years' time). But the inverse is also true. If it is possible to tell the future then there must be a considerable degree of causality. I personally know of several cases of people having foretold the future so definitely that coincidence can be totally ruled out. It therefore follows that there must be a considerable degree of causality in the non-physical world. Neither of the two causalities is absolute. That in the physical world is limited by the wave mechanical uncertainty, which leaves room for that in the non-physical world, which is also limited. However, the law of Karma is hard for most people to accept, because their minds operate like children's and they therefore believe they will be rewarded or punished for being good or bad. Therefore Karma tends to be misinterpreted.

At a personal level I am very concerned about the laws of Karma and I am very careful going down the stairs, especially when I am not feeling well because according to the law of Karma, carelessness can make you fall. On the other hand I do in life that which I feel I should do or must do. Therefore I have put severe curses upon God the Father, God the Son, God the Holy Ghost and all that goes along with them including Mary, Mother of God. This is because I consider them to be demons of a rather nasty kind, and certainly not friends of mankind.

I was involved in exploring hypnosis when I was much younger. I have never been successfully hypnotized myself. It is well known that only certain people can be subjected to it with any degree of success. I think you are right - in nearly all cases there is an element of make-believe or pretence.

I cannot remember saying that I did not trust you, but I had the feeling, that you were terribly obsessed with the Christina-Bernadette and child business. I am quite happy to talk about Christina. In any case she concerns you because she was your friend. Bernadette and the child are another matter. I would rather not re-energize any memories of them at all. That more or less answers your questions. It is late and I would like to send this to-night. So with lots of love until we speak again after your duty at the teenage camp, your Vanith.

Infuriating though it might be he was not to be moved from his position of feeling that any decision he had made in the past, now or in the future, was right and proper no matter how at odds it might be with what the rest of the world considered fitting and appropriate. Therefore the idea of harvesting any vestige of culpability for the misery he had heaped upon my younger self was not even on the periphery of his vision. His grandiosity took my breath away but probably it was no worse now than it had been in the 1960s; I simply had not been associated with him in the interim. It was easy to forget how merciless some of his attitudes were, how confident he was in his own worth.

On 14th October whilst still astounded at the extent of his total belief in himself, we wrote to say Faith had returned from her duties at the camp and we told him what an egocentric group young males are, describing generally and under the guise of a 'group' of teenage boys, himself to himself, using his own words, outlining his worst faults and frailties in no uncertain terms. Faith also spoke of Narcissism and wondered if it might be his brother's problem and sought his opinion on this. And then we told him we were glad to hear that his earlier anger was not directed towards us directly, and that the subject of our friend Christina was not to be off limits. We also agreed with him that we had definitely become far too involved with the subject of Bernadette but on the other hand, talk about Christina again we now would.

So because she had been Faith's friend and not mine, it was she who then wrote, reiterating that Christina had been a good friend to her during a period in her life when friends were of utmost importance. She spoke once again of that obsessive love she bore for Vanith, the delusion that they were destined to be together. Then because Bernadette was armed with evidence of more than one relationship between close women friends that Vanith Lefarge had not exactly forbidden but at least forced a choice to be made, I urged her to dig deeper and perhaps more dangerously. She was uneasy and asked what actual evidence I had, what friendships had he deemed not permissible? So then I reminded her of poor Sukey Horowitz and Rona, the closest of friends through schooldays and would be still if Vanith had not issued an ultimatum: Which relationship was more important he had wanted to know. Each with him - or with each other? And it was Sukey who tearfully told Rona that their friendship must cease because it was destroying an important bond with Vanith. This I had heard reiterated from Rona's own lips and recently. Faith sighed, fingers hesitating just above the keyboard. So I prompted further. What about Miriam and myself? Had we not been able to associate freely with each other until Vanith put a stop to it, making poor Miriam fearful in her own home if I should visit on my infrequent trips to London? So Faith, whilst biting her lower lip, determinedly tapped the keyboard. She suggested that he might have had at times a divisive and disruptive effect upon relationships between his women friends. She sensed there had been some difficulty for Rona and a woman with a name that began with S. They had been close but began to distrust each other and the catalyst appeared to have been Vanith himself. The S woman came from a wealthy Jewish family but had a poor self-image because of being grossly overweight. Faith wondered if any of this made sense to him. In fact he would have had to be rather dense for it not to make perfect sense.

Sukey was the youngest of three sisters with whom Vanith and I became acquainted long ago. I knew from Miriam, who had been quite horrified at the time, that he had begun an effective grooming process upon her at the tender age of thirteen which a year later had progressed successfully to an affair that had some consequence for her mental health. Her weight dismayed him but her age was thrilling and he made weekly drives through the Sussex countryside to take her on visits to village teashops followed by prolonged amorous encounters in the back of his car, the Mini Station Wagon I had paid for. I anticipated with some pleasure his astonishment that Faith, who had never been anywhere near any of the Horowitz sisters, appeared to know so much about them. Her telepathic powers grew ever more astonishing.

But in essence his reply of 16th October was to some extent disappointing. He spoke a great deal of some friends he had visited in Hampshire, with much detail about the woman's early life growing up with her grandfather who had built state coaches for his Imperial Majesty the Emperor Franz Joseph of Austria. The fact that she ran away to become a dancer and was henceforth cast out by her entire family and later married an English sailor who tried to sell her to a brothel in the Middle East. All this would have been quite amusing under normal circumstances but Faith and Bernadette found it tedious on that particular day. Neither of them knew her after all. He sneered a little more regarding his brother and revealed that the foolish fellow used to collect autographs of famous opera singers as a teenager, but despite that he would still be going to see him from 29th October returning on 6th November with any luck, a trip his brother was generously paying for. He again commented that Faith's telepathic interest in Bernadette and her child had produced powerful and dangerous waves that had been hard to control. He spoke of Christina and just a little of Sukey. He revealed that she had been a child of twelve when he met her. Later her mother, a Zionist, maintained upon discovering that he had seduced each one of her daughters, that she hated Vanith Lefarge more than Yasser Arafat. He said he had been quite flattered at the time. He confirmed that poor overweight Sukey had been in love with him for many painful years and that Faith's powers were quite astonishing.

Faith had been reluctant to believe me when I first revealed how he had preyed upon the child Sukey causing her so much emotional damage. She shook her head and said back when she had known him he simply had not been that bad a person. She looked reproachfully at me almost as if his downward spiral was somehow or other my fault. When I remonstrated with her she nodded faintly and gave a despondent shake of her head.

We sent our reply on 20th October and spoke of the pleasure he gave us with his interesting stories, adding as a reminder that we looked forward to the next gripping episode of the yarn concerning Sukey and her sisters. We complimented him for his charm and charisma and unfailing ability to draw around him a group of fascinating women who invariably fell in love – and we commiserated in that this very attribute might well make his own path through life more arduous than was necessary. Poor luckless Vanith. Did he perhaps ever feel responsible for the extent of the sufferings of these lovesick females? Faith confessed that she had herself at times fallen from the straight and narrow and cashed in on the devotion of another, almost using them for her own ends. She was not proud of this. She pointed out that the one-sided relationship conducted with Christina had all but destroyed that particular devotee. And oddly Faith seemed to sense another young woman whose life had been devastated by obsessive love for Vanith Lefarge. A young woman who had been at the time when they met, excessively vulnerable, and he had charged into her life on a white horse and rescued her from a difficult situation... because of her vulnerability she fell precipitously in love and this caused her ongoing grief. A dark haired woman who now obscured her identity as if somehow fearful of completely revealing herself. Did this ring any bells for him?

And feeling confident and almost invincible, at my urging she stepped further onto thin and cracking ice. She apologized that her telepathic involvement in his relationship with Bernadette had produced such powerful waves and said that this outcome was as disturbing to her as it was to him. It was a nasty business and poor Rudy was indeed also inextricably caught up in it and at times envied his brother for fathering the child, referring to him frequently as their father's only grandchild. This was almost understandable as the boy was his nephew and at one stage he had also envied Vanith's relationship with the mother. She then spoke a little of Plato and his comments on frank discussion , the need at times for the use of obscurantism. Did not Jacques Lacan once say that he intentionally made his lectures hard to understand so that students would concentrate. She generously told him not to simply endure her comments if he felt uncomfortable. He must tell her and she would make adjustments.

Finally a mention of poor Josef was made, how he failed to improve and was taking a new drug which it was hoped would help him. Larissa's birthday party was also spoken of, and the number of friends she had invited, and all the preparation it would need. Faith was indeed a busy woman. She and Josef might also go away for a month or two to see if a trip might be recuperative for him.

Vanith's reply that exasperatingly arrived within hours was long, meandering and talked a great deal once more about his difficulties at school before the skull fracture when he found it almost impossible to learn to read and write and he felt this might have been because no-one really seemed to appreciate that even highly intelligent children need to reach a certain level of maturity before some skills can be accomplished; and of course he was quite correct. He spoke with some fondness of the private tutors he had, and explored further the problems at Trinity College, Dublin. He asked if Faith could somehow find, via telepathy perhaps, Christina's address on Exmoor and admitted that he had tried to find it without success but he would so like to meet up with her again. Importantly he assured Faith that no subjects were taboo for discussion between them and that, tiresome as ever, he could not understand who the mystery woman was that she spoke of, the one who was obscured and had been so vulnerable. He suggested he give her a list of his most important girlfriends and she should see if she could pick her out from the group. The names were:

Noreen, Pamela, Biddy, Faith, Paula, Davina, Maudie, Jane, Christina, Irena, Marianne, Bernadette, Kim, Jenny, Yolanda, Sukey, Anne, Rona, Milly, Brigitte, Carrie, Heather.

He said he did not think he had left anyone out and these were the women who had all fallen head over heels in love with him over the years. He went on to talk about Rudy and maintained that his brother had never wanted children because he thought that the family was tainted with madness. He agreed, however, that he would want contact with his nephew although it had to be borne in mind that this person was only an illegitimate nephew and therefore not of any enormous consequence. He admitted that their mother had been greatly taken with Bernadette and had urged Rudy to marry her if Vanith did not want her. She had, of course, been most anxious to have contact with that bastard child. He had to inform her that if she ever did so then he, Vanith, would have nothing further to do with her as long as she lived. Although not in any way surprised by these revelations both Bernadette and Faith admitted to feeling just a tiny bit traumatized.

He added that it would be very sad if he did not hear from Faith whilst she was away with Josef. How long would she be gone? And when would she leave? He urged her to write as soon as possible with more news of her life and added that their correspondence was enormously important to him and that he had not written so much in his entire life. He sent a great deal of love, genuine love, to her. The two women thought that was actually very nice of him.

A long reply was sent to him on the twenty fifth of October in which Faith described the very busy week she had just had and how the two girls went to too many parties, the inadequate education system, Josef's state of health and other details concerning the minutia of daily life. Then the question of Christina was examined and she told him that sadly she had been quite unable to find an address on Exmoor either telepathically or via more mundane means, but she now remembered having a conversation with that woman's older sister at some stage in which it was disclosed that poor Christina thought she must stay near to Vanith in order to protect him from a woman who was keeping him under lock and key because when he was able to escape she and he would run away together into golden days of happiness.

The mystery woman still obscured from full vision was to the forefront once more. She had been naïve and emotionally disadvantaged Faith told him, and strangely she insisted that she was cruelly manipulated by him throughout their attachment. Taking another leap towards the frozen pond she added more clues and said he had been living in the home of another woman when they first met. She had been involved in some kind of paid activity that disturbed her and had to work at night.

Surely he could not be totally stupid, I said to Faith and she agreed though rather disapprovingly. If he could not be seduced back into a conversation with regard to Bernadette so that a degree of culpability for his past actions could be inculcated within him, then it was hardly worth the trouble of writing all these interminable emails. The novelty value of the situation was wearing a little thin. Both of us agreed that it was time consuming. Faith wandered into a long discourse on infidelity and the boundaries of sex and love, even stating that the desire for monogamy was an artifact of culture. And fancying that his guard was down sufficiently as he read and absorbed this psycho-babble, she moved towards the jugular with an extended catalogue of telepathic tit-bits concerning people and situations that she could not possibly have any knowledge of, but if he only stopped to consider, he would realise that Bernadette knew these things very well.

She cautiously spoke of his son and suggested that possibly his brother left all contact with him to his wife in order that he could say quite honestly, with hand on heart that he at least had not strayed from the straight and narrow. Faith felt that the relationship with his nephew had grown in importance for Rudy and what is more she strongly believed that there had been a visit to Germany by this young man some time previously, and even a visit to the castle in Saxony. She ended the letter with hope that he would have a good visit with his brother. She and I both felt they would have much to discuss.

Then there was a welcome hiatus during which Jack and I entertained a number of his old university friends to a fine lunch party. The preparation went on for several days because I was determined that the food should be worthy of the occasion. And although she protested, whilst this took place Faith was folded up like an old shirt and placed on a shelf at the very back of the linen cupboard and the door was firmly shut on her.

Vanith himself did not emerge once more from the inbox until 13th November with a long and tedious letter telling us that the trip had been a success apart from the fact that he had suffered an inconvenient accident whilst stepping back to take a photograph and he thought he might have cracked a rib. He spoke at length on the pain and how he was dealing with it. He progressed then to discussion on his many girlfriends and their love for him and again, frustratingly, said he had no idea who the mystery woman might be. He commented that Faith seemed to keep picking up on Bernadette again and he could not understand why because she had not been all that important to him from an emotional point of view. There were, after all, more interesting topics for them to discuss together.

I was then more than indignant at the dismissive tone with regard to myself, being better pleased when he spoke of me with unease and trepidation. Faith, newly emerged from the cupboard and blinking at the sudden bright daylight, simply shrugged her shoulders and made no comment. We stared at each other disapprovingly across the office desk and I wondered if she should be dismissed for a further few days then she suddenly exclaimed and pointed to the Inbox screen where a second message had appeared, sent within an hour of the first.

'It's from Him!' She pronounced. And it was.

I AM VERY ANGRY WITH YOU!
From: Vanith Lefarge (Vanith@inthesky.co.uk)

To: PersephoneFaith@highmail.com

13th November

I just wanted you to know that I am exceedingly angry with you for breaking the seals I had put on that business of Bernadette and her child by your incessant focusing on the matter. I now have severe chest pain and at the moment I feel out of breath and shaky. With the seals damaged I am forced to renew them and also remake the curses I placed so many years ago. Yet all was well until you came along with your insatiable desire to find out all there was to know about the matter. Do you realise that this is only likely to bring fresh trouble onto all who are concerned in the business? This is the last thing I wanted. I have warned you and pleaded with you but to no avail. You simply ignore my instructions. The best thing would be for that bloody child to drop dead and the sooner the better. Vanith.

Vanith the Remarkable, the Illustrious, the Eminent – and astonishingly the elderly Persephone Faith Callahan from Israel, was daring to disobey. I rocked back in my typist's chair and laughed but softly. Faith shook her head to and fro and said she did not think it was all that funny. What, after all, was going to happen next? I told her she was foolish if she actually believed that his curses might work. This was a notion even I had discarded. Faith looked apprehensive and half whispered something about just needing to be careful that's all and what was the point of totally upsetting him and then she slid away.

I shouted at her retreating figure in its neat tweed skirt, 'Don't forget that I'm powerful too.' But she had gone.

Later when we spoke again I insisted that he should wait nearly three weeks for a reply. And it was during this hiatus that I first suggested to myself and to Faith that it might be time to reveal to him the Truth. I initially broached the idea when I noticed her drifting along the window sill as I packed the dishwasher one Saturday evening.

'But why?' she asked feebly. 'Why do something that will make him so incredibly angry?'

'I don't think you quite understand the depth of the misery he heaped upon me.' Strangely I found myself easily dissolving into tears. 'Decades later it just doesn't go away.'

Her voice grew bolder and the pale blue of her cardigan marginally brighter.

'But it all happened such a very long time ago. Surely it's too late for that. Unleashing Truth can cause destructive and overwhelming effects. You should understand that it's not something we could easily control.'

Truth was emerging as an amorphous group of savage and primordial canines, impatient to tear into whatever place the slumbering conscience of Vanith Lefarge inhabited. I found the thought exhilarating, the idea liberating, but Faith was sitting quiet and still, Madonna-like, her cardigan becoming bluer and bluer.

'Perhaps,' she suggested at last, 'we should simply compose a draft when we have both calmed down a little. That way it will be conveniently on hand if and when you decide we actually should send it.'

I found myself agreeing to this proposal although in fact more than three weeks elapsed before The Draft itself was constructed, after Faith had eventually sent off the following reply to his venomous message of 13th November.

From: PersephoneFaith@highmail.com
To: Vanith@inthesky.co.uk
2nd December
First I must thank you for your honesty; as you know I have been urging honesty for several months. From that perspective perhaps I have only myself to blame for the unpalatable things you have said to me. I have found this tirade especially wounding but I am sure you know that well enough.

At various stages in our lives unpleasant things – like pain and ill health for instance – just happen... no-one is to blame. It is simply what life doles out to us, particularly as we age and I know it only too well. We cannot reach old age without experiencing bouts of poor health and it is foolish in the extreme to imagine that we can take part in this human existence and yet somehow remain unscathed by the ravages of time. In this matter of your health, the fault lies in your genetic inheritance. Whatever I wrote...or did not write, this inherent blemish was there in your genetic profile to emerge eventually and cause you concern.

After receipt of your last email I sat for some time feeling bewildered and also of course, worried about your health – but far too angry to respond. Had I done so I would have possibly used the same kind of language you employed yourself and I did not want to do that. Instead I have made strenuous efforts psychically to ensure that you sort out the current health problem with your heart.

In the interim I would most strenuously urge you to believe the following: When you accuse me of 'an insatiable desire to know' you are quite, quite wrong and if only you had stopped momentarily to think before sending that message you would have realised that I have not initiated discussion in this matter at all recently but merely commented on information YOU have offered yourself (for example your mother's desire to see Rollo married to the woman, etc.) All of us sometimes simply get things wrong, even you.

I am confused as to where we go from here but it is undeniably foolish for us to maintain a stubborn silence for any length of time. Whatever comes of this I want to tell you that I shall always carry with me and close to my heart, a great deal of love for you and it is my wish to at all times think of you with true affection no matter how badly you may have come to think of me. This life is short and if we allow ourselves to be imprudently torn from important relationships the subsequent separation and silence can be so complete that we only then realise that we can never make enough of the links that we have with the living. Faith.

And as we had come to predict, his response was immediate.

I AM SO HAPPY TO HEAR FROM YOU!
From: Vanith Lefarge (Vanith@inthesky.co.uk)
To: PersephoneFaith@highmail.com
2nd December
Dearest Faith, thank you very much for your email. I have been feeling very sad, because I feared that you would not write again after my last message. So I was terribly pleased to hear from you again! I have had a lot to do, silly things like applying for a new driving license, because mine expires shortly and other nonsense work like that, but by the week end I will be able to write to you properly. This is just to let you know how very pleased I am to hear from you. Love and good wishes to you and to your family. I have so much love for you, from Vanith.

I felt very satisfied with this and even Faith looked less worried. We wrote back a sentence or two telling him not to worry, simply to write when he had more time – and of course he did.

ANGER
From: Vanith Lefarge (Vanith@inthesky.co.uk)
To: PersephoneFaith@highmail.com
5th December

My Dearest Faith, it is Saturday evening and at last the troubles of the last week or so are over. No, you misunderstand if you think that my anger was directed against you, in particular. I think this is partly because I express myself badly when I am angry. I am truly sorry about that. On the contrary, my anger is partly against myself, because I am well aware of the fact that I told you more things about Bernadette and thereby encouraged you to reply to what I had said and that I am in that sense equally to blame, if blame is the right word. But my chief anger is towards the 'Bernadette and her child' business, which is bad and powerful and manages to force its way into your thoughts and mine and thereby draw energy. In any case I am more concerned for you because I fear that you may become enmeshed in a potentially dangerous set of forces. She is a nasty and dangerous entity.

And I certainly do not blame you for my health problems, which started two or three years ago. I slightly injured my knee, which provoked pain in my lower leg. It was very painful and so I took a lot of Codis (Aspirin with Codeine) which I had taken from time to time all my life with impunity. I now realise I took too much for too long and got a nasty gastritis which caused that awful pain. It did not really heal until about June this year. It is now better but all this masked the onset of Angina Pectoris which I am now trying to sort out. I have had a scan and am waiting to see if an operation can help me.

I repeat that I am not blaming you for any of this. However the Bernadette business is serious for me, and at present I am particularly anxious to avoid stress of any kind, and opening up that nasty business is very stressful - do let us both try to avoid it.

I am sorry I accused you of an insatiable desire to know about her. It is not you. It is the matter itself, which has a powerful energy to suck one in, like an eddy. I think I told you that even I, who had lived with her for several years, vastly underestimated what she was capable of. You are no more at fault than I am. I also allowed the matter to prey on my mind again recently. About twelve years ago the whole thing began to totally consume my brother and his wife and her mother though I begged them to leave it alone, telling them it was dangerous, that there was powerful magic involved. They did not believe me of course. No-one ever does.

I very much hope, that I have expressed myself better today and that you will realise, that I am not blaming you for anything. On the contrary, I have a great deal of love and affection for you and I am aware that I owe you a great deal, and that you have always wanted the best for me. I hope very much that we will now carry on our friendship without more of these problems. Much love always, Vanith.

I showed this to Faith rather proudly and asked, 'Is this not a satisfyingly grovelling little letter?' But Faith said uncertainly, 'It does not bode well.'

What nonsense she spoke at times. He deserved a nice long letter. We told him that the doctor had been to see Josef and that his drug regime was going to be adjusted, and that Tamzin who had been wanting more pocket money, had taken some junior maths students on two evenings a week and was now earning a little which pleased her. We spoke a great deal about the Israeli education system modelling it on the current New Zealand one, and hoped we were correct but decided that even if we were not, he would hardly know any better. And Faith quoted John Stuart Mill from time to time and then C.S. Lewis. We thanked him for his profound apology and agreed that all of us from time to time express ourselves badly and possibly incur the wrath of others. We recommended some historical recordings on the Pearl label that he should listen to – the young Ida Haendel. This I felt would definitely interest him so I also directed him to an internet site where he could see the more elderly Haendel performing and Josef Hassid also if he cared to search. It was a very nice letter – and then somewhat capriciously I allotted Faith another telepathic incident involving a woman called Lila Andhurst, whom he had once known well and visited often with Bernadette in tow, a woman completely unknown to Faith. Nevertheless it came to her in a dream during their time of estrangement, a rather nice house in Edgware Road. The woman was in distress at the death of her husband and Vanith had sat with her on the lawn, offering comfort and playing with her two little boys. Miriam had seemed to live somewhere nearby.

Then, because I had not entirely forgiven him for his anger towards Faith, I ordered that it should not be sent until at least December 12th. His reply arrived on December 13th and he thanked them for their long and very interesting email and told them he was sorry that poor Josef was not doing well. He spoke a great deal about the education system, saying he was a little surprised that it was so mediocre in Israel because he had thought it might be better than in England. In his opinion this general lack of education spilled over into every area. He pointed out that even educated people make mistakes. He had often felt that Bertrand Russell would have been more sensible to hold marches to support the banning of television and using the bomb. He announced that he was soon to be 84 years old and that his mother had died at 88. He once again waxed lyrical about Faith's gifts of telepathy and agreed that he certainly knew Lila and her two sons and that he had an affair with her although she was at the time a great deal older than him.

And he ended by telling Faith that he had enormous love for her, for being his friend and for being herself. I was quite touched by that. Faith was pleased too but she looked pensive all the same. I knew she was worried about The Draft waiting, ready to be sent and sometimes late at night reworded here and there. Often at those times when a sentence was restructured, I saw the shadow of her loitering on the periphery of the Drafts Folder.

FIFTEEN

On 14th of December full of enthusiasm and excitement after hours in front of the computer screen viewing Ida Haendel, he wrote:

HAENDEL AND HASSID
From: Vanith Lefarge (Vanith@inthesky.co.uk)
To: PersephoneFaith@highmail.com
14th December
Dearest Faith, I can't write for long because Christmas is coming and I must buy, write and send cards, etc. I just wanted to let you know that I followed your directions and found Hassid and Haendel and I found them so mind blowing, I got to bed 3 hours later than intended. Especially Haendel. She is beyond description. As Gerald Moore said 'a Heifetz comes every 100 years, a Haendel every 200.' There are lots of good violinists and quite a few very good ones, but the greats are rare. Thank you so very much for introducing me.

I also watched Lawrence Krauss, who is Professor of theoretical physics and astro-physics and the best I have come across since Gentner. There is a Krauss video on the opening panel at the Quantum to Cosmo Festival which you can find a link to, if you put 'Lawrence Krauss' into Google and bring up the Wikipedia entry. It is a lecture primarily for lay people – I get about 80 percent of it.

More love (one can never get enough of it, at least I can't) for today. Vanith.

Faith looked vaguely dissatisfied and when asked why she said that she thought it was a disappointingly short message but Bernadette could not altogether agree and pointed out that it rather let them off the hook in that their reply could be equally brief; they could also claim that the forthcoming festive season was responsible.

Faith disagreed. 'But we live in Israel – and Josef at least is Jewish'.

'I don't think you are though,' she was reminded, 'And the girls are a kind of mix. In any event none of them have to be religious do they?'

They both wondered what was customary in modern Israel as far as Christmas was concerned. Did department stores have decorations and a Santa's Grotto for example? There must be a reasonable number of Christians in the country. They could come to no sensible conclusion and so Bernadette instructed Faith to begin work on a lengthy reply if she so wished, by herself, but warned that it should consist mostly of generalities, perhaps a lot more about education – could she be trusted to do that? Faith said she could and began to type diligently.

So the message he received on 17th December contained some rather dull facts and figures about modern education and an enthusiastic expansion on the relating cultural aspects pertaining to loss of language in some North American Indian tribes or renaissance of language in the case of the New Zealand Maori. At least Bernadette knew something about that and now so did Faith having lived with us in Auckland for the best part of that year. And then, just for fun, and as an afterthought, they included part of an Eleven Plus Arithmetic Paper aimed at eleven year olds from 1924 and compared it with a Mathematics Grading Test from Teachers' Training College 1988. These had been discovered in a book about school failure picked up in a second-hand shop when Daniel was nine and had been relegated briefly to the Tortoises Mathematics Group at St. Joseph's Primary School.

In order to further fan the flames Bernadette suggested including a number of telepathic incidents which she listed for Faith, involving events and people Faith agreed she had no previous knowledge of. However, they were closely connected to Bernadette herself and Clive of the Holland Park orgies and dinners and meeting Rona and Rosalinda, a long-dead nightclub colleague who had owned a determinedly incontinent white poodle, Angel. They ended by telling him how glad they were that he had enjoyed Haendel and Hassid so much. Bernadette knew Daniel at least would be pleased because it was his suggestion that his father be introduced to these two greats; a definite linking of father and son that the former would recoil from in some horror if only he should become aware of it.

In the days leading up to Christmas he did not write but sent an internet link to the Chinese Circus and Bernadette sent him a link to Feng Ning playing Paganini Caprices. But on Christmas Eve a proper letter arrived and Faith was unfolded so they could read it together. They felt quite Christmassy as they did so.

GODS & DEMONS
From: Vanith Lefarge (Vanith@inthesky.co.uk)
To: PersephoneFaith@highmail.com
24th December
My Very Dearest Faith, The things you picked up telepathically are, all correct, but a bit of a jumble of what various people said and did at various times. What you say about Clive is correct. I met him, because I used to go to swinging parties, and he was one of the original Christine Keeler, Stephen Ward crowd I got involved with. He had been a naval officer. Rona did indeed meet him. She was very class conscious, and as Clive was a QC and of good family and very well off, she would have liked to marry him. The little white dog you speak of called Angel belonged to a Jewish friend of Bernadette's whose name was Rosalinda just as you say! As I have said previously, I am totally blown away by your ability in this area. I have never come across anyone who had such a well-developed gift!

I found what you say about education extremely interesting and also quite shocking, because you live in Israel and I thought that things would be slightly better there than here.

I would now like to turn to something else and perhaps my following thoughts will shock you. I want your comments. I will begin in ancient Egypt where according to mythology Osiris was married to Isis. He had an evil brother called Set. Eventually there was a great battle between the brothers which Set won and he cut his brother into 12 or 13 pieces, and laid them in the four corners of the world. Isis went to look for the pieces and found all of them except the penis.

She assembled the pieces on the banks of the Nile and uttering the secret name of Rah, brought Osiris back to life. It is my belief that Set, in his great fury, magically produced an Avatar called Moses some 3300 years ago. Moses was brought up by a royal princess and received the education of a Pharaoh. However, he was probably deeply ashamed of being from Jewish slave stock and he hated the Egyptians. At some stage he came into conflict with an Egyptian and killed him and so he had to flee, but returned after some years. Moses created a Tutelary Deity for the Jews, called Yahweh. Because of all the hatred involved in his creation this god turned out to be a truly terrible demon.

During his exile Moses had lived with a farmer near the Sinai desert, and in all likelihood it was there he discovered a place where it was possible to survive. He then exhorted the Jews to kill all the Egyptian first born and to steal as much gold and jewellery as they could. When this had been accomplished he led them into the Sinai desert to the place he knew. The Egyptians were taken by surprise and by the time they got a posse of soldiers to go in pursuit the route was impassable (maybe because of tides?) and the officer in charge decided that without substantial provisions it would be too dangerous to follow into the desert, and in any case, as far as he was concerned, there was no way to survive there. So he let them go. Moses kept the Jews in the desert and there re-enforced Yahweh's strength with his tablets of Commandments and stories of burning bushes etc. There was no way they could return into Egypt after what they had done.

Moses died in the desert and later Joshua led the people into the Promised Land. When they got there Yahweh urged them to attack Jericho and massacre the entire population - men, women and children. So the Jews did so and Yahweh said 'well done, now do the same to the city of Ai.' And again they did so, sparing only the town prostitute who had betrayed the city

You may now begin to understand why I am inclined to regard this particular Tutelary Deity as a demon. Judaism was not actually a monotheistic religion in the beginning. (see Judaism in the Encyclopaedia Britannica). But this particular God was a male chauvinist pig, judging from the first commandment. In time the Egyptians heard about the descendants of the Jews, who had fled some decades previously, now turning up in Palestine and they promptly sent an army. At any rate an Egyptian victory column was found dating from about 1200 BC celebrating the fact that they had wiped out the Jews completely though obviously some would have survived. I will skip the history of the Jews for the next thousand years.

In due course this demon Yahweh had children – all demons, and arguably far worse and more sinister than Yahweh himself, who was simply the lord and protector of slaves. One of his children, Jesus, favoured all slaves and in fact anyone who was inferior. You only have to read the Sermon on the Mount to realise this. 'Blessed are the poor... the feeble minded, the criminals, etc.'. On the other hand he hated the rich, the successful, the upper classes and warned them, 'It is easier for a camel to go through the eye of a needle' etc.

I find it difficult to ascertain exactly what sort of a man Jesus was. All we know about him is from the gospels, and they were written a long time after his death from hearsay by not very well educated people. The actual founders of Christianity were the not terribly bright fisherman Peter and the schizophrenic Paul, along with one or two other nonentities. Christianity introduced the idea of a kind of Divine Socialism. God loves sinners, etc.

I think God would be greatly displeased if you claimed righteousness in any shape or form. The only thing that will mollify that monstrous demon is kissing his backside very, very diligently, and admitting that you are the most unworthy of sinners. If you cringe sufficiently this particular Lord of Justice will make an exception and let you into Heaven (unjustly, because you would not deserve it - after all you will still be tainted with original sin). But on the other hand he simply cannot resist flattery, adulation, cringing and backside kissing. What a repulsive and filthy demon!!!

After the Reformation and the bloody wars associated with it people began to lose some faith in Christianity (and the Kingdom of God on Earth) and while the intelligent ones conceived modern science, the not so clever ones (who could nevertheless read and write) created in its place, Temporal Christianity - i.e. Socialism. This is worse than religious Christianity because now all people immediately become equal. So with time man has become more stupid and more criminal.

To say this is of course terribly shocking and politically incorrect. We identify giving to the poor with goodness. In the ancient world, the idea of giving money from the public purse to beggars would have seemed absurd. Money from the public purse was given to people of special merit in the same way as an OBE. However, we are now in the grip of a vast swathe of demonic and idiotic ideas we are undoubtedly heading for horrendous disaster. Have a look at our present population explosion. The graph is progressing towards infinity, and as nothing can become infinite, it can only mean one thing – disaster!

To reiterate what I said earlier on about Yahweh and Jesus: it is these demon Gods that are the problem and not their innocent victims. The Jews and the Christians are simply that – victims. They have been duped by demonic entities that threaten to destroy mankind, and one disaster after another will overcome humanity. Throwing Christians to the lions unfortunately creates martyrs, and only strengthens the deity. As you know Nero failed miserably in this respect and so did Hitler.

Madame Blavatsky was as we have discussed previously, a Magician of consequence, and she skilfully created the Masters, designed as an antidote. They are doing well and multiplying but is it too little too late I wonder?

Now to other matters: I have been to my doctor, he is very nice and from Bangladesh but unfortunately he does not know a lot about medicine. He did not have my report and said I would have to wait until I see the cardiologist at the North Middlesex Hospital. However Rona, who is a nurse, managed to get hold of the report and sent me a copy. I will attach the file and you can make of it what you like. It would appear, that I have had a very slight heart attack at some point, without realising it and that it did a little damage. I am going to Germany to see my brother again shortly for a week or two so it could be a while before I see the cardiologist as this will now have to take place when I get back.

There is lots more I would like to say, but this must suffice for today. I am very interested what you have to say about the matters I have discussed with you in this letter.

I wish you a merry Xmas and a happy New Year. With love, Vanith.

Faith seemed quite beguiled by the diatribe against organised religion and read the history of the Jews several times, nodding sagely and saying she quite understood where he was coming from. Bernadette privately thought her a fool but said nothing as she was itching to put her away for Christmas. Jonah was arriving from Shanghai and was to stay several weeks. His room had to be made ready for him and there was still food shopping to be done. So Faith, protesting just a little, was put away, the medical report hurriedly printed off and left for Jack to find when he awoke and Bernadette sped off to the supermarket, feeling satisfied with the work of the past months. Possibly, she thought, as she dallied between the frozen food aisles, he would actually become critically ill if the heart condition was indeed serious. The thought gave her pleasure. And if he should actually die, it might be fun to wander through his flat, looking at the evidence of his life over the past forty years.

She gave serious thought to when The Draft should be sent. Should it perhaps arrive as a Christmas surprise?

'I don't think there's much chance of you getting into his flat,' Daniel said when he made real coffee an hour or two later and they sat drinking it at the kitchen bench.

'Never say never,' Bernadette advised. Later that evening Jack did look at the cardiology report and all he said was that it was not terribly significant though it did show that he had some slight damage to his heart. This, of course, he had told us.

Then Christmas intervened and she roasted a goose that had been remarkably difficult to come by during a hot Auckland summer. She had made a traditional Christmas pudding in honour of Jonah who was fussy about such things, and he made rum butter himself on Christmas morning, he and Daniel drinking beer in the kitchen together, the latter informing his brother of every single good point Salome had and how outstanding her marks were and that she was going to get a scholarship to Oxford. And everything around them was Christmassy and smelling of goodwill.

On 27th December somewhat annoyingly Faith began to insist that a reply should be sent to Vanith's last message. Bernadette had shown considerable reluctance when she contemplated his tirade of abuse towards religion, the ongoing rant that she barely understood and his demands for comment, suggesting that The Draft should be sent in its stead. Faith greeted this idea with horror and so after considerable argument between them a compromise was reached. Faith eventually agreed that she was willing to talk more about Rosalinda, her Italian husband, the East End criminal she was once in love with and the adopted daughter, Beverly. And because the substance of his last message was of such extreme importance, Faith herself would set her mind to a suitable response.

From: PersephoneFaith@highmail.com
To: Vanith@inthesky.co.uk
27th December

My Dear Vanith – It was so good to hear from you before the dreadful 'festive' season really and truly began. I must tell you that I am not fond of this strange and obligatory festive time of year when we extend hospitality and offer gifts to those we are not terribly fond of at all. One would imagine that in this country we would be able to get away from the whole thing but not so and the smallest Jewish child will be aware, however orthodox his family, that it is something to do with the birthday of Mary's son Jesus and in the local kindergarten they have been known to sing 'Happy Birthday Dear Jesus' in his honour!!!

I am pleased that the things I picked up on telepathically are for the most part correct albeit a jumble. This was in fact what I had begun to understand myself. I would see things very clearly and then realise that my interpretation was not totally correct and I was superimposing one event upon another like bits of film fading in and out.

That man Clive seems to have loomed quite large in your life at one stage and from what you now say about Rona I can quite see why she was fond of him in fact. Clearly he would have made a better husband for her than the man she has ended up with.

Sorry to seem to leap from topic to topic but I am still going through your own letter and have it in front of me. The Jewish girl Rosalinda –I have had a few images of her and in fact one strong one at this very moment. I see her as extremely pretty and maybe just a bit overweight (curvy)... with an Italian husband at one stage – certainly he was not Jewish... and then she is inconsolable because she is unable to conceive a child and so she makes plans to adopt one (a private adoption and not through the social services or whatever they are called in England) and then ends up with a daughter and she gives the girl a name that can fit either sex - it is most probably Beverly. But her husband leaves and then she is alone with the child and she gets involved somehow with a criminal type of man who causes her extreme anguish and treats the poor child very badly. I think that she worked at some stage in her life as a courtesan of some kind, perhaps a hostess. What became of her? I feel she might get a form of cancer eventually which of course kills her.

I am not shocked by your theories at all. I think you are probably right when you say that Jesus favoured the inferior, the criminals and the feeble minded. Nowadays we don't have to look too far around ourselves to find similar 'leaders' do we? I think I certainly agree with you that this Jesus is most certainly the enemy of civilized man in more ways than one. For my part I am however, far more wary of socialism than I am of any form of organized religion. I hate socialism in all its forms and find especially terrifying the insidious language changes that come with it – men and women no longer have husbands and wives, they have 'partners' instead. The socialists simply love partners because the term manages to deftly debase the state of commitment that might (or might not) exist between two people, thus giving the State just a little more control than it should have. Your partner is essentially a temporary arrangement.

And quite apart from that, can be male, female, what you will. Our children too are fast heading towards belonging to the State rather than to their parents – something the socialists have long desired. Schools no longer send home newsletters to parents, they are instead sent to 'caregivers' so that the child without parents does not feel disenfranchised and the State becomes ever more powerful. Of course long ago Aldous Huxley warned us of this in 'Brave New World' where one of the most disgusting words a child could utter was 'mother' or 'father' (is my memory correct here? It is years since I read the book). But then George Orwell gave us more than a few warnings too in '1984' where cameras followed Winston Smith, our hero, everywhere. I remember reading this as a teenager and thinking how simply dreadful it would be if that state of always being watched actually eventuated – but again decided it would be most unlikely – and now of course we are quite at ease to be followed around our cities by CCTV cameras and give it not a thought.

In connection with your forthcoming trip to Germany. At this very moment I can see and hear your brother and his wife close by me and they are discussing this proposed trip within my hearing. The good news seems to be that you will be allowed to visit the house once again because the mother-in-law will not be there as she and her daughter plan a trip away. Not in Germany or even in Europe but thousands of miles away to somewhere like India possibly. You will have Rudy to yourself once again. He seems to be totally consumed with writing his book (the autobiography?) and you are the person who can help him most with some part of this project. He is still very anxious that you two keep on good terms so I have no doubt that the trip will once again be a good one.

Before I finish, just a little about magic. I have become more and more interested in magic as it has always been practiced by ordinary people. Paganism seems to be returning all over Europe and elsewhere and although it fills the average Church Pastor's heart with dread, I find I cannot see it as such a terrible thing. The old religions had an established focus and intensity that to me was/is far more acceptable than what replaced them. They engendered a basic respect for ritual that has been largely absent from society for generations. The ordinary man and woman living their ordinary lives have the tools for practicing basic magic always at hand and to a greater or lesser extent might be successful. All thoughts have a tendency to materialize ...intense thoughts might certainly have a greater tendency to do so.

I should say that since the inception of my resurrected interest in these matters, my ability to tune in on events in the lives of others has increased one thousand fold. In more recent times I have even heard the actual voices of people both dead and alive, and they have seemed to be quite close to me – those of your brother and his wife discussing your impending visit for example which I described earlier. And during the writing of this letter to you I seem to have heard your friend Rosalinda discussing matters both mundane and significant – from the training of a

*poodle puppy to something far more serious in her life -
'Franco has left...Franco has left!' (and whoever Franco
might be I know not.)*

*Anyhow, I must stop writing for it grows darker
and I have much to do with what is left of the daylight.
Much love, Faith.*

With Jonah being home and with the fulfilment of
all the usual traditions of Christmas and New Year,
Faith was now left in charge of the correspondence
which she enjoyed. We were aware that Vanith was
once again to be allowed inside Rudy's house because
this helpful information had arrived in the form of a
Christmas message from Rudy's wife Angela.
Bernadette knew that he would be enormously
impressed with this particular piece of telepathic
intelligence. It was a day or two before he replied.

MAGIC
From: Vanith Lefarge (Vanith@inthesky.co.uk)
To: PersephoneFaith@highmail.com
2nd January
*Very Dearest Faith, I have to leave the house at 12
noon to get my coach to Munich. I was hoping to write
to you properly before I go, but I don't have time. I am
allowed to visit my brother, because his wife and her
mother have gone away to Sri Lanka until the 15th.
You overheard this!!!! Astonishing!!! I am very, very
impressed and almost reduced to tears when I
contemplate this colossal gift of yours.*

What you say about Rosalinda is remarkable. Her adopted daughter was called Beverly. Franco was her husband, and she married him simply so she could adopt a child. Then she got rid of him. I can't remember the name of the man she tried to possess, but she was very upset when he left her and she asked me to advise her how to get him back with magic. I advised her very much against it but she went ahead and of course it worked, but it was horrible with shouting, violence, police intervention etc. She died about 10 years ago of lung cancer, just as you said. Your power is mind blowing!

As I discussed in my last email, of course Socialism is a form of Temporal Christianity. Charlemagne wanted the Kingdom of God on earth. So he thought, that if he forcibly converted everybody to Christ. The Kingdom would appear in a short space of time. It did not. Then people thought it was because the Holy Land was in the hands of non-Christians. They initiated The Crusades. The Kingdom of God still did not arrive. Then they decided it was because we tolerated witches amongst us, and so began the Inquisition. Still no Kingdom, however! Then came the Reformation, and after the Reformation people were so sick of bloodshed, they became increasingly tolerant and they lost faith in the Church's ability to deliver the Kingdom of God. They created Temporal Christianity or Socialism. This has failed to bring about the universal brotherhood of all men.

I am in agreement with you largely in what you say about magic. I have managed to sort of reply to you. It is late and must go to bed. Write to me in time for my return. Lots of love from Vanith.

And then he went off to visit once again with his brother and it was indirectly as a result of this trip that his health problems multiplied. In the latter part of January they wrote him a welcome home message because they felt he surely must have arrived back in London by that time. And Faith obligingly tempted him into dialogue with information about a woman Bernadette knew he had been in email contact with in recent weeks. Bernadette knew of his renewed friendship with Alexa because she had created her resurrection personally, bringing her from the dim, dark past, and placing her in Northern England in front of a school computer where, when researching mythology for her students she had suddenly happened upon his webpage. Naturally enough when she realised this was the very Vanith Lefarge from her childhood, she sent him a message at once and asked if he remembered her.

She had been a child of fourteen when they last met, the daughter of a friend Bernadette had worked with in a night club. And true to form, as she knew he would, recalling Alexa at her most tempting, with long golden hair and slender limbs, he replied to her at once. She had then given her a whole new life – albeit one with problems. A determined ex-lover with mental health problems was stalking her which meant she was obliged to move about the North of England from school to school. Sadly this also meant she was never in one place long enough for Vanith to visit and she was between cell phones because Alan (the stalker) had recently managed to inveigle her number from a mutual friend. Anybody would agree that life was not straightforward for Alexa.

Vanith, now more accustomed than ever to writing emails, swallowed his disappointment that she was not available to meet with him or even talk on the telephone. He enquired about her mother and also her brother and even told her how alluring she had been to him at the age of fourteen. And of course Persephone Faith Callahan was able to tune in to their associations both past and present with no trouble at all. And so upon his return from Germany he was to become astonished afresh at his old friend's ability to tap into situations he knew for sure she could not possibly have previous knowledge of.

'Good,' said Bernadette then added, 'How easily he's fooled.' At this Faith looked uncertain and said she continued to be just a little surprised that he was able to accept the authenticity of otherworldly internet friends and acquaintances without undue scrutiny. And Bernadette advised, 'That's what over-confidence does for you. You begin to lose caution.'

Their next letter expressed nonchalant pleasure that the newcomer in their midst, Alexa, was in fact not a figment of their imagination. Then Bernadette, aghast at his lack of propriety concerning his sexual designs on the girl, demanded to know a little more about that other teenage child he had emotionally damaged, poor overweight little Sukey. But infuriatingly his reply told her little though he noted that the Headmistress of the school Sukey attended would no doubt still be turning in her grave at the ramifications of the affair. He would prefer to know from Faith if she had any thoughts about the Future of Mankind and where Western Society was heading? His own concerns were very serious and although he knew the progress towards disaster was inevitable, he was very keen to know her feelings. He believed that Armageddon or Ragnarok or Gotterdammerung was imminent. This overpopulated planet had to get rid of vast rafts of the useless from society... but how? Personally he favoured totally obliterating criminals and liars in the first instance because this particular human refuse was flourishing. He now believed that although some of Adolf Hitler's ideas had been expressed somewhat offensively, they were not as flawed as the values by which we now all lived.

He told her that he had now had more medical investigations and that he was essentially suffering from heart failure. He also had some urinary problems but they were of a minor nature. The Cardiologist he had seen a day or two previously had thought it would be wise to do a heart by-pass operation. He emphasised that he valued his relationship with her enormously. Friends were very important to him, particularly those from the past.

Faith was very worried about all this and wrote back at once saying that he should take care of himself and think carefully about the wisdom of having such a serious operation. Bernadette thought he should go ahead because she knew he loved to be the centre of attention as far as the medical profession was concerned and that it would give him the opportunity to show off his own medical knowledge, generally disagree with advice and become as difficult a patient as possible.

'Now is the time to send The Draft,' she said in some excitement but Faith looked quite horrified.

'No, no, no it is not a good time!'

So on 27th January they wrote him a rather nice letter a lot of which was very complimentary concerning friendship because like the Christian God he so despised, he loved flattery and adulation. They added a number of telepathic passages into the mix throwing caution to the wind, but although Faith disapproved, Bernadette now cared little about that because she knew now how dependent he had become upon that which tied them together. They told him that they wholeheartedly agreed with him regarding the importance of friends especially as one grew older. They complimented him as someone who had a gift for friendship, attracting around him many fascinating people, all eager for the comradeship of a charismatic person such as himself. There was a buzz of excitement in being his friend, he was like a glass of champagne, a beacon of light attracting creatures of the night. His appeal made him irresistible and particularly so to the women who had been part of his life over the years. His magnetism made it impossible for them to totally release him. And for his part he had become accustomed to the adulation of these women and from time to time he would underestimate the consequences upon them of the great love they had for him. Sadly at times such a situation would result in a desire in them for retribution, ugly though that was. One woman in particular felt a compelling and specific need that he should suffer for the harm he had done her.

Then straying from the subject of friendships he was reminded of a dinner party attended at Christmastime decades ago where the young woman he was then living with met her future husband, a man with whom she would eventually live on the other side of the world. Yet in that moment when they met she felt only pain because she knew he would become her husband, and with him she would live in domestic harmony and raise a family, yet her love for Vanith was so great that the thought left her desolate. And in yet another flash of telepathic genius poor Sukey is seen crying bitterly for some reason. Then some complaint has been made about his visits to the child's school and there is talk of a police complaint.

Bernadette was pleased with the tone of the last paragraphs but Faith made no comment and just typed on with a grim look on her face. Looking over her shoulder, Bernadette could read easily the several elongated and dull paragraphs about what was to become of the world they lived in, how best to cull the planet's population, this matter that so seemed to preoccupy him. And it had been Faith who was left to the monotonous and dreary research that facilitated these comments. Bernadette was becoming more and more frustrated by the mere dribble of information he was prepared to give concerning more important topics such as the child he so astonishingly managed to seduce and furthermore apparently got away with it and whose teenage heart he so effectively broke. And she even allowed herself further meditation on the titanic suffering he had heaped upon her own younger self during the years she had known him though she knew this would lead to more discussion about when to send The Draft.

'He totally corrupted me,' she said to Faith. 'He turned me into a person I should not have been.'

But Faith, predictably, said something about most women having disappointments in their lives with regard to men and that there came a time in which it was better by far to move on.

Accordingly Bernadette hurtled them into vigorous discussion about the tightly worded little paragraph they both knew would have at least as much devastating effect upon his psyche as the news all those years ago about twins and triplets in utero. After fruitless debate a truce was reached and Faith allowed the minor punishment of having Alexa, whom he had so coveted as a fourteen –year-old, go into hiding from her stalker somewhere in Leeds and refuse to reply to his emails. Exasperatingly, when he wrote back to Faith he firmly claimed to have no knowledge of the Christmas party in Clive's Campden Hill house where the twenty-five-year-old Bernadette had first met the man with the tantalising initials who was to become her husband some years later.

'He's just being difficult,' she said to Faith as they read his latest reply together. 'He cannot possibly have forgotten that party.' But Faith said that she believed him and that in those days one party was very much like another and after all it was just so long ago; he was now an old man and he was sick – he couldn't be expected to remember all these trivial details.

PUTTING JIGSAW PIECES TOGETHER
From: Vanith Lefarge (Vanith@inthesky.co.uk)
To: PersephoneFaith@highmail.com
28th January
My Dearest Faith, I was very pleased to hear from you, partly because I became worried that all was not well with you or rather with Joseph and the girls. You speak of relationships and indeed all relationships are difficult, especially at the end. I suppose the most difficult and damaging one for me was that with my mother, who as I have said to you, was determined to possess me. Possessiveness is a terrible thing. Another problem in relationships is the implied meaning of one's actions. In pre-first world war Germany the gift of a ring was considered in law to be tantamount to a promise of marriage for example. How things have changed.

Most people are too foolish to be capable of thinking coherently about their effect upon those around them. Mostly they project their own faults onto others and then criticize them. It took me a long time to develop this confidence about the stupidity of those around me, which in turn is of course interpreted by the moronic majority as arrogance.

To your telepathy instances: The Christmas party in the house with high ceilings and the girl you describe rings absolutely no bells whatsoever.

As for poor Sukey, she cried a lot of the time, and mostly to do with me. Contrary to rumour I never forbade her to do anything or meet with anyone. She was free to make her own decisions. I merely reminded her of the consequences of her actions. However, somehow or other that bitch Bernadette must have heard about us because she attempted to tell Sukey's mother who was fortunately away in Singapore when she rang. One of Sukey's sisters answered and Bernadette warned her against me. It was a very close shave and shows just how dangerous Bernadette could be. It could have done me an enormous amount of damage because Sukey was only fourteen at the time and at boarding school. I could have ended up charged by the police! Bernadette would still do me harm if she could, of that I am convinced.

I have decided to have the heart operation that was suggested and I now wait for this to be organised. Afterwards I should be a new man! I will update you with details in this regard.

You know I can sense your own love for me and I am grateful for it. You were able to turn me from a boy into a man. Very few women could have done that. Your letters mean a very great deal to me. The document of our correspondence is now bigger than ever! Vanith.

An hour or so later the document arrived and as he had said, it was quite large, the largest attachment they had ever received.

SIXTEEN

By the middle of February we were all becoming concerned about his silence and Jack said on more than one occasion that it was his opinion that his health problems had become worse. Faith looked gloomy and said it was clear that things were not going well at all. I wallowed in the strangely liberating space where there were no regular messages with their self-obsessed monologues spreading from paragraph to paragraph and sometimes from page to page.

'It's a little like a holiday,' I told Faith. 'Like years ago when he suddenly decided to go away for a few days, because after the initial misery of being without him there was elation.' But Faith who had become considerably less substantial during recent weeks, was not able to reply.

Finally it was Rudy who provided the answer with a nice email to Daniel informing him that his father had finally had a heart operation at the beginning of the month, which had gone very well, but that in the following days he had deteriorated with severe stomach spasms and had to be taken to another hospital where a further extensive operation was performed on his bowel. He was now, however, recovering as well as could be expected. Daniel looked at once alarmed and explained a little helplessly that the thought that this father who rejected him might actually die, made him feel strangely uneasy. He wanted to know if he should rush to London to visit him in the hospital whilst he still lived. Both Jack and I thought such a visit would be unproductive.

The now regenerated Faith took the opportunity to write a concerned little message based on information she had received in a dream. Predictably though, she pursed her lips and hunched her shoulders, and muttered a little as she did so. She had woken quite terrified one night knowing he had indeed had his heart operation and that it had been uneventful. He should have been recovering and would have been so but for those demons he had fought for so many years. They took the opportunity to strike him when his defences were at their lowest point. She sent great love.

A CLOSE SHAVE
From: Vanith Lefarge (Vanith@inthesky.co.uk)
To: PersephoneFaith@highmail.com
18th March
Dearest Faith, Again, amazingly, you are quite right! I have had a very close shave with death and I am very weak after two operations. On 2nd February I had sudden heart failure and needed emergency quad-bypass. The next day they discovered I had strangulated intestines and therefore I had a further operation. They warned me my chances of survival were less than 50/50. But I am still here. I am going to stay with Paula for a week or two and I will try to write

*to you from her place. I am out of danger but it will be
a long recovery. Love, V.*

He added contact details for Paula; her address,
telephone number and also an email address, which
was thoughtful. A month went by before we heard
from him again though Rudy kept in touch with
Daniel telling him that his father was hopefully on the
road to recovery and Paula herself wrote to Faith at
least once saying much the same thing. This gave
Paula and I the opportunity to exchange pleasantries
and get to know one another just a little. I could not
help feeling that she was being a little reserved with
Faith which was unnecessary under the circumstances. We sent him a very pleasant letter early in
April, detailing the importance of ties of friends and
family. In retrospect I suppose it was designed
primarily to fortify the idea that there could be no
escaping those sons and daughters indiscriminately
spawned and like it or not errant parents were linked
to them through all eternity. It quoted Bertrand
Russell as well as Plato and Socrates and finally noted
the endurance of the parent-child tie which persists
when all others fade away. It was possibly just a little
over the top, especially if he chose to show it to Paula,
though I did think that unlikely. The good thing was
that it was a long letter, possibly the longest we had
ever sent him, and it would nicely pre-occupy him
during his convalescence. Just before I pressed the
send button I added a paragraph, in case he grew to
expect a plethora of such letters: we were off to the

vineyard again to visit Josef's wine growing friend and I would contact him when we returned. In late April Paula sent news that Vanith had returned to his own flat, because he now felt he could manage alone. She did not sound confident and added that she thought he still had a lot of healing to do.

May began stormily in Auckland that year. The wind churned the incoming tide and whirled its way up the beach towards the house. It was just before the office clock ticked relentlessly towards midnight and without further consultation with Faith on the matter that I then chose to send The Draft. It had long been itching to escape the confines of the Drafts Folder, straining the parameters of its own Arial 11 Bold Font and when I examined it I had intended merely to read it once more before tucking it away again for whatever 'the time being' actually meant. But instead, surprisingly, I sent it. It was April Fools' Day.

From: Bernadette@xtrasaints.co.nz
To: Vanith@inthesky.co.uk
1st April
Dear Vanith, At long last I have decided to reveal something that you will undoubtedly find hard to believe. You have been deceived by Persephone Faith Callahan. She never was the woman you thought she was, being largely a figment of Bernadette's imagination. All things considered she and I did very well though wouldn't you agree? You seemed to grow more and more fond of her over time which was touching because it allowed you to send her just a little

of the love I always hoped you would bestow upon me and perhaps also upon our son, Daniel.

You would get on very well with Daniel. He's a musician, a violinist and like you, at times quite preoccupied with music. He and I both knew you would enjoy the playing of Ida Haendel.

All things considered I think you were wise to underestimate me. Bernadette.

After it had gone I checked several times to make absolutely certain I had completed the procedure. There could now be no going back. Poor Faith, aroused from her current corner of the shelf by the spare toner cartridge made several wildly agitated circles of the laptop desk.

'What have you done? Oh WHAT have you done?' Her voice bounced from the office walls and fractured into silvery fragments, shivering little broken pieces of 26/6 staples from the stapling machine. As I watched, her image shuddered and trembled until with a final spasm she simply disappeared into the wall calendar above the desk. The last part of her to melt away was the pale blue cardigan.

His final message came at the end of May when Faith and her family should have well and truly returned from their vineyard holiday.

HEALTH
From: Vanith Lefarge (Vanith@inthesky.co.uk)
To: PersephoneFaith@highmail.com
28th May

Der fiath, I am still veree poorly but over a fuw weekes you cann sea thr impruvment. It wul tak a longe time to get betltar. Luv V.

When he read this strange little note Jack said he had probably had a stroke. Much later I heard from Rudy, and from Paula, and also from Rona that in all likelihood that is what did happen although at the time it had not been properly recognised. He went on to have urinary troubles, and to be hospitalized several more times. Eventually he excelled in the role of the Exceedingly Difficult Patient and then of course, I did not hear from him again. I was relieved to finally be rid of the burden of the ongoing non-productive email correspondence but just occasionally I wondered if in fact he had already had the stroke before he received The Draft. Was he ever able to actually read The Draft and properly understand the significance of it?

Over the following months, his dwindling energies were taken up with trying to regain a degree of health and strength but because of his impenetrable belief that he was a Very Special Being, he found it increasingly difficult to take advice. He insisted on changing his own catheters, he decided in his wisdom, whether or not he should continue to take the drugs he had been discharged from hospital with, or whether in fact he should double the dose. He demanded opiates to help him sleep and when they were not forthcoming he sent Paula in search of prescription-free substitutes at a more and more elevated cost.

All these developments were related to us by Rudy and Angela over the next three months. Daniel, deprived for years of a relationship with his father, now enjoyed an active telephone and email relationship with his uncle where the focus of discussion at least, was his father. And during this time even Salome was made to retreat from the forefront of his attention.

Once, strangely, a little note appeared in the Persephone Faith Callahan Inbox. It was from Paula, telling her how he was faring. I wondered for a moment if Faith was still somewhere in the vicinity and from time to time, when the house was quiet and still, still writing her own anxious missives of enquiry. And did that mean he had not been able to read or comprehend The Draft? Or did it mean he had simply chosen not to reveal to Paula the manner in which he had been so utterly deceived?

He began to make increasing demands upon her and she, like the long suffering Christina before her, continued to offer on-going sanctuary and support without complaint. Several times on a whim he left the Essex village where she lived and drove himself back to North London. On these occasions another hospital admission invariably followed.

At the beginning of August, he agreed he would return to Paula but only on his terms. Those terms included her giving over to him her sunny downstairs living room adjacent to the kitchen. That was where he would like his bed to be, with a computer set up nearby. He no longer wanted to be relegated to the upstairs guest room. Strangely, this is when Paula dug her toes in and told him, and apparently Rudy and Angela also, that she was very happy to look after him for as long as was necessary, but she wanted to have her sitting room remain just that, a place where she could entertain an occasional visitor; she did not want Vanith sleeping there and that if he insisted upon doing so she would feel banished from within her own surroundings.

He was most displeased, explaining to his brother via Skype at some length, that he liked her sitting room very much. It was sun drenched by eleven am when he usually awoke and he enjoyed the view of what remained of the village green (the pump was still there). He liked lying on the day bed in that warm sunlight, reading the newspaper and perhaps using Paula's laptop which was a much more handy device than his own rather cumbersome machine. In fact he was thinking of buying himself a laptop in order to make his convalescence more agreeable; there were people he needed to keep in touch with. If Paula wanted to entertain a visitor privately why could she not do so upstairs? She could be as private as she liked up there. The guest room could easily be turned into a very acceptable little sitting room for her whilst of course the bed could be moved downstairs for him. Strangely, Paula did not capitulate but continued to insist that she would be delighted for him to become a permanent house guest, but he had to accept the guest room.

So the argument went on until the middle of August when Rudy travelled to London to visit him in hospital where he had once more been taken for treatment of an infection due to an improperly inserted or extracted catheter. He was thus able to explain more fully his position without the constraints of time or the distortion of Skype and he made it clear that he was not simply being difficult. What is more he was fully cognizant of the fact that Paula was a true and generous friend and cared deeply about him. He pointed out not for the first time that she had once upon a time been very much in love with him, long ago after he had rid himself of Bernadette and got over the stress of that bloody child business. She had even said she wished to marry him and in his opinion she was still perhaps more than a little in love with him. He knew that she would prefer to keep that downstairs sitting room as it was and did not really want it turned into a bed sitter to accommodate him. But on the other hand that was not only what would suit him best, but also was the most sensible solution to the space problem. It was, after all, just a small cottage. He could be close to the kitchen so that when he wanted a cup of coffee late at night, he could simply shuffle over and make it himself and would not have to call for her. Poor Paula was very willing but he did at times feel guilty about putting so many demands on her, for coffee, for new batteries for the laptop mouse, to go on endless trips to buy newspapers, etc. And apart from all that she would be able to keep the upstairs rooms as tidy as she wanted. He had found that Paula was fond of tidy rooms and this was in fact something he did not personally admire in her, but anyway if he confined himself to the downstairs area then his papers and coffee cups, etc. would not worry her so much. It was a win-win situation. They could both be happy.

But Paula became unpredictably difficult and continued to say: No.

Finally Vanith told his brother, 'If you do not put pressure on her to give me the room I want, then I will never leave this hospital alive. I will henceforth refuse all food and all drug treatment. Both you and she will be responsible for my death!'

And in short that is what he did. It took two or three weeks and I was not made aware of all the details until later because in the first instance Paula certainly did not choose to reveal these facts to long since absent Faith. It was close to Christmas that year, when Jack and I had already been to London and back, before Rudy spoke to me at any length about what had happened.

Vanith had died on the fifth of September in a North London hospital with a dark clutch of female friends at his bedside, Paula, Rona, Sukey and Katya, a Polish woman he had never mentioned to Faith. Martha had done quite a good job on behalf of Daniel and myself in trying to keep in touch with what the arrangements for his funeral might be. Rudy, recently returned to Germany decided he did not have the strength to attend. Daniel was keen to go but Martha suggested that it might be more appropriate if she acted as the official family representative. I thought this to be by far the best option as far as the conflicting emotions of the gaggle of female followers was concerned and she could simply appear as yet another obsessed admirer.

Disappointingly, we discovered from Paula and Rudy, that there would be no funeral to go to. His wishes had been that his body was simply to be cremated without ceremony and his ashes scattered in the forest at Epping. Paula was in full charge of this procedure as he had nominated her his next of kin. It was not until we got to London later in the month that the full magnitude of his undiminished determination and resolve with regard to Daniel and myself unfolded.

His principal concern was that Daniel should not become heir to any of his earthly possessions. Clearly he thought that this was most likely to happen if the normal procedures and rituals of dying were allowed to develop. Wisely, he did not trust his brother in this matter and so he left instructions with each one of the attendant women, that nothing of his must go to his brother and furthermore that his family, Rudy and Angela, should not even be told of his death until several days had elapsed. In the interim, Paula would be relieved of responsibility in this regard and everything he owned was left to the mysterious Katya who was to ensure that his possessions should be removed from his flat as fast as humanly possible.

This, with the help of her two sons, Katya did over the space of a weekend.

Poor Rudy was baffled because Vanith still held a large number of family photographs and documents together with several paintings of ancestors that he had anticipated retrieving. Even Martha was surprised and observed that Katya might well find it challenging in future years when making decisions regarding storage space, to hold on to memorabilia that related to a family other than her own. But no-one knew, or at least they maintained they did not know, where to get hold of the mysterious Katya. It was rumoured that she had recently moved to somewhere in the North of England and was only available at the end of a mobile telephone which she did not seem to answer.

It was in the final two days of our London visit that I eventually summoned the courage to go to the address in Wood Green where he had lived. It was a beautiful morning when the sunshine was almost as penetrating as that I had become so accustomed to in Auckland, when the sky becomes impossibly blue and the trees impossibly green. I was acutely aware that penetrating his domain after his death was the final terrible assault on this man for whom such an event had become the stuff from which nightmares were made. Had I not been so propelled by the obsessive earlier passion and had his kind and caring upstairs neighbour, Steve, had not so swiftly answered the door I might have simply walked away and never returned because we were departing once more for New Zealand the next day.

But it was difficult to walk away from Steve, standing on the doorstep looking only slightly bedraggled at ten fifteen a.m. and not really like the chronic alcoholic described to Faith on more than one occasion. I told him I had once been very close to Vanith and in fact we had a son together and he then assumed a marital union and told me though he had known him more than twenty years he never revealed that he had a wife and child. Vanith always kept a lot to himself, he added, it was part of his nature. He took me upstairs and told me the long story of his neighbour's slow demise and finally of 'the bloody daft nonsense' of Rudy not being allowed inside the flat and not permitted to retrieve family items. He told me how he had watched Katya and her sons burning documents late into the night in the bins at the front of the house and that at times the flames were so high he wondered that nobody made a complaint to the council. He did not think the ancestor paintings had been burned, however.

Then somewhat surprisingly he revealed that he still held a set of keys to Vanith's flat and asked me if I would like to have a look around and of course, with palpitating heart, I said I would love to and tried to sound casual. And so we then stood together in the almost bare bed-sitting room with shafts of sunlight streaming through the narrow window, making the exposed floorboards look sadly barren. Steve seemed to know what I was thinking, and commented that they'd been determined buggers, even taking away the carpet and perhaps that had been because it still had a lot of wear in it. The new carpet he had purchased with part of the cash discovered in Miriam's flat after her death and as that thought nuzzled into memory there followed behind an unexpected wave of compassion for poor, dead Vanith. Recall of the long years during which I had so devotedly adored him was odd standing there in the silence of his recently vacated kingdom, the very place where not so long ago he laboriously typed emails to Faith hour after hour, pouring forth philosophy and vitriol.

His custom-made bed was still there, the bed we had slept on together in Clerkenwell, the bed upon which Daniel had been conceived. It looked somehow smaller than I remembered it now it was without its mattress. On it was a pile of books – German textbooks on mostly maths and physics and here and there were scattered CDs. I picked one up and because it was Ricci playing Paganini I asked Steve's permission to take it. He said to take whatever I wanted and then observed that there was precious little left in any case and it had been a crying shame and he wished he had been able to stop them. He opened a cupboard door and retrieved from its depths a walking cane made from a length of bamboo, cut precisely to Vanith's height and from a hook in the kitchen he recovered an apron and told me Vanith was careful to wear it each time he cooked and what a fair Jamie Oliver he looked in it. Just a couple of odds

327

and ends the bastards had missed, he said as he handed them to me.

Poised on the verge of tears I could say nothing because the flesh and blood part of me was quite unable to believe that I now actually stood within the North London home of the dead and already scattered Vanith Lefarge, wondering what to take with me of the paltry few items that remained, left presumably because Katya and her helpers had simply run out of time, or of room, or of energy. Finally Steve led me upstairs again to collect a little copper lamp he had been cleaning and I recognised it immediately as an item that long ago we had used during one long Clerkenwell winter of power cuts. He then produced a couple of monogrammed hand towels from a laundry basket saying that they needed ironing and he had taken over Vanith's laundry arrangements whilst he was sick. He urged me to take them and I did so with gratitude.

Walking back to the tube station, after promises to keep in touch with the increasingly helpful and likeable Steve, I felt shaky as if I had only recently descended rapidly in a modern glass elevator from at least the thirtieth floor. But there were also little swells and surges of triumph. A growing sense of achievement because I had done the unthinkable and moreover it delighted me to reflect upon Vanith's undoubted disquiet and discomposure, his unease and distress should he somehow be made aware of what had happened. It was unthinkable that within a short time of his death the much-hated Bernadette would so effortlessly accomplish the unimaginable. That she would, no doubt with the aid of her Black Gypsy Magic, dally a while in the little fortress of his home, mostly unhurried and idly deciding what to misappropriate for that demon son who filled him with so much odium.

Safely back in New Zealand, there were of course hours of re-examination and scrutiny of these events with Daniel and with Jack and to a lesser extent and long distance, with Martha and Jonah. And to be totally fair, and because she had played such a pivotal part in the deception, I also tried to discuss it with Faith. But she was hard to locate and when she wrote to Paula acknowledging all the effort she had put into attempting to bring him back to good health, and thanking her, it was largely Bernadette at the keyboard. Paula wrote back a somewhat prim little missive that did not invite further fellowship or involvement, thanking her for her thanks. I wondered what Faith would say to that and thought it might be, 'Thank God we didn't have to have too much to do with her - there's something about us she doesn't like. It's almost as if she suspects something.'

And had Faith been there in the room it would have been my turn to call her paranoid but I wouldn't because I was feeling magnanimous towards her, knowing she could be easily dismissed and folded away again and be for all time primeval and pristine in her tweed skirt and cashmere cardigan yet also the kind of woman who could turn boys into men overnight; a real woman.

No matter which way I examined the events of the preceding eighteen months, in the final analysis, I could only view the deception wreaked upon Vanith Lefarge via the alter ego of Faith, as the ultimate victory of Good over Evil or at least that is how I chose to view it. As had happened with him on more than one occasion, he had called for her and she came. Possibly he should have taken more care for whom he called, taken precautions that the Faith he had ended up corresponding so intimately with, was the real Faith. He who knew so much more than most of us about the possible consequences of admitting a gatecrasher into the confidence, or an extra fairy to a christening, had somehow made a perilous error of judgment in his eagerness to unearth an old friend.

From time to time a softer woman within me had felt more than a twinge of regret at the burgeoning extent of the duplicity. Frequently I had shivered with embarrassment at his self- importance, felt horror at his naked narcissism and then sat in wonder at his eagerness to be defrauded whilst all the time insisting that he was a Fully Enlightened Being. And on more than one occasion I wondered if it would have been possible for The Draft to have caused The Stroke.

THE END

ABOUT THE AUTHOR

JEAN HENDY-HARRIS is a free-lance writer who was born in England and now lives in New Zealand. She developed a keen interest in writing as a child but went on to work in a number of different fields including office worker, nurse and night club hostess. Her writing includes short stories and articles in health and education, a book on home education and several on developing literature themes in junior classrooms. She has three completely grown up children and now lives with her retired Medical Practitioner husband in Auckland.

Printed in Great Britain
by Amazon